NAM

My dear friends
Pat e Mark
Hope you enjoy

Maurice
xxx

NAM

Someone Else's War

Maurice Tudor

Writers Club Press
San Jose New York Lincoln Shanghai

NAM
Someone Else's War

Writers Club Press
an imprint of iUniverse.com, Inc.

For information address:
iUniverse.com, Inc.
620 North 48th Street, Suite 201
Lincoln, NE 68504-3467
www.iuniverse.com

ISBN: 0-595-13981-7

Printed in the United States of America

To my wife Elizabeth for her undying support in writing this book

FOREWORD

MALARIA

This is a deadly disease, caused by certain Parasites in the blood, which are carried by the Mosquito. Its name is derived from 'Mala Aria' (Italian for bad air).

BREEDING AREAS

Most Tropical Countries, where the population is poorly fed, swampy areas, and rank vegetation.

Its chief seats are, The East Indies, South China, and Central America. But the most dangerous Malaria-carrier Mosquito named 'Anopheles Gambiae' is rife on the Mediterranean shores, and Tropical Africa.

PARASITES

They are three in number, namely the 'Tertian Fever', the 'Quartan fever', and the 'Aestivo-Autumnal Fever', or Subtertian, or Malignant Tertian Malaria.

The Parasites penetrate the blood cells, forming a ring around the red cells,they then enlarge, and split into numerous small Parasites, which burst out into the main bloodstream, then they attack other red corpuscles. repeating the whole cycle again.

SYMPTOMS

The affected person experiences three stages, known as 'The Cold Stage' 'The Hot Stage' and 'The Sweating Stage'.

If the Parasite is the 'Quartan Fever' there is an intermission of three days between attacks, thus allowing the body to prepare a defence.

If the Parasites is the 'Tertian Fever' there is only two days intermission between attacks, so the body doesn't have as much time to prepare its defences.

But if the Parasite is the 'Subtertian Fever' each attack could last considerably over a day, giving no intermission, each attack overlapping the previous one, thus creating a continued state of fever, the body has no time to prepare any defence. Death can occur at this stage, the affected person *must* have constant nursing care.

Insensibility often occurs at this stage, and a person can die, due to a blockage of the small vessels in the brain, caused by huge the amount of numbers of Parasites.

OTHER COMPLICATIONS

At this stage referred to above,the dreaded 'Black Water Fever' often occurs, symptoms of this are, heavy body weight loss, yellow discoloration of the skin, spleen enlargement and liver damage.

TREATMENT is in two forms.

PREVENTIVE Could be directed either against the Parasite or the Mosquito which convey them. 'MEPACRINE', 'PROGUANIL', 'PYRIMETHAMMINE', 'CHLORO-QUINE', and 'AMODIAQUINE', are effective Prophycactics. One of these tablets should be taken regularly by all white people living in Malaria areas.

CURATIVE

Depends on 'QUINIE', 'MEPACRINE', 'PROGUANIL-HYDROCHLO-RIDE', 'CHLOROQUINE', and 'AMODIAQUINE'.

ACKNOWLEDGEMENTS

I would like to mention one or two people who, by their encouragement made this book possible. I had nursed this sore on my mind for over fifty years, and by and with the help, of the following people and organisations. I would never have laid the ghost to rest.

Helen and Keith for their encouragement and Keith for keeping my computer from overheating.

Southport Technical College UK, and my tutor in word processing *********for her patience with an older pupil, who knew nothing about computers.

The Readers Digest for their kindness in sorting out useful information concerning one of their 1954 issues. Which helped enormously in jogging my memory of that horrific year.

Last but not least, my computer widow wife Elizabeth who uncomplainingly, kept my teacup full!

CHAPTER ONE

I awoke to find myself laying face down on an uncomfortable bed, and hearing sounds like rumbling thunder. Through closed eyes I could sense light but could also sense darkness. Keeping quite still I wondered about this, first light then dark? As I wondered about this, other noises crept into my head, muted voices as if from a distance. Footsteps, some like boots on a hard floor others more soft, almost like slippers, making a shushing sound, as if telling the noises to be quiet. More rumbling. More noises. Getting louder and louder, like an orchestra reaching a crescendo it made my head want to explode.

I cried out opening my eyes. Harsh light seared through them into my brain, causing such pain that I clenched them shut again. *Where am I?* I asked myself. *What has happened to me?* Feeling weak and tired and unable to cope with the noises and the pain in my head. I felt myself drifting into a welcome void of darkness.

I was very reluctant to wake up, I only wanted to stay in the safe cocoon of sleep without the pain and noise, until I could figure out what it all meant. But no matter how hard I tried to shut everything out, my brain accepted the noises.

Someone very near to me was making groaning sounds; I wished he would shut up and let me sleep. But no! So I tried to roll over onto my back but the effort was too much. The groans became louder. Then, and only then, did I realise the groans were coming from me.

Cautiously opening one eye and more than ready to close it again if the pain returned. I tried to take stock of where I was. The light and dark, which confused me before, was the overhead lights that were swinging with each rumble of thunder? Outside the window white flashes of light could be seen. With each rumble the overhead lights danced casting weird shadows on the wall, shadows that resembled other beds similar to mine with muffled shapes on them.

Bang! Flash! Bang! Flash! *Christ! Must be a hell of a storm.* I thought. *Glad I'm not out in it.* To my horror I found that any movement of my head caused fireworks to go off, so I just lay there with one eye open looking at the floor and whatever else that came into my vision. *What a pretty red stream going past my bed, or am I floating on it? Wait a minute! Water in streams are clear or muddy not red.*

My mind couldn't grasp this puzzle because it had another to solve. Why was I sweating so much but feeling very cold? My heart started to race. *Calm down Maurice you are having a nightmare* my mind said. But I didn't believe that. Oh yes I wanted too. To wake up with everything Ok. But I knew it wasn't to be when in the dim swinging light I saw opposite me what I had thought earlier to be shadows resembling beds, were beds!

A soldier lay on one, my mind recoiled in horror to what my eyes were seeing, and it was all that I should imagine an Abattoir to look like. Everywhere I looked men, some not much older than myself, lay on stretchers like mine, bloodied beyond imagination, blood everywhere, blood dripping through the canvas of the stretchers adding to the red stream! Moans and whimpering sounds could be heard in between the noises from outside making a spectacle to horrific to comprehend for my shocked mind.

My lips felt swollen and my tongue seemed to fill my mouth, my head was still throbbing! I needed a drink of water desperately. Panic set in, *what if this is a living nightmare? You never wake up from? The noises and headaches are always there.* Thoughts were flashing through my mind too fast for me to dwell on. As I tried to fasten any reason to them they were superseded by others just like a kaleidoscope I used to have as a child.

Seeing a light coming my way different to the overhead lights and again that swishing type of footsteps, I mustered all my strength to shout.

"Over here help me." But the words only passing my lips in a croaking whisper. The light swept over me and I could just make out a white shape leaning and placing a cool hand on my forehead, my arm was lifted and I felt a prick, gratefully I felt myself swimming back into the safe black void.

With a start I awoke. The loud bangs seemed nearer, briefly the room seemed to be shaking, and reluctantly I opened my eyes, remembering the red stream! Pictures flashed through my head like a cine camera, ship, guns, soldiers, and bombs, so fast that I could not concentrate on any one picture. I lay there thinking. *This is stupid, the lads have spiked my drinks and I'm having an almighty hangover* what else could it be? *What do I know of guns and bombs? Christ I'm only nineteen!* An alarming thought crossed my mind. *God if the Skipper sees me like this I'll be logged again.* Panic set in. *I must get up and show willing.*

Attempting to sit up, was when I realised that I was laying on my back, a pillow was under my head, I thought I could hear a voice saying something in a language I couldn't understand, seeming to waft over me then fading away-near-far-near-far. I felt the sides of my bed it didn't feel like my bunk; in fact I thought, *this is not my ship.* I cried out. My eyes, although open, didn't seem to focus properly, everything seemed to float and was distorted, and the overhead light was still on and swaying causing the room to appear to be swaying too. *Just like my ship* I was thinking, then felt gentle hands going under my shoulders raising me up and a cold welcome refreshing drink soaked my parched lips. I couldn't see who was giving me the drink but was so grateful. As my head was placed gently back on the pillow all I wanted was to go back to sleep, a cool cloth was pressed to my face. Thanks mum I mumbled and drifted back to sleep.

I kept waking for minutes then seemingly sleeping for hours. At times on awakening my mind was lucid, other times I was feverish, at these times I couldn't grasp anything that was going on around me. Gradually I began to put the puzzle together, enough for me to under-stand that I was very ill, that I was in some kind of hospital, although it wasn't like any hospital I had known or seen back in England.

The beds were not beds but stretchers raised on blocks (so they can move you quickly I later learned.) These stretchers were placed in lines; I appeared to be in the middle line with other lines on either side of me. There seemed a lack of hospital things, like lockers, flowers, trolleys etc, but I didn't dwell on these things my mind had more important things to dwell on, hundreds of questions needed answering before lockers and things.

The main questions. Were and why was I here in the first place? What was wrong with me? Why was I so thirsty but not hungry? Why was I sweating profusely and shivering with cold? *These are the questions I want answering* I thought. Not the absence of lockers!

Looking around at my neighbours, I took in the sights that were to haunt me for years to come. Sights that earlier my mind had tried unsuccessfully to blot out. Men and boys so horribly wounded, limbs amputated, wounds so horrific to me that even then seeing them, my mind refused to register them. Some with tubes going into their arms from hanging plastic pouches others swathed in bloodstained bandages that made them look mummified. The stench of human waste, blood and sweat, couldn't be disguised completely by disinfectant. The cacophony of sobbing, groaning and sheer terror of these wounded men struck real fear into my heart causing me to sweat more profusely, my heart pumping so furiously at times I thought it would explode through my chest. *Christ!* I thought. *I want out of here and quick.*

I was afraid to examine myself for wounds like the other wounded. *Why else would I be here if I wasn't wounded?* I thought. Gritting my teeth I eventually raised, ever so gingerly the blanket covering my legs, as I was flat on my back and found that I was too weak to raise myself to a sitting position I had to squint over my chest to see. To my utter relief I saw that I still had two legs! Tentatively feeling my groin I found that was Ok too! The sound of my relief surprised even me, to anyone listening it probably sounded on a par with a football fan after a goal was scored.

A smiling face loomed into my vision saying in French accented English.

"You are back with us then?" I peered at what was obviously a nurse, my vision was still blurred but I could see that she was in a white uniform with a white cap on her head. Just to hear my own language made my eyes prick with tears.

"Where am I?" I asked, my mouth was so dry it was difficult to speak. I didn't know if she could hear me, for I could hardly hear myself. "What happened to me?" A little louder this time.

Putting her finger to her lips she said. "Shush, you 'ave been very ill, I go now to bring doctor he will explain to you, you rest now, I will be quick." With that she raised my head and gave me a drink of water which I gulped greedily down, thanking her as she gently laid my head back onto the pillow, smiling again she went away. lay there waiting in anticipation for her and the doctor to return. My thoughts were still jumbled but some memories were beginning to return, slowly pieces of the jigsaw puzzle began to form a picture.

I was in the crews quarters with my shipmates, playing stud poker and drinking beer. It was very hot and stuffy, even though one of my shipmates had cut a huge piece of cardboard from a cereal outer package, and stuffed it through the open porthole, to form a wind trap to funnel any air back into the cabin. We found to our regret it wasn't working. The air was hot and muggy.

We were all sitting around the table, which was set in the centre of the cabin. All of us in the cabin were stripped to shorts and sandals. The heat just bounced off the steel bulkhead and mixed gleefully with the heat generated off our hot clammy bodies as if to say, GOTTCHA, even the beer joined in, it too was warm!

Bloody Hell, it's hot. Taffy grumbled wiping his brow and tossing down the damp cards onto the table in disgust. Taffy was two years older than I was, being 21 his job was Junior Engineer but he preferred to mix socially with his own age group as we all did!

It must be a hundred degree's and its nighttime! He went on. This was Taffy's third trip on the ' HARTISMERE' and he liked to let us first timers on the ship know it. He seemed to adopt the role of leader of the pack and we all let him.

Steve was with us in the card school, as was Chas, both were from Liverpool. We were a mixed British crew, Welsh. Scottish. Irish. North and South of England, but we all got on well with each other, not like other ships I'd been on where cliques were formed. On the whole we were a happy ship which was good because being a Tramp Cargo shi, meant that there was no set time for the voyage, we just carried cargo's from port to port until we got one that fitted in with going back to England. So one never knew which was the Going Home Cargo until the last moment.

A voyage could be three months or two years. It was the Captain's job or 'Skipper' as they are called by the crew, in obtaining Cargo's. The better the Skipper was, in obtaining Cargo's, the longer the voyage, and our Skipper was good!

Oh you'll only be away for three months. The company rep said. Back in Liverpool four at the most. He added grinning as he stamped my seaman's book. That was twelve months ago!

What a joke, I thought. Being stuck here in this rathole in a war which has nothing to do with us! VIETNAM? I'd never heard of it before, now here I was? Getting up from the table and walking towards the porthole meaning to get some air, I felt woozy, in fact I'd felt off colour for a day or two, but felt really awful now. Must be coming down with something, I thought. My head was hurting and I felt sick to my stomach.

Hey Mo, are you playing or what? Shouted Taffy.

No, I'm going to my bunk I don't feel so good. I was surprised to hear my speech was slurred. Yet I'd only had two drinks. I'm bitten all over. That repellent doesn't work Steve.

I seem to remember having to grab a chair for support for my legs were like jelly, my heart was pounding and sweat was dripping off me. I thought my skin was shrinking, getting tight ready to split open like a ripe peach.

Help me to my bunk. I vaguely recall saying. Everything was spinning around; there was a loud buzzing in my ears.

I felt arms supporting me. I knew I was going to faint, voices around me, friendly concerned voices, seemingly from a distance.

Get him on deck. Someone said. It must be that fucking prickly heat! My body was burning; my head felt like it had been blown up like a balloon, everything was going dark…

CHAPTER TWO

The doctor arrived with the same smiling nurse. She mopped my brow whilst the doctor took my temperature. As he was taking my pulse he spoke rapidly in French to the nurse, she in turn was writing it down on a chart. I couldn't understand a word he was saying, except the odd word like 'Medicine, Quinine' I cursed myself for not taking my French teachers seriously enough at school, now when I needed it most, I couldn't understand a word of it.

The doctor still talking to the nurse turned me over onto my stomach saying as he did so. "Pardon" tapping my back with his fingers then turning me back again making me comfortable. He said something to me in French smiling as he turned away, briefly touching my shoulder and walking quickly away. The nurse was still writing on the chart.

"What did he say?" I asked her.

"You are to have Quinine to help bring your fever down," she replied, with a smile that was to captivate me for the rest of my life.

"You have been close to death with Malaria and still very ill, you were in a coma for three days and it was touch and go as to whether you would pull through—" She put down the chart on the foot of the bed. "—but you are recovering now and with plenty of rest and Quinine you should make a full recovery." She fluffed my pillow and straightened my sheet. I felt exhausted after all the pulling and pushing from the doctor and just wanted to go back to sleep, but first I needed to know were I was.

"What sort of Hospital is this?" I asked.

"This is a Military Field Hospital for the Legionnaires." She replied.

"But why am I here, and not in a proper Hospital?" I wanted to know. She laughed. "This is a proper Hospital Cheri, anyway you have a French name 'no? Maurice?" Pronouncing it 'Moor-ise.

"I'm English." I muttered.

"I'm English," she mimicked. "Poor Moor-ise" She was laughing. "I will come back with soup, then you must try to get some sleep." I called after her as she walked away. "Please contact the British Embassy for me."

When she brought the soup, she spoon fed me smiling all the time. I could not take my eyes off her. The way she said Moor-ise sent shivers through me, her accent was like music that you never want to switch off. *Behave yourself lad; just eat your soup!* went through my mind. I was sorry when the soup was finished and she went away.

Slowly my strength began to return. I was awake for longer periods, my mind was accepting more and more each day of what was happening around me was for real, and preparing an acceptable defence for the horror of my situation. My headaches were becoming less severe. But now and then without warning they returned to remind me that they could still pack a punch! I had no idea how long I had been absent from my ship. I could only guess, maybe one week or two weeks? This worried me because how long would my ship wait for me? If it obtained another cargo and went off to another port I could be stuck here for God only knows when.

I lay there these thoughts going through my head searching for an answer. If only I could speak to a fellow Englishman maybe I could get some answers. *Oh my God, what if my ship was already on its way home with a cargo? What happens to me? Would I just disappear in this God Forsaken country?* I fretted about my plight, so much so that I constantly asked for the British Consul to any of the nurses who came to attend to me, or were in earshot of me. Not knowing all the facts made what was an awful situation for me into a bloody awful situation!

I couldn't get up and was uncomfortable on the stretcher, I seemed to be living on tablets and injections interspaced with soup. Sometimes after an injection, I would feel sleepy, yet other times I felt that I wanted to get up, even if only to walk around my stretcher just to exercise my limbs. Thoughts, although jumbled, constantly Flashed—Died—Flashed through my mind, confused thoughts, a lot of whys? *Why didn't my teachers at school warn me of dangers like this? Why didn't someone prepare me for the suddenness of crossing over from Teenager to Adult?*

It wasn't fair. Back home, my school friends were enjoying their 'Teens', girlfriends, dances, music, not a care in the world. Yet here I was thrust into a mad mans world and couldn't do anything about it, wasn't given a choice, couldn't even converse with the people around me. I was wallowing in self-pity. I knew it but I couldn't or didn't want to do anything about it. Tears came often without warning just flowed. When this happened I got angry with myself. Me. self styled tough guy. Always in fights around the world, trained in 'Snowballs' Gym back home in Southport as a boxer. Blubbering like a schoolboy. When these self-pity moods engulfed me I was glad to some extent, that my shipmates couldn't see me.

Because of the stifling heat and my feverish condition it was necessary for the nurses to sponge me down, sometimes more than once a day. It was on these occasions that I wished more than ever to be able to stand on my own two feet and fend for myself, especially when I needed a bed pan. It was very embarrassing for me with no privacy, no screens to hide me. Not being able to sit up, having a nurse do everything. I knew I blushed on these occasions, yet they didn't seem to notice just smiled, they were to me all, 'Florence Nightingales.' Although they must have been tired and frightened for their own safety, yet never showed it, they could have been back in France in the safety of a hospital there, for all the concern they showed. Truly Angels.

One day my smiling nurse brought my soup and said. "Would you like to get up today and walk around a little?" I still didn't know her name, in my mind I referred to her as 'Smiler.'

"You bet." I replied eagerly.

"OK" she said. "After your soup, I will help you stand up." When she helped me to sit up I felt light-headed, the room swam in front of my eyes, and the soup I had just drunk wanted to part company with me. Two heads were in front of me one pair of arms holding me. My mind thought it funny, my stomach didn't!

"Let me sit awhile." I groaned. "Don't let go of me."

She laughed. It sounded like water running over stones in a stream, clean and fresh. I wanted to hear her laugh, again and again.

"You've spiked my soup!" I said. Squinting at her trying to get her into focus. Again that tinkling laugh.

"Hold on to the bed, I will get you some walking sticks." She said letting go of me and walking away. Grimly holding on I called after her "Don't—be—long—" Within a short time she returned with the walking sticks saying.

"Here you are Cheri, these will help." They did. I found it much easier keeping my balance with the sticks and the room didn't sway so much. Having spied in the corner at the bottom of the room 'The Latrine' I decided above all else that's where I wanted to go! Without further ado I steered a tottering course towards my goal, stopping for a rest every few yards to get my breath back. My goal seemed to be getting further away not nearer. It was whilst having these rests, that I noticed the room was in fact a Nissan Hut, the dome shaped kind which accounted for the shadows that shifted into weird shapes from the swinging lights I had seen when I first became conscious, how many days before?

As I neared the 'Latrine' I noticed it was typical French type as I had seen on my previous visits to France. A corner screen open at the top and bottom with a small swing door. Peering over the door, my stomach lurched, my nose rebelled seeing the large bucket type toilet from which emitted an awful stench. My resolve faltered, but thinking of the long walk back for nothing made me grit my teeth,. Breathing through my mouth, I entered and gingerly lowering my pyjamas, I positioned myself over the bucket. Looking over the top of the screen at the beds nearby, I thought *God it must be awful for those poor sods being so near to this smell.* Not fancying sitting down on the bucket, I turned and back pedalled leaning on my sticks, backside in the air, hoping that I was over the target area, when to my dismay and horror I broke wind! It seemed to go on and on, in desperation I tried to clench my buttocks but all I succeeded in doing was to produce a gargling sound and a series of 'Phut, 'Phut, 'Phut's, like a two stroke engine!

"Oh God let me die." I groaned. I looked through the slats in the screen to see if anyone in the nearby beds had heard me. I couldn't be sure so just in case I decided to stay where I was for a minute or two, if they had heard they would have forgotten by the time I came out I reasoned. Agonising moments went by, seemingly an eternity crouched over the bucket my legs protested, so giving up I pulled up my pyjama legs, took a deep breath and walked out from behind the screen, nearly knocking the tray out of her hands, I bumped into Smiler!

"'Allo Moor-ise" she said. "Good walk eh?" I didn't say anything just hurried away head down.

CHAPTER THREE

Now that I could move about a little with the aid of my walking sticks, I was able to speak with some of the less seriously wounded soldiers, who could speak a little English. With plenty of hand movements I was able to determine many answers to my unlimited questions. Most of the wounded were Foreign Legionaries, made up mostly of Germans, Italians, Africans and Belgians. It seemed to me that the only French were Officers, Doctors, and Nurses. The legionaries came from all walks of life, deserters from the last World War, criminals on the run, failures of life either through business or love or just adventurers. But all with a common bond Loyalty to the French Legion.

Speaking with these soldiers I gradually built up a picture of what I was mixed up in. it wasn't a pretty picture by any means and confirmed my worst fears of my predicament, strengthening my determination to get in contact with the British Consul. A nasty war was going on between the North and South of Vietnam. The South Vietnamese against the Communist North was supporting the French.

One of the soldiers I talked to a lot. *Call me Tommy* He said. *No one in the Legion uses real names makes it harder to check you out.* He explained with a laugh. He was Italian. His wounds were internal, but he was very cheerful, considering the pain he must have been in. He smoked a lot which caused him to cough constantly whilst he smoked. Because his hands were heavily bandaged I sat with him and held his cigarette to his lips, we talked a lot or rather Tommy talked. I listened.

He told me that he had been wounded in an ambush in the jungle. "We were on patrol." He said. "Eight Legionaries and twenty South Vietnamese, we got pinned down, they, the South Vietnamese panicked and ran for it we couldn't stop them—" He paused making a disgusted face. "—they are cowards, always run when under fire, we have complained time and time again but no one listens, we can do better without them, if we have to fight I want to be with Legionaries who will look after my back." He lay quiet. I just sat watching him I could see the turmoil in his face. Suddenly he burst out. "That's how I got all this! Because they panicked, we can't win this war with cowards." This he said vehemently. I told him to rest and that I would return later. I waited until he closed his eyes then returned to my bed to ponder on what I had just learned.

Another time talking to a German named Hans, for him the war was over; he had lost a leg by stepping on a land mine. He was very bitter and talked contemptuously of other Legionaries, in particular the South Vietnamese Army, who he described as, Farmers in Uniform, who were not trained properly.

"Don't know how to fight, no heart for it." He said. "Not like us Germans, we are fighting men don't run away like them."

From talking to Hans I learnt that most of the German Legionaries were from the SS in World War Two, and that they formed their own regiment. I didn't like Hans as much as the others, he was arrogant making me feel uncomfortable, but nevertheless I had sympathy for him as I did for all of them.

A bond grew between Tommy and me. He thought it both funny and sad that I was amongst them, wounded by an insect not a bullet! He wanted to know all about England. I wanted to know about the war.

Because he was flat on his back and I was standing, albeit with sticks to aid me. I won! "My friend," he said. "More than the bullets that are killing us, morale is our enemy too. We have been fighting to long, this war has been going on since the Thirty's, I've been here three years now and seen lots of my friends killed, for what…? "Nothing…!" "—Because nothing has changed, nothing will ever change, the food is poor, we are out in the jungle for days on end." He stopped. I could see anger and frustration in his eyes.

"Who is the enemy Tommy?" I asked.

"Who knows my friend—" He looked at me with troubled eyes, "—you can't see them, Women, Children, they all shoot you, no uniforms to identify friend from foe. Can you see that's why we can't win, to win you must know your enemy…" He tailed off. A tear seeped out of his closed eyes slowly trickling down his cheek finally soaking into his pillow.

"I lit another cigarette and held it to his lips he dragged on it gratefully, smiling when I also took a lung full. Friends Eh?" He gasped painfully.

"Yes." I replied. "Friends," taking one of his bandaged hands gently into mine. We smoked in silence, when suddenly very quietly, he said. "Communists! I will tell you my friend but not today, I'm tired now maybe tomorrow eh?"

"Ok Tommy, thank you." I said. Getting up and going back to my bed lying there thinking over what I'd been told. The communists were fighting the French in the North of Vietnam. The French were losing men in great numbers. Losing them in jungle warfare, which they were not properly trained for, but the enemy was! Seemed to me to be a somewhat one-sided affair.

Later that day after asking permission from Smiler. I sat outside the Clinic, which was situated near to the front of the Hospital. I was in the shade because the heat was so unbearable; sweat was continually pouring from every pore in my body. There was no breeze to bring relief and flies buzzed around me causing more discomfort. Smiler had given me strict orders not to be out for more than fifteen minutes. I was eager to see part of the outside world after being cooped up inside the constant half darkness of the ward.

The Clinic was set a little nearer to the public road, whereas the Hospital and grounds were set immediately behind the Clinic, hidden from the main road by both the Clinic frontage and the dense foliage of bamboo and palm shrubs. From the main road, a turning into the Clinic grounds led straight to the main entrance, either side of this pathway were neatly set flower beds of all colours and near to the gateway were rickshaws, the drivers in a huddle talking, laughing, smoking, seemingly without a care in world.

Looking at this scene made it almost unbelievable that a war was going on, until I looked away back into the hospital grounds, and saw the heavy military presence, the gun positions, the trucks and soldiers everywhere.

Standing up swatting flies off me, I went closer to the entrance of the clinic where I had seen a shady spot hidden to the road by shrubbery. It obviously was a favourite place for the staff to take a break judging by the cigarette ends scattered in the flowerbeds. A table and chairs were set out in the shade. I sat down with relief to be out of the relentless sun for a moment. After a few minutes of relaxing listening to the sounds of insects, birds twittering, traffic on the road, I started to doze off.

A voice startled me. I squinted up into the glare of the sun and could just make out a shadowy figure standing at the table.

"I am sorry if I startled you. My name is Doctor Jean-Etienne. May I sit down and join you?" I was still a little flustered, but sitting up in my chair replied. "Of course you may, my pleasure." Thanking me he sat down placing a cup of coffee onto the table, and taking out of his pocket, a pack of cigarettes offering me one, which I accepted. After lighting our cigarettes I was just about to introduce myself, he stayed me with his hand saying. "I know who you are, when you were first brought here I was one of your doctors." Sipping his coffee he went on. "I can see a big difference now, you very nearly died on us. But…" smiling now jokingly. "—we are good at our job, no?" I didn't disagree

I asked him how he thought the war was going good or bad? He thought a moment before replying.

"Er, how do you say in English, 'Stalemate?'"

"Yes" I replied. Nodding he said. "We are now in a position where we are not going forward and not going backwards, you understand?"

I nodded. "I think so."

"Well," he continued. "we are an army too far away from our Politicians. They can't make up their minds what to do, so we stand still until they do, and this is what happens…" Pointing to the hospital.

"We need more troops from France, but have to wait until our Government makes its mind up whilst our enemy Ho-Chin-Minh. has many more soldiers than us maybe five to ten against our one in some area's—"

"You mean they out-number you up to ten to one?" I interrupted.

He nodded his head glumly. "Yes maybe more, our strongest troops are mixed German and French, they are fighting in Haiphong in the north, here in the south we have to rely on the south Vietnamese army to support our legionnaires." He went on to explain in an embittered tone that most of the south Vietnamese had family here, and often took off their uniforms and went back to their families with pilfered rations.

"You can't recognise them, their officers won't, because they do the same! Most of the soldiers couldn't care less who wins as long as they can feed their families. I don't really blame them." With this he got up to go remarking of how nice it was to talk to me and would see me again no doubt and that I shouldn't over do things as I was still a long way off a full recovery. "Plenty of rest and medicine." Was his parting shot.

Everyone I talked to didn't seem to think that they would win this war! This didn't make me feel any easier, what made me more uneasy still, was when Tommy told me that around the perimeter of the hospital on the edge of the jungle, the French had strung empty tin cans as a form of an early warning system against Guerrilla attacks!

Tommy had lent me a shirt because the shirt I had been wearing when I had been brought here was now yellow with sweat, and stank.

"Borrow one of my shirts whilst yours gets washed." He had said. Probably so as not to embarrass me, that was the type of man he was. I was grateful because I was aware that my clothes, for what they were worth, did pong a little! It was too big for me; we both laughed when I was unsuccessfully trying to roll the sleeves up.

"You're too fat and I'm too thin." I said. "Anyway thanks Tommy how about a tie!" Our laughter attracted Smiler to come over; she joined in laughing as she helped me to roll my sleeves up. It was an army issue shirt. I remarked that by wearing it didn't mean I'd joined the army! We all laughed at my joke.

It was times like this when she was helping me to do things, like washing, combing my hair, giving me medicine that my thoughts went back to my childhood…

My mother used to smile whilst doing these things for me. I loved to see my mum smile, she would smile with delight when I brought home, after a long weekend on the local Golf course caddying, the princely sum of Two Shillings and Sixpence. I experienced enormous pleasure sitting at the table counting all the coins; these were some of the few times my mum looked happy.

Other times by searching the Golf course for lost balls then selling them back at the Club House I was able to bring more money home, I would get back ' One Shilling' pocket money. On these occasions I felt quite grown up helping with the wages! Having five children to bring up with only my Fathers wage every little bit helped my parents. So I looked forward to the ritual of counting the weekend money at the table…

CHAPTER FOUR

Little by little my strength returned, but the doctor insisted that rest, and more rest was the order of the day. Explaining that the Malaria strain affecting me was the worst of three strains of Malaria called 'Subtertian Malaria.' Unlike the other two strains, which had remission stages of two or three days between each attack allowing the body to fight it. This strain, I had, didn't! So not allowing the body to defend itself. Apparently the parasite carried by this mosquito, enters the blood stream and attacks the liver, spleen and the brain, together with rapid body weight loss. Without immediate and constant medical care death can result. Quinine by tablet or injection is the only means of controlling the disease. He went on at length about Malaria, but I could only grasp enough to know that I was very lucky to be alive and now knew why I felt as I did. Especially after he told me that I had had Pneumonia on top of everything else.

"You are not better yet, but you are over the crisis stage, it will take some time before your body heals. You will need your medication for some time yet to allow your body to heal and put back the body weight you have lost. But above all else to help speed up your recovery, you must not exert yourself and get plenty of rest." He said firmly.

I was full of admiration for the way the hospital staff could converse with me in my own language, but was disgusted with myself for not being able to converse with them in theirs. But I'll learn I told myself.

Parts of days, and all of some, the outside noises of bombs and aero-
planes overhead ceased as if someone had called half time, the quietness
to my ears was in itself deafening! It was in these moments of silence
that gave me time to put together all that I had seen and heard concerning this war. To try to understand why a country divided into two halves
wanted to fight and kill each other? The horrors I had witnessed of
these soldiers here in this hospital, who only a day or so ago, I had held
their hands in mutual comfort, helped them smoke a cigarette, some
had died alone on a dirty stretcher, not able to see or hear their loved
ones.

The thought of me dying out here without seeing my parents again
engulfed me in such sorrow that without realising it I was crying, tears
running into the sweat already drenching my body. I felt so alone, even
with all these people around me couldn't alter this feeling of loneliness.

Why don't Politicians who want war pick a champion from each
country put them in a boxing ring to slug it out winner takes all? No
more needless futile bloodletting! *Your kidding yourself lad there is no
money to be made in that idea*! My mind told m

The next day I felt unwell. My head was at bursting point and my
heart was racing, the nurse had insisted that I stayed on my stretcher
bed. I lay there for most of the morning until the call of nature made me
struggle to rise. Reaching for my sticks, intending to talk some more
with the soldiers, on the way back from the latrine. I made my way to
the end of the ward to the latrine. As I passed Tommy's bed space I
noticed it was empty. Spotting a nurse I beckoned her over and asked
where Tommy was, she looked at me for a moment then taking my arm
in hers said quietly that he had died in the night.

I was devastated, if the nurse had not been holding me I would have
collapsed. I felt my legs giving way and my lungs seize up, as I struggled
for air. Tommy? Who only yesterday had laughed with me as we
smoked, who had lent me his shirt, gone…Died? I had not said goodbye

my friend. Numb with shock I struggled to my bed sat down and cried vowing to keep his shirt forever.

Smiler's seeing me distressed and knowing how close Tommy and I had become, came over to me and suggested that I went outside into the grounds and have a cool drink and a cigarette. She insisted that I had a blanket over my shoulders even though it was extremely hot outside, when I started to protest she said fussily.

"You must not stay out there too long and keep this blanket over you even though its hot your body with all the sweating can catch a cold very easy." She helped me outside to a shady spot, as she was about to go back into the hospital, I put my hand on her arm to stop her saying. "I don't know your name."

"Genevieve-Marie." She replied. I rolled the name over in my head, but knew I would have difficulty remembering it, let alone saying it. Instead I said.

"That is hard for me to pronounce I've always thought of you as Smiler because of your smile. Do you mind if I just call you Smiler?" "Oui Cheri." She said. Ruffling my hair, smiling as she went inside.

Looking around me I could see dense green jungle. Palm trees stood about ten feet tall; the fronds were possibly four feet across swaying gently in the hot breeze. *I am a sitting target if anyone is hiding behind those.* I thought. Towering above the Palms, were trees thick in the trunk with heavy boughs laden with masses of green leaves shimmering in the sunlight. As far as the eye could see there wasn't a break in the dense and thick wooded jungle.

I could hear the birds calling to each other, just another peaceful day. *This could be a beautiful place if you didn't know a war was going on.* I mused. But glancing around the grounds, shattered that thought. Everywhere there was evidence of a heavy military presence, gun positions all pointing at the jungle, trucks dotted about, soldiers busy doing many things, a scene of high tension activity.

I noticed that my ward wasn't the only one. More Nissan type huts were clustered in-groups. I counted six from where I was sitting and calculated that if they all had the same number of wounded as my ward, which I estimated as fifty, then this was a major field hospital and that the casualty rate was very high. Some soldiers with arms in slings, or just bandaged were like me, sitting in the sun enjoying the respite. Distant rumblings were the only reminders that this peace and solitude couldn't last.

I must have dozed off because a voice abruptly brought me back to earth saying. "Moor-ise, this is Monsieur Evans from the Embassy." Excited anticipation must have shown in my face because on looking up, I saw Smiler looking at me, a strange expression on her face, was it my imagination or did she look a little sad? I had no time to dwell on it as my eyes fell eagerly on the man with her.

He was a rather agitated looking man very thin. He was dressed in a Tropical lightweight suit. He was going bald and was mopping his face with a rather large damp looking handkerchief with one hand, clutching a Panama hat with the other.

Smiler placed a tray containing a jug of iced orange juice onto the table, I saw that there was only two glasses. Sitting down opposite me Mr Evans began to speak in a nervous rapid voice, which made me want to say. *Hey, slow down what's the rush?* He kept glancing over his shoulder whilst talking as if he expected someone to sneak up behind him and pinch his hat or something. This at first amused me, but amusement soon turned to dismay when he told me that my ship had been forced to leave. *Because it was very dangerous to stay.* Was how he put it. It was at this point that I protested, that being a British subject I wanted to be moved to somewhere safer than here, or better still to rejoin my ship no matter where it was. He shook his head, glancing over his shoulder, saying that it wasn't possible at the moment because the Vietminh were too close. But in the mean time until he could arrange something I would have to stay here, assuring me that better accommodation would be found as soon as possible, and when the time came he would arrange with the doctors for my treatment to continue. "Be patient." he almost pleaded. "I'll be in touch." He didn't walk away he scurried away. I immediately nick named him Twitchy!

After he had gone I just slouched in my chair thinking of what he had said. So I was going to be here longer than I had thought! This didn't make me feel any better, the excitement I had felt when Smiler had introduced us had gone, and only apprehension remained.

My head was starting to ache again. *It's this heat, I feel as though I'm in the shower all the time.* I thought. Wiping my face on my shirtsleeve I closed my eyes feeling drowsy…

There were shouts, people were screaming, I looked in the direction of the commotion in alarm. Two Vietnamese soldiers were running towards me. Rifles pointed and shouting something that I couldn't understand. I tried to shout back but no sound passed my lips. What I had thought as two soldiers, was now more, they had appeared without my noticing. Their broad squat faces were twisted snarling masks of hate; they were shooting at the wounded soldiers who were sitting quietly in the sun.

Horrified, unable to move I looked on seeing bandaged heads already blood stained spurting more blood. Blood…forming a stream as it merged together. The stream was gathering speed rushing towards me; the soldiers were also rushing towards me as though they were trying to get to me before the blood stream did! I knew I was moaning but couldn't hear myself. The faces of the onrushing soldiers seemed to be changing; first squat with flattened noses, then elongated with long antenna like hairs protruding from their noses, and black egg-shaped eyes. As they came nearer, their rifles seemed to be changing too, getting thinner waving about. I must be imagining this, it's a trick of the sun, a heat haze or some-thing making them look like that. I wanted to believe it, but most of all I wanted to get out of my chair and hide.

I struggled with all my strength to rise from my chair shouting Go back. Go back. Leave me alone. I seemed to be glued to my chair. The black eyes just glared at me, one of the bendy arms reached out to grab me...

I shouted out. 'Nyaah.' Jolting upright pressing back into my chair...

"Ssshhh." A voice said in my ear hands on my shoulders. "You were having a bad dream, everything is all right now." Opening my eyes I saw Smiler bending over me. I looked at the floor fully expecting to see my heart pumping away in all the blood, because I was certain that my heart had jumped out of my chest. Instead all I saw was the green grass. My heart was still pumping away furiously in my chest, my relief was so great, that I felt a warm feeling between my legs. Miserably with tears in my eyes, I looked up at her and said. "Smiler. I've wet myself." She helped me to my feet pulling my head onto her shoulder, I felt so unhappy and embarrassed and just wanted to bury my face in her bosom and never let go. The only time I felt safe and secure was when I was with her, when she wasn't around I found myself looking amongst the other nurses for her.

CHAPTER FIVE

Back inside the ward after having a good strip wash and a clean pair of pyjamas, I was still feeling uneasy and remembering the dream. I couldn't help wondering if my mind would heal or would I go through this all my life. Having these nightmares? Smiler brought me my clothes which I had been wearing when I was taken ill on board ship, she had washed and ironed them herself she told me.

"Better to sit outside in your own clothes." She said. I agreed. Looking at the white linen shirt and shorts neatly pressed reminded me of when I used to do it for the Skipper. Laying his daily 'whites' out on his bunk. Being his personal valet, commonly known as the Skippers Tiger. It also helped me to believe that I was on the road to recovery. "Feeling better now Moor-ise?" she asked.

I looked at her, seeing her really for the first time. She was perhaps five foot six I guessed. I was five foot nine and she was a few inches smaller than I was. Her face was round with a pert nose, full lips with a hint of a pout. She was lightly tanned with just a suggestion of lipstick. The kind of lips you couldn't help but want to kiss! But her eyes…they were brown pools that I would have willingly drowned in, the corners crinkled when she smiled, her teeth were white and even, emphasised by her tan, she had light brown hair tucked under a white cap. Not like the caps the other nurses wore, they looked like the paper boats I used to make for my younger brother to sail on the boating lake when I was at school. No hers was more like a pillbox hat. Maybe she was an officer nurse?

I reminded myself to ask her later. Under her loose white coat I couldn't be sure as to whether she was full figured or not, but did notice that her legs were tanned and shapely with small feet in open toed sandals. All this probably only took seconds, but to me it seemed an age as I committed her image to memory. She seemed uncomfortable with my staring at her, and fussed with my laundry on the bed. I could feel myself blushing and felt awkward. *What's the matter with me?* I wondered. *Your in love you idiot that's what's the matter!*

"Will you sit outside with me for a little while?" I asked her rather timidly. "I need to talk to you."

"Later." She replied. "I have a lot to do, but when I have some free time I will come and talk with you, Okay Cheri?" "Okay" I replied.

Going outside we found a shady spot under a large tree; I sat with my back to the wall of the ward. Placing a glass jug of lemonade down onto the table, she poured me a glass. The ice chinked as she poured and the sun shone through the ice cubes, making them sparkle like diamonds; creating a miniature rainbow effect. Together with the birds chirping in the trees, making this a little patch of paradise. *If only this moment was in another place, another time another world!* I thought. *The suns gone to your head lad, you're going soft.* My mind told me.

"I don't care." I blurted out.

"Pardon Cheri?" I looked up startled, I hadn't meant to say anything. Just thinking aloud about how lovely this spot is and what a beautiful place this could be." I said still flustered."

"Yes it was once, but not any more." She said sadly.

"I meant this spot here with you." Cursing inwardly for blushing.

"Thank you sir." This said coyly. "Enjoy your drink I will come back shortly." I watched her back as she walked away. Feelings I'd never experienced before coursed through me. My heart was tat-tooing, and my mouth was dry. I raised my glass taking a sip of the cold lemonade.

Feeling more relaxed I sat staring into space remembering how I had arrived in Saigon…

On entering the Mekong Delta, I was on deck with some of the crew. We watched in awe, the spectacle of the shells arcing across the sky, listening to loud explosions as shells falling short of their targets, exploded on the banks sending earth and debris high into the sky! We instinctively ducked our heads as seemingly shells were heading directly at us.

Christ! said Taffy, as a shell exploded with tremendous force nearby sending great gouts of water up into the air, the wind carrying it over the ship as spray. We are sitting ducks! What happens if one of them hit the hold? He meant that our two forward holds had bombs in one and detonators in the other. The after holds had shells, whilst lashed on deck were trucks and jeeps.

You won't know anything about it, we would be blown clear out of the water, I answered a little shakily. You're a bloody good comforter. Taffy muttered.

It was a hairy experience. It seemed to go on for hours, but was probably only about an hour. I was mesmerised by this gigantic fireworks display and the deafening crescendo it orchestrated. I had to clap my hands over my ears to stop the vibration of my eardrums. I was both fascinated and afraid, my heart was thumping and my bowels were grinding!

As the ship neared the entrance to the docks of Saigon, I could see large ammunition dumps like small hillocks every few yards apart, as far as the eye could see, lining the quayside, and military everywhere. It was then that realisation sunk in that we were really and truly, no going back, in a real war! In trepidation I went below deck to prepare for docking duties.

Docking was always pleasurable for me. I loved the excitement of seeing new sights, and listening to the noises of the ship docking. The muted shouts of command, the ringing of bells from bridge to engine room, the trembling of the deck as the big engines go into reverse, giving off a high pitched whine, making the whole ship shudder and the sea broiling from the huge props. The sound of the winches playing out the mooring ropes, thicker than ones arm, steel chains on steel decks. I loved all these sounds, they were beautiful sounds to me, and I loved them almost as much as I loved the sea its self. This was my life I wouldn't change it. The feel of a moving deck under my feet and the ocean spray in my face, giving me the feeling of complete freedom, was all I wanted.

I made my way to the galley thinking Skipper will be ready for his cup of coffee now. Being Captains Tiger meant, that apart from my normal duties as steward in the officer's mess, I looked after the Skipper as a personal valet. Cleaned his cabin, laid his uniform of the day out on his bunk, pressed his whites that sort of thing. I enjoyed my job because I liked and respected my Skipper full stop. He was a fair and just man, not like some Skipper's I've sailed under.

As in all ports, the first opportunity to go ashore was uppermost in our thoughts, however we were informed by the first officer that we had to be in groups of six accompanied by two soldiers and we were not to leave the dock area or the soldiers. Taffy, my other shipmates, and myself Steve, Chas, Harry, and Big Brummie formed our expedition band, being that we were all in the same age group. Our two-soldier escort didn't seem much older than us, one hardly shaved! They were French Legionnaires and spoke understandable broken English, enough for us to understand the dangers that could befall us.

One soldier pointing to the Ammo dumps said. Saboteurs. Boom—and pulling his finger across his throat said with a laugh.—we watch for Commie! As we walked along the dockside they explained why. The Vietminh, Commies, as they referred to them, were all around and it was hard to spot the Guerrilla's from the local population. Pointing to our clothes, one said. No uniform, hard-to-tell, come-quick, kills then-vanish. Hearing this we decided to stay near our ship.

First bar we come to then eh lads? Said. Taffy

There's one over there. Pointed out Big Brummie. We headed towards it; it looked no different to all dockside bars the world over. Shabby front, loud music, raucous voices.

Yes this will do me cocker. I said going in. The air was like a blue fog with cigarette smoke. The blaring music was deafening. Glasses everywhere, on the tables, the floor, full, half full; the crowded bar was, besieged by noisy drinkers wanting refills. The sweating barmen, cigarettes hanging from their mouths, seemingly unconcerned at the chaos at the bar. Drunks were lolling around with their heads down on their chests, others with their arms buried to their elbows up the skirts of the local bar belles, who didn't seem to care as long as they had a drink in their hand. Someone was trying to sing, to a chorus from the bar of Put a sock in it. Another was trying to follow the singer off key and a beat behind!

Up-righting a table, we sat near to the open door because it was cooler, and to some extent spared us the cloying choking smoke. The soldiers stayed outside refusing our offered drink with gestures meaning no thanks.

Dick-bloody-Turpin prices grumbled Taffy, putting down on the table the bottles of beer. Ten Bob a bottle. We all chipped in to a kitty so that Taffy could get his money back; the beer was almost a week's wages for most of us.

We sat there a cold beer in our hands not saying much just eyeing up the talent, with only one thought in our minds, to get our leg over! Looking around the bar saying the same tired old remark, said a thousand times, don't like the look of yours! The night was progressing nicely. By now we were sharing a bottle between two of us to keep the cost down, we were mellow and even joining in with the off key singer, forgetting all that was going on around us.

Our soldiers bursting in abruptly brought us back into the real world. Quick. Quick. They shouted. Come quick. Pulling at our arms. Big Brummie grabbed me, I was a little tipsy, he was from the Midlands, big chap over six feet. For some unknown reason he always came ashore with me, we had become good mates; he was deck crew not catering like me, and he was a bloody good scrapper! Came in handy having Big Brummie behind me as I was always getting involved in bar brawls.

Outside people were running about shouting and screaming. I could hear gunfire. The soldiers with us were pushing and shoving us back in the direction of our shi, shouting to each other in rapid French. Moments later a loud bang from behind us followed by a hot rushing wind sweeping over us, causing me to stumble, looking back all we could see was thick smoke and dust.

Later back on board ship we learnt that, next door to the bar we had been in, was the police station, the guerrilla's had blown it up, taking our bar with it. This was a sobering thought. What if we hadn't had our soldiers with us?

CHAPTER SIX

I jerked upright; a hand touching my head brought me out of my day dreaming, looking up I saw 'Smiler.' "I am on my break now." she smiled. "Would you like some coffee?" Still drowsy I just nodded. Whilst she was away getting the coffee, I absently combed my hair with my fingers, and became frustrated, when I found I hadn't got a tie on, when I attempted to straighten it.

She returned placing a tray with a coffeepot, cream, sugar and two cups. When we were settled she offered me a cigarette, leaning over the table to light it for me. We sat sipping coffee and smoking not saying anything, I looked at her she seemed more relaxed but tired, she was absently tapping her cigarette into the ashtray. I was content just to look at her, the little mannerisms, like when she blew smoke from her cigarette she tilted her head slightly blowing smoke from the side of her mouth, I could have sat there saying nothing just having her with me was enough.

But I needed to know so much more about this war, about my illness. She reached across the table to crush out her cigarette in the ashtray, I also reached out taking her hand in mine, saying as I did so. "I need you to explain to me why all these jumbled thoughts and nightmares are constantly with me, why all this is happening and for what—?" I stopped. Looking down at her hand my heart sank.

My world slowly started to crumble like a sandcastle when the tide comes in. She was wearing a *wedding* ring. Looking up at her I saw that she was staring intently into my eyes.

"What is the matter Cheri?" She withdrew her hand gently. I noticed it was shaking slightly. I sat still watching her numbly; emotions washing over me that I'd never experienced before. She poured us both another coffee whilst I lit a cigarette with a shaking hand. My mind was racing with this shattering discovery. I was outraged that *anyone*, someone, could share my Smiler. The thought made me clench my fists so tightly that my nails dug into my palms.

"You are married!" I almost sobbed

"Moor-ise" she said gently. "Why does it make you upset?"

"Because." I blurted. "I love you!" I felt so miserable. All the girls I had ever known in all the ports I'd been too, I'd never felt like this with any of them, it had always been a drink, a girl, a good time. But with Smiler it was different; I couldn't put into words, if anyone asked me how I felt about her. I didn't want to take her to bed and forget about it the next day. I wanted to be with her, talk with her, hold her hand, comfort her, like she comforts me.

She laughed that lovely laugh like tinkling waterfalls! "Cheri all or most patients fall in love with their nurse." I started to protest, but she put up her hand to silence me, and said in a soft and gentle voice.

"I was married for five years and was nursing in a big hospital in Lyon. My husband was sent here to fight—" she paused, her lips trembled. "—and he was killed here in Saigon." This was said quietly. I could see she was becoming distressed. Rising from my side of the table I went to her, putting my arms around her shoulders holding her, inwardly sharing her pain and cursing myself for being selfish.

Moments later tossing her head and smiling through eyes, glistening with unshed tears; she looked at me and said simply.

"That's why I am here to be near him and help our soldiers." I lit two cigarettes handing one to her not knowing what to say, and decided not to say anything now, or in the future about her husband, unless she brought the subject up.

Trying to lighten the tension of the moment, I asked the only thing that came into my head. Why she wore a different hat to the other nurses? She explained that she was the senior nurse and was in charge of all medicines, part of her duties was to train the junior nurses, mainly South Vietnamese, so if she had to leave this hospital the nurses would be capable of tending to the more serious of the wounded.

"Are you planing on going back to France then?" I asked.

"Yes, soon I hope." She replied. "I have been here two years now and am sick of all the killing." She blew smoke from the side of her mouth. "I don't think we are winning this war, all those wasted lives, I just want to return home to France."

"Mr Evans said he will arrange for me to be transferred to some safer place." I said. "Do you know when that may be and where?"

She shook her head. "I don't know 'Moor-ise, but it must be arranged with the doctors, you are still very sick you know. "You will need plenty of medicine yet, it will take time for your body to heal, also your head."

"What do you mean? I feel stronger already." I protested.

"You think you are but believe me you are not." She said with a smile.

"You must have regular injections to help your blood cells beat the Malaria disease, also your daily Quinine tablets, otherwise you would have a relapse and be back where you started and we wouldn't want that would we?"

"But I could keep coming to the Clinic for my medication." I countered.

"Saigon City is more than a mile away from here, it would be too tiring for you to come that distance each day until you are stronger and can travel. Anyway I thought you liked being here with me?" She said coyly.

I didn't know how to reply. I wanted to get as far away from the hospital as I could, away from all the sick and dying, but on the other hand I couldn't bear the thought that this would mean leaving Smiler. She glanced at her watch, exclaiming "Goodness. Look at the time I must go, we will sit again another time, and have a chat." She rose leaning over me and brushed her lips to my cheek saying. "Au revoir Cheri."

Watching her walk away I felt sad, and elated, sad about her husband and why she was here, but elated that I could see her as I first saw her, before I knew about her husband. *She is much older than I am but what the heck I love her!*

Over the next few days I just wandered about the hospital grounds aimlessly. Smiler had gone to the airport to supervise the transfer of the more serious wounded to be flown out to a bigger hospital in a safer place. I didn't learn about this, until she had gone. It was only when another nurse was giving me my injection, I had casually asked where she was, the nurse told me that she had gone in the night, that this was a regular thing. She was on call at a moment's notice, but she will be back in a day or so the nurse assured me. Did I detect amusement in her glance?

Did she and the other nurses know how I felt about Smiler? I worried about her safety and felt very much alone.

It was whilst I was wandering about, and thinking about her that I strayed further away from the hospital than I had ever before. I had passed gun posts, the soldiers manning them nodding to me cheerfully. The guns to me looked massive. The soldiers had obviously recognised my hospital pyjamas. *Probably think I'm one of them.*

In the distance I could see dense green bushes with what I thought looked like water sparkling in the sunlight, so making my way towards it I came upon the tin cans on string which I had been told about. *The early warning system!* Stepping over them I walked across a flat strip of grassy land towards the bushes, but hadn't taken more than a few steps, when I heard shouting behind me. Looking back I could see soldiers from the gun post running towards me waving their arms and shouting. Stop! Stop!

I stood still. Perplexed! *Must be out of bounds, now I'll get told off.* The soldiers stopped at the cans on string shouting "Be careful, walk slowly back in a straight line, look at us don't look down." Not wanting to upset them any more but not knowing what all the fuss was about, I did as they asked feeling a little stupid because it was only a few yards back to them. I was grabbed and hauled over the string, then pointing to the grassy strip one said. "No. No very dangerous. Landmines! I went numb with shock remembering Hans who had lost his leg through landmines.

Oh God! What will 'Smiler say? I looked back at the bushes thinking, *How many ghosts are out there staring at me, silently screaming, Stop! Our ranks can't take any more!* Shuddering at my lucky escape, I thanked the soldiers and unsteadily made my way back to the ward. I remained there for the rest of the day on my bed, just thinking about it, and thinking that, not only was I lucky in my narrow escape, but how stupid I'd been in the first place. I felt ill and was coughing so much that my chest hurt, my head pounded, I lay there willing sleep to overcome me.

I spent more time in the ward after my lucky escape; just waiting for Smiler to return it was four days now since I had last seen her and it felt like Eternity. I now knew for sure that I wanted to be with her always. *Even if I have to join the French Army.* I told myself. *When I get better I will take her out to dances and things; she may then fall in love with me.* I tried to convince myself that age didn't matter that I knew people back home who had big age differences and they were happy. My head hurt I wished she would come back soon.

Staying in the ward made me more aware of what went on, on a daily basis and to acquaint myself with its lay out. The walls being steel and a complete curve retained the heat. The only air that desultory swirled about, came from the only doorway at the front of the ward. Originally this would have opened to the outside but an annex had been built to house the clinic and staff rooms. This meant that the outside air had to circulate through the clinic before it came into the ward very little did. Maybe it was the stench that kept it out! Although at least once or sometimes twice a day depending on the strength of the smell. The concrete floors were swilled down with disinfectant water. It was a losing battle against the latrine at the far end, and the body sweat of the sick and dying.

On really bad days I had learnt to breath through my mouth which helped in a small way. I never did figure out how they emptied the bucket without being seen, they would have to carry it the length of the ward past us all, but not once did I see them, I couldn't work that out at all! But what I did work out was, if I arose early in the morning the bucket was empty and smelled strongly of disinfectant, so I could dwell awhile in comparative comfort. Even the flies didn't get up early because they didn't like the smell of disinfectant! Once the disinfectant had worn off, the flies were out in droves and seemed to begrudge you sitting amongst them on the bucket, by angrily buzzing around. The more daring ones tried to bite you, which is why I went early. Later in the day if I were outside I would go behind a bush or the side of the hut. No flies on me, so to speak!

My stretcher had been moved nearer to the door because more and more stretchers were coming in and going out. The dead was moved at night, so I was seeing new faces all the time. I was grateful for being moved nearer to the door, letting myself believe that Smiler had, had something to do with it. It was slightly cooler, but I needed to be, for the sweat just dripped of me constantly, like rain dripping off the trees, and I was eating salt tablets like sweets.

The nurses had assured me that the sweating would ease off once my fever subsided. Yet I felt most days that I was better than the previous day, until Mother Nature said. Sorry Kid,' time to sweat again, and laid me on my back for a day. It was one of those, Sorry Kid, days when I first met Garlic Breath. I was dozing when my nose twitched. *Ah! caught you emptying the bucket.* I thought gleefully, but on opening my eyes, which instantly started to water, I saw an uniformed figure with his back to me in the doorway talking to a nurse, the smell of garlic was so strong that my stomach nudged me saying. *Sorry mate, this is where we part company.* I gurgled, Aghh. Or something like that which made him turn towards me. Beaming all over his face, he made his way towards me with his hand out saying. "English Eh?" He was quite tall, going bald. He had medals on his chest, which I'm sure, if I could have read French, one would have said. French Champion Garlic Eater! He had a florid face red cheeks, but a redder bulbous nose. *Bet I know what your job is at Christmas.* I thought to myself. On the end of his nose was a big dew-drop that dangled precariously, I watched fascinated hoping it wouldn't land on me when he leant over, suddenly, magically, it disappeared up his nostril! "Hope you are okay, getting better yes?" Grabbing my hand and pumping it. I moved my head, desperately seeking downwind of him but it was useless, it hammered at me from all angles. I wondered how long I could hold my breath before my face looked like his! I pretended, by clutching my groin that I needed to go to the latrine and hastily beat a retreat in that direction, his voice followed on the garlic wave. "See you again Eh?" *Not if I can bloody help it.* I said under my breath.

Later one of the nurses, who had witnessed our encounter, gave me a cloth soaked in disinfectant which I kept draped over the handle of my stretcher. If Mr Garlic Breath came back again I was going to clamp it over my mouth and pretend to have a coughing fit, then beat the retreat to the latrine. *Yes sir that's what I'm going to do.* I told my stomach!

CHAPTER SEVEN

I was sitting outside one afternoon with a Coolie hat tipped over my eyes against the suns relentless rays. I had borrowed it from one of the cleaning staff from the clinic. One of the nurses had told me that the local people wore these hats to keep the sun off them whilst working in the Paddy Fields. Rice is the main food supply. In fact I had been told that the Vietminh soldiers in the North were being paid in rice because the Piastre, the local currency was practically worthless. The French had devalued it so often, that even services and supplies to the army were being paid for with rice. With the population being so poor it was easy for the Vietminh to recruit the peasants to be Guerrillas by night for hit and run ambushes, and paying them with rice so they could feed their families.

The French paid dearly in casualties all over Vietnam, I had learnt, so did the Vietminh, but their advantage over the French was they had an unlimited supply of men, women and even children. The French didn't!

I thought it a cruel world we lived in. These people go to bed at night and wake up to the sounds and reality of war, after a while it must become normal to them that's the frightening part of it all. Tears pricked my eyes as I was thinking of this. *'Hey'* I scolded myself, men *don't cry!*

"'Allo Moor-ise." I looked up. Joy flooded through me there she was smiling down at me. I couldn't help myself, jumping up I clasped her in my arms hugging her tightly. Feeling her soft body against mine sent thrills through me, I could only murmur her name over and over again, and despite myself I felt aroused. Freeing herself, by gently pushing me away, I could see in her eyes that she too was experiencing something. In a slightly husky voice she asked if I would like some coffee, or lemonade.

"Lemonade please." I replied in an unsteady voice.

"Ok, I have some time off, you can tell me what has been going on here whilst I've been away."

When she returned with the tray of iced lemonade and we were settled with our drinks, she gave me a cigarette. Not having any money, I had to rely on having cigarettes given to me. *Once I'm out of here, I'll get 'Twitchy to give me a sub, then I can repay her for all these cigarettes.* I promised myself. I longed for a Woodbine. The cigarettes I was having were either French or local, both were harsh to my throat, but I wasn't complaining.

She was horrified when I told her of the incident with the minefield. "You must be careful Moor-ise, when the Japanese were defeated here in 1946 they left all of Vietnam mined, there are many thousands all over the country, many people especially children, are killed every day with mines." She took my hand in hers. "Promise me you will not do that again." She looked very seriously at me.

"I promise." I said wishing I hadn't told her. But she went into a fit of giggling when I told her about Garlic Breath. Between giggles she told me that he was the Padre. This set me off; we both sat there with tears in our eyes. Gulping some lemonade and wiping my eyes I said.

"God help the soldiers taking Communion!" We both roared. It was nice to see her relaxed and happy.

"What have you been doing for five days?" I asked. "I've been going crazy thinking I wouldn't see you again." She touched my hand for a moment. "It hasn't been a happy time for me." Explaining that she had been moving the badly wounded to bigger hospitals, where they could be tended better than in a field hospital, some had to be flown out to

Cambodia, or Korea. Then when they were strong enough repatriated back to France.

She talked of attacks to the airfield which made it difficult for the aircraft to take off, and of planes trying to land to pick up the wounded being shot at, a lot having to crash land, meaning that fewer planes were available to ferry the wounded to safety.

"For every fit fighting soldier, we have three or four wounded." She added. "That's what we know of—out there." Pointing to the jungle. "Who really knows for sure!"

Looking in the direction of the jungle digesting her words I couldn't help thinking. *Nature was the biggest reclaimer in this war. For it was impossible for either side to remove their dead from the numerous battlefields, in the jungle in particular. So they just lay there rotting, until nature embraces them to her bosom…Earth!*

I'd heard tales from the soldiers in the hospital, who said that they often had to leave their dead in the jungle, or they themselves would have died. Which saddened me to think of all the families, who would never know where their loved ones really were, couldn't lay them to rest in peace. The Futile Reality of All Wars!

Lighting us both another cigarette. I prompted her to carry on talking now that she seemed in the mood to do so.

"Tell me something about this war." I said. "How it started and why?"

"To do that, I will have to start at the beginning." She replied. I poured her another glass of lemonade as she began to talk; her voice changed key often from soft, to impassioned, as her emotions varied.

"Vietnam has been a French Colony since the Eighteen Hundreds. In 1930 the Communists led by the self-styled leader calling himself Ho-Chi-Min. Instigated an uprising against French rule, and tried to declare independence for North Vietnam. France would not agree, sending troops to quell the uprising, they succeeded and an uneasy truce prevailed. Then World War Two came to Asia. 'Ho-Chi-Minh faded into obscurity during this war. The enemy now was the Japanese.

In 1945, supported by America. Ho-Chi-Minh re-amerged as a force to be reckoned with, defeating the Japanese in a fierce battle, capturing Hanoi, and declaring North Vietnam an independent nation—" She paused lighting another cigarette. Blowing smoke out of the corner of her mouth she continued. "—again my Government would not accept this—" She paused again. Looking directly at me carried on. "—nor would yours Moor-ise, your country supported the South for fear of losing the strategic position of Saigon and jeopardise their attempt to re-colonise Burma, Malaya, and Singapore. The threat of Ho-Chi-Minh' was so strong to their plans that your country re-armed the Japanese to hold back the communist

Vietminh, to defend and hold Saigon. But this failed because the Vietminh were too strong and the result was hundreds of hostages were taken by the Vietminh—" Pausing again she said. "—For you to understand Moor-ise I must tell you our history here, it will help you to understand why this war is still going on Okay?"

I nodded. "I do understand please go on this is very interesting for me."

Reaching for the cigarettes, and lighting for both of us. We smoked in silence for a while, I could see in her face that she was having an inward battle with herself. Some memories must have been painful for her and I admired her for her courage to relate all this to me including her personal involvement.

Whilst she was composing herself I thought about what she had told me so far and realised that worse was to come. With a sigh she went on with her story.

"My Country was forced to have talks with Ho-Chi-Minh, who still wanted Vietnam to be a free state within the French Union. Reluctantly my country agreed, but the agreement couldn't hold, and the fighting began yet again with French cruisers shelling Haiphong, resulting in all out war which is still going on after all these years." She paused again. "So now we not only have Ho-Chi-Minh to contend with Politically, we now have General Vo Nguyen Giap, who is an expert in jungle and guerrilla warfare, and he is making it very hard for us. We are not very expert in jungle fighting, and are losing too many of our men to unseen enemies. Hit and run tactics not only in the jungle but also in our cities, are filling our hospitals to overflowing, that is why I am always having to go away to help evacuate our soldiers…" Her eyes glistened with held back tears. "…So you see Cheri it is not safe to go far anywhere in this country, that is why I want you to be careful." I wanted to cry for her, in my heart I did.

"What are the ordinary people like?" I enquired. Trying to change the mood as I could see she was getting upset again.

"They are passive and peaceful people, all they want is to tend their Paddy fields, and look after their families, but are unwittingly helping the Vietminh, who mingle with them killing our soldiers in one's and two's. Here one minute gone the next" She stopped and lit another cigarette with a shaking hand.

Shaking my head in wonder of what she had told me said. "I have heard a lot of what you have said, from the soldiers I've spoken to in the hospital. Now I know what this war is about…Politics…" she nodded saying. "Its history repeating itself, and will continue to repeat itself long after we have gone. No one ever learns!" Sighing and shaking her head she added. "That's why I want to go back to my country Moor-ise, because I think we will lose this war." By this time the sun was casting long shadows, we decided to go back inside the hospital.

On my own in the ward, what Smiler had told me churned around in my mind, in a way betrayal was a key feature here and to a certain degree I also had been betrayed. *By my own country!*

I started to think back, as to how it started for me, to being here in this hospital almost dying, waiting in a field hospital sick in body and mind to be reunited with my ship…

CHAPTER EIGHT

The rumours had started in India. We were docked in Calcutta. Going to Indo china, was one. Carrying Bombs, was another. A war is going on there. Was said. What's that got to do with us? Someone asked. England's not at war! Rumours were being bandied around from all sources

If we do go we will get danger money whilst in territorial waters just like we did in the Korean War. Said with some authority by Sparks. He was our radio officer. Although a big man he was running to fat, with receding hair. He was a heavy drinker and talked in a Hoity Toity way, but had knowledge of what went on and what was said on the bridge. He was our ear to officer's talk. Because of his drinking habit his fellow officers didn't tolerate him so well, so he used to come down to the crews deck to sit, drink and talk with us. He was worldly wise told all who would listen of his Connections, as he put it, of his involvement with Show Biz; of his wrecked marriage with Dorothy Squires, all through drink he admitted.

He used to be on the Cruise Liners in a prestigious position Wireless Operator earning good money, until drink pulled me down to this! was his favourite expression. By this, he meant it as a demotion to Cargo Ships, less salary and very little to do but drink. But we could tolerate him, his usefulness in gaining information for us from the officers quarters, more than made up for having to listen to his tales more than once! He could get us up-to-date information about these Indo China rumours.

All Ships crews have an unofficial spokesman who acts, I suppose as a union spokesman. Commonly known as the 'Ships Lawyer.' usually the cook! In our case though it was Taffy.

If we don't get danger money we don't sail, simple as that. He said.

Go on strike you mean? I asked. He nodded.

We will be in deep shit if we do that! Said Steve.

We got it in the Korean War. Replied Taffy.

How much? We chorused.

Thirty Shillings whilst in territorial waters. He replied.

A day? This from Steve.

No, you Burke a week. Snorted Taffy.

A noticeable gloom had settled over the crew deck like a sea mist, just creeping up on you...

I was abruptly brought out of my reverie by shouts of Nurse! Nurse! from the far end of the ward. I peered towards the shouting but couldn't make out what the fuss was about. Two nurses hurried past me. I was curious and just sat there peering down the ward. Because out of here soon for fear that I would lose my mind altogether.the ward didn't have windows and was always dim it was difficult to see clearly what was happening at the other end.

One of the nurses came back walking quickly disappearing into the clinic, returning almost immediately followed by two orderlies and a doctor. *Someone's having a bad time poor bugger!* I thought. Necks were craning from other beds a low muttering started, rising in volume as more heads were raised. The orderlies went past me carrying a stretcher covered by a bed sheet, the nurses and doctor in file behind. I still hadn't got used to being so close to dead people and my stomach knotted. Yet just being here you were always aware of death around you, you smelt it on the wind, you tasted it in your food, it engulfed your waking thoughts, even in sleep you were not spared...you dreamt it! I silently prayed that Twitchy would get me.

I didn't see much of Smiler over the next few days, she and the other nurses were very busy with the constant flow of wounded that flowed through the doors. We spoke briefly to each other, more in passing, than a sit down conversation. I missed our talks, I missed Smiler, I missed sitting with her watching the corners of her eyes crinkling as she smiled, I often thought to myself that this love sickness was worse than the Malaria Sickness!

The food was becoming monotonous it was so bland, soup and rice, the only way I could eat it was to mix it together to give it some bulk. I had to eat as much as I could to try and put some of the lost weight back on, but I found it hard to swallow and almost drowned myself with water just to get it down. I could never swallow tablets having to gulp large quantities of water that seemed to stay in my mouth as though a shutter had come down over my tonsils gradually seeping down my throat leaving the tablet dissolved on my tongue. This was the same with my food I wished I could have some chips, just thinking of chips made my mouth water. Miserably looking down at my rice-soup I could hear my Mum saying. *Eat it all up because as sure as eggs are eggs, you won't grow into a nice big boy!* Just thinking of my mother made me smile and wishing that I were with her now even if she was always scolding me for things I'd done, or not done.

I found myself fantasising about Smiler and myself in better times far away from all this. Going out together to dances or the cinema, these were good moments for me, If someone had said to me. *Right Maurice I'm going to pick you and Smiler up, put you down on a desert island and leave you there together. I would have said. I can live with that.* But deep down my heart said. *That's not about to happen my lad, face up to it when you get out of here you won't see her again and that's that.* Then I would protest strongly that I would get her address in France and write to her, I would join a ship that goes there, and visit her, take her out to the cinema or something….Deep down but not wanting to believe I knew it was wishful thinking.

"Your Mr Evans may call today." We were sitting outside in what I liked to think as our spot. Looking at her feeling my spirits lift said. "'Twitchy? You mean, what did he say?" She replied in her tinkling laughing voice. "Oh, Moor-ise why do you call him that name?" "Well, he twitches all the time, haven't you noticed?" I said a little testily. Laughing at me she took my hand saying.

"Cheri, you are so maussade today."

"What does that mean?" I demanded.

She pulled her mouth down with her fingers, laughed saying. "How do you say in English?" Again pulling her mouth down. "Grumpy I replied.

She was right, I had been feeling grumpy lately, irritable was probably the correct word. It was this waiting not knowing, that was getting me down, not seeing Smiler for a few days didn't help either. But she was here now so I should be happy not grumpy I smiled at her. "Sorry love I'm not grumpy as you call it, with you, it's this waiting not knowing, it's getting to me." I reached for her hand and told her of my fears that once I left here I would not see her again or that I would not get better and finish up on a stretcher covered up just like I'd seen on the ward. That I wanted to visit her in France take her to the pictures, that I wanted to protect her never to let her go. All this just tumbled out I knew I was crying but didn't care, I felt my heart cracking "I could leave the sea get a job in Lyon work in a hotel anything, I could look after you." I sobbed. "I love you, I don't want to lose you." She got up putting her arms around me pulling my head to her bosom saying. "Do not upset yourself Cheri we will not lose each other." I took that to mean that she also cared for me, my heart lifted I clung to her, smelling her special smells until I composed myself.

Twitchy came later that day mopping his head with his overlarge handkerchief, sitting down in the chair with a grunt and accepting a glass of lemonade gratefully exclaiming. "I'll never get used to this heat." gulping down half of his glass. "Ah! That's better." And glancing over his shoulder

I had gone back to the ward after my little outburst with Smiler, to try and pull myself together. What she had said when she held me close, gave me hope that we had some kind of a future together, and feeling a lot better I had gone back outside to *our* spot to await the arrival of Twitchy.

He was rattling on about something; I hadn't really been listening, my mind still being on Smiler.

"I'm sorry what did you say?" I asked apologetically. He looked at me a little flustered glancing nervously over his shoulder, as though he had rehearsed his lines and hadn't expected to have to repeat them. He mopped his brow poured another lemonade then sighing said. "I was explaining what I have arranged, you will go to a hotel in Saigon until your treatment here is completed—"

"How long will that be?" I interrupted.

"—Umph, about a week or so—" glancing over his shoulder. "—Then we will try to fly you out to a port that is safe to rejoin your ship. "Putting up his hands to stop me saying anything added. "This is the hard bit, because Saigon's main airfield is under constant attack and planes coming and going are being shot at making life hard for everyone—" Another glance over his shoulder. "—so when there is a lull in the fighting you will be on the first flight out Okay?" I nodded.

"Any questions?" He demanded. Taking another gulp of lemonade and holding the glass up to the light. Probably *wishing it was a gin and tonic!* I thought.

"Yes." I said. "What do I do about money and clothes? I've only got what I stand in." He looked at me with what passed for a smile.

"You must get rid of that shirt for a start." Meaning Tommy's shirt.

"If you are seen outside of here with that on, you could be mistaken for a soldier and shot at." I hadn't thought of that. Moving his head from side to side he seemed to be looking over my shoulder, involuntary

I glanced over my shoulder to see what he was looking at. Nothing there. *I don't want to get into his habit. I thought.*

Sniffing, he continued. "Well I have arranged with the hotel for you to sign receipts for anything you buy, refreshments, clothes, whatever but—" holding up a finger. "—don't overdo it, your Company will be paying the bill, if you go mad spending on other than necessities you may end up paying the excess. Do you understand me?" This last bit like a schoolmaster.

"Yes" I replied, nearly adding Sir! "But what if I buy something outside of the hotel? How do I pay?"

"Outside! Outside! What do you mean, Outside?" He was really twitching now, mopping his brow, gulping his drink, and glancing over his shoulder almost in one motion. I half expected him to fall off his chair; he was getting so agitated. *What is he getting into such a state for? I only asked a simple question!*

"The only time you leave the hotel is when you have to go to the clinic and that should be about twice a week." He said a little breathlessly.

"Okay then, how do I get to the clinic? And how do I pay?" Now I did expect him to fall out of his chair, as this was a harder question.

He disappointed me on two counts; he didn't fall out of his chair, or twitch! But just looked at me in a calculating way.

"Ah…I will arrange with the clinic and the hotel to pay either end, then it can all go on your hotel bill. I thought I would try once more for him to fall out of his chair saying. "Wouldn't be simpler for you to give me some cash? Save everyone signing Chitty's all the time say…Er…Twenty pounds?"

I stared intently at him, under my breath I said. *Now fall off your chair you silly twat!* But he just sniffed and said. "Ha Ha, very funny." Looking at his watch and rising said. "No! We will do it my way receipts all the time. I must go now I will contact the hospital as soon as the final arrangements are made Goodbye."

I didn't reply or get up from the table, just watched him walk away thinking. *God! I wouldn't like to work with him all day, I'd be as nutty as he is!*

The following day, meaning to go outside and sit in front of the clinic where I had spoken to the young doctor, how long ago was it? Days? Weeks? I could not remember it seemed so long ago. To do this would need going through the clinic, instead of out through the side of the ward into the hospital grounds, and walking around to the front of the clinic. I had never done this before so being very cautious in case I was challenged. I made my way through the clinic keeping as quiet as possible. The few nurses I passed didn't seemed concerned, one or two smiled at me, so getting bolder I carried on glancing in open doorways, as I passed. Some were obviously operating rooms judging by the equipment, whilst others were storerooms filled with blankets and sheets with stretchers stacked against the walls.

One room I passed appeared to be a rest room; chairs scattered about, low tables with overflowing ashtrays, papers tossed onto chairs. A nurse reading a book looked up, on seeing me waved. I waved back hoping to give the impression that this was normal for me to be walking around the clinic, because by this time I was too far into the clinic to turn back so I kept on going towards what I hoped was the front door.

The clinic was bigger than what I had imagined. I was passing yet another open doorway. Glancing in I stopped in my tracks; this was clearly an office carpeted in a rich green colour, pictures on the walls a large desk in the centre with chairs scattered around the walls. All this I took in with a glance, but what riveted my attention and made my heart race, was seeing Smiler with her back to me, bending over the desk so absorbed in what she was doing that she wasn't aware of me being there at the doorway watching her. Silently I watched her for a few moments taking in the curve of her back as she leant over the desk; her uniform was hitched up at the back by her leaning over the desk, showing shapely legs. The sunlight pouring through the window in front of her seemed to cast an aura around her making her look like some mythical goddess.

CHAPTER NINE

My heart was thumping madly as I crept up to her and putting my arms around her, feeling her soft body against mine almost made me swoon. She jerked with an almost inaudible cry of surprise turning quickly in my arms. When she recognized me she relaxed. "You startled me Cheri." She said a little breathlessly. Looking down into her eyes, I knew without a shadow of a doubt that I loved this woman. She half lay in my arms pressed against me, I could feel her soft breasts and the warmth of her through my shirt. I tried to read her eyes, which just looked at me, the corners starting to crinkle as she smiled up at me. Bending my head to hers, still looking into her eyes. I kissed her. She didn't resist. Her lips tasted so sweet. A chorus of angels was singing softly in my ears, cupid was sitting on my heart grinning triumphantly, making no attempt to retrieve his arrow. She gently but firmly pushed me away. I tried to hold her not wanting this moment to pass.

"Let me go Moor-ise." She whispered in a strange voice. "Someone may see us."

Reluctantly I moved away and groped for a chair and sat down, still not taking my eyes off her. Was she blushing? I couldn't tell, did she kiss me back? I couldn't remember, I couldn't think straight, all I knew was that I was happy, happier than I'd been in years.

I wanted to shout out to anyone who would listen. *I Love This Woman! Bring Out Your Biggest Opponent to Love And I Will Fight Him!* I was brought back to earth hearing her say.

"Go outside and I will come and sit with you." Handing me a packet of cigarettes she added. "I will bring you some coffee." I floated out of the office on cloud nine joining in with the birds singing in the trees, or where they in my head? I didn't much care. Sitting outside waiting for her I thought musingly. 'Love gives strength to the weakest breast.'

She poured the coffee, and then sitting down taking the proffered cigarette from me remained silent. I thought she looked a little chastened, keeping quiet I waited for her to speak. Puffing on her cigarette and sipping coffee saying nothing, she looked at me. No. Stared at me. I squirmed uncomfortably anticipating the worst. She must have seen the anguish in my face for she started to smile. Reaching across the table, taking my hand into hers, looked searchingly into my eyes then said.

"Moor-ise that was dangerous for me what you did in my office, if someone had seen us I could be in trouble with my job." I mumbled an apology feeling very abject, still holding hands I played with the ring on her finger slowly turning it around and around. "When you are in love you don't always think clearly." My hands felt sweaty, yet hers felt cool, I wished the table wasn't there between us because I wanted to kiss her again.

Christ lad you've got it bad! Steady up old son; don't show all your hand, you don't know how she feels yet! I wasn't listening, I knew what I knew, and my mind could go tell someone else. She spoke. Slowly tentatively. "You have put me in a position which is confusing me, you say that you love me, now you believe that you do, yet you don't even know anything about me—" She sipped her coffee.

"—when you go back to your ship and see your friends…do all the things you do together—" She stopped pulling her hand free and lighting another cigarette. "You will, and must, forget all this…" Then very quietly. "…and me."

"No I won't, I will prove it to you, don't reject me please." I said desperately. I wanted her to believe me, I needed her to believe me, never being in this situation before I didn't know the right words to say and frantically searched my mind for the right words.

"Don't you feel a little for me?" Was all I could say.

"Yes I care for you, of course I do but everything is going too fast for me." She looked so sad. I felt bad, so much so, that I wished that I hadn't kissed her and that everything was as it was before, laughing together, happy together, why was love so painful? I always thought it would be joyful.

Taking her hand once more I said. "Smiler if my heart was four times as big, it couldn't hold anymore love than it does now. When I leave here I will only see you twice a week when I come here for my injection." I lit another cigarette with a shaking hand. "And if Twitchy can arrange a plane to get me out of here, maybe I've only got a week or two at the most. Can't you see I have to know your address in France to reach you, but only you can give me that, and that will keep my hopes alive that you may learn to love me back." This was a long speech for me but inside I knew that I might never get the chance again to say it. My head ached with the thought that I may lose her.

For a long time we remained silent, then she took hold of my hand and looking at me in a way she hadn't before, said. "How old are you Moor-ise."

"Nearly twenty why?"

"I am nearly thirty two."

"So what! What does it matter what our ages are, I will still love you when I'm eighty two." She smiled that Smiler smile saying.

"Oh, Cheri if only I was nearly twenty!" I knew I was losing so changed the subject by telling her what Twitchy had said about all the arrangements he was making, she was nearly her old self again laughing and asked me what Chitty meant. I told her adding. "I would sign any Chitty if it would make you feel the same way about me as I do about you."

Getting up to go she lightly brushed her lips to mine whispering. "Au revoir Cheri." and went inside. I sat a moment longer, then taking the longer route back, I returned to the ward my mind in turmoil.

Twitchy came the following day. One of the orderlies came to me telling me to get ready and come to the office in the clinic. With mixed feelings I got dressed in my whites, carefully folding Tommy's shirt putting it into my bag...*Bugger what Twitchy says I'm keeping it.* I looked at the space Tommy had occupied, remembering sharing a cigarette him saying. *Friends Eh!* "Yes" I whispered "Goodbye my friend."

In the office Twitchy was with the doctor who on seeing me said.

"Mr Evans has got your tablets and medicine sheet, remember to take two tablets a day get plenty of rest and eat properly we will see you here twice a week any questions?"

"No thank you." I replied. He shook my hand and ushered me to the door. I looked around hoping to see Smiler. She wasn't there.

As I went out to the car I did Twitchy's trick glancing over my shoulder peering at the windows in case she was there but she wasn't.

Placing my meagre possessions on the back seat of the car I got into the front passenger seat and whilst Twitchy was having a last word with the doctor I had a last look for Smiler.

As he reversed the car and started to drive out of the clinic I twisted myself around and never took my eyes off the clinic until it was out of sight, no sign of Smiler.

My eyes were like a camera, recording everything on the journey. I had not seen anything of Saigon, only the hospital. So I didn't know what to expect, I was so engrossed in what I was seeing that I was only half listening to what Twitchy was saying, as he weaved the car in and out of potholes in the road, or to be more precise tracks strewn with rocks.

"Monsoon's are a curse here." He remarked in answer to a question that I was about to ask.

"When they come they last for months." He went on. "Makes the 'Mekong' overflow and floods the land causing landslides and this is what happens to the road." Pointing to the rocks and holes. "Makes driving difficult." He grumbled.

I watched people trudging alongside high slatted carts pulled by Oxen piled high with green vegetation of some kind. They all seemed alike all dressed in what could be termed a Civilian uniform I thought.

The men wore long black trousers with a loose fitting white shirt. On their feet they had a sort of thick sandal, almost all had the 'Coolie' hat like the one I had worn at the hospital, which the nurse had lent me. Their faces were almost hidden by the large conical straw like hat. They all looked alike to me no matter who I looked at; Squat broad faces with high cheekbones looked back. All had straight black hair.

"Make those sandals out of used car tyres." Answered Twitchy to my question. "They're very poor you see."

The women didn't differ much from the men, only in that they dressed in long loose white tunic type smocks with either black or brown wide bottomed trousers, some were barefoot whilst others wore the thick sandals made from car tyres, but all had the 'Coolie' hats.

CHAPTER TEN

I thought back to what the young French doctor had said at the clinic. *You can't recognise them; anyone of these people could be a 'Commie Guerrilla' and could pull out a gun and shoot you.* I shuddered at the thought. "—don't forget to sign receipts—" Twitchy was talking to himself I was too busy drinking in the sights and the landscape to bother with his ramblings, just saying yes and no, whenever I thought appropriate.

The lush green vegetation was a sight to see. Bamboo shrubs towering above Palms with wide drooping fronds, other places it was reversed with the Palms towering above the Bamboo. But towering above them all, were the majestic trees of the jungle. Occasionally through gaps in the dense wall of green, I glimpsed people stooped over as if gathering something into large baskets.

"Paddy fields, main source of food." Twitchy informed me, swerving to avoid a rather large pothole, and narrowingly missing a collision with a cart, the man trudging alongside the cart didn't as much as glance at us his face impassive.

As we neared the city of Saigon. Twitchy was still muttering to himself, I tried to blot out his voice by concentrating on what was going on outside of the car. "—refreshments—don't go outside or—" under my breath I said, shut *up you silly sod!* The road started to widen I could see shops some quite modern made of brick, in the gaps between the shops were makeshift shops made from bamboo with palm leaves for the roof, fruit and vegetables displayed outside, more like a market than a shop.

Everything seemed to be on top of each other, but the people didn't seem to mind. The noise of the traders shouting to each other was deafening, reminding me of the chattering of the monkeys back home in the Zoo but considerable louder.

The sun was beating down remorselessly causing a heat haze to shimmer over everything and everyone, giving the illusion of steam rising from the dusty ground. A policeman was trying vainly to direct traffic blowing a whistle and waving his arms, but the traffic seemed oblivious to his efforts and directed itself. I had at this point wound my window up, the noise, the smell of traffic fumes and bad drains was overpowering and my head was aching, a hammer was beating in my temple I was feeling sick and just wanted to lay down out of this heat.

The hotel was situated on a corner; two wide roads ran past it at angles, which created a seemingly impossible curve. As we approached the hotel, Twitchy slowed right down to almost a crawl to negotiate the curve, which led into the hotel grounds. My first impression was how grand it looked; the approach to the main entrance was sprawling. The large forecourt was dotted with cars, and one or two military vehicles. Groups of rickshaws were just inside the main gates with their drivers lolling about in the shade. But what struck me the most was the colour! It was breathtaking, masses of flowers and shrubs were neatly laid out, and each competing with the other to produce the most vibrant colours I had ever seen. *My Mum would love this.* I was thinking. The French Tricolour was lazily fluttering from a flag post near the main entrance. My thoughts were, *if this is the outside what must the inside be like?* Glancing at the rickshaw men, I saw that they were wearing what looked to me a sort of wrap around garment, bare chested and bare feet. *Don't look strong enough to pull those heavy rickshaws, they are too small! I suppose I will have to use them when I go to the clinic so I'll soon know.* Twitchy must have read my thoughts because on entering the hotel he commented for me to use the foot rickshaws not the pedal ones. "It's cheaper." He said. *Penny pinching again!*

Entering the foyer, I marvelled at the sheer splendour and spacious-
ness of it. Huge fans in the ceiling were creating a pleasant cooling air;
my skin reacted favourably to it. I stood there implanting in my brain,
the memory of what I was seeing. Ahead of me stretching across the
whole wall was the reception area, a long highly polished counter with
smartly dressed receptionists in attendance. To the left of the reception
desk was an area set out with comfy looking cushioned chairs and low
glass topped coffee tables. A large bar, all mirrors and lights ran the
length of the wall. The front of the bar was set out in chrome, and red
topped stools. Flowery chintz curtains hung from the tall windows
complimenting the fabric of the chairs scattered about. Strategically
placed were large potted Palms that gave an illusion of privacy to anyone drinking at the bar yet allowed them to see the reception area. In
the corner immediately to the left as you entered the hotel, sat a large
grand piano. Sunlight through the window glinted off its raised polished lid. Seated on a low stool was a Vietnamese man. He was crooning
to himself, whilst lovingly caressing the keys, producing a melodious
sound that blended with the other sounds of voices, both from the bar
and reception, but not being intrusive. He was wearing a white shirt
with a black bow tie and dark trousers, on his feet were open toed sandals. The scene reminded me of the film 'Casablanca' with Humphrey
Bogart and I very nearly said. *'Play it again Sam'*. But stopped myself,
smiling at the thought. On the other side to my right was a large stair-
case with lifts to the side, it looked without closer inspection that there
were three lifts with flashing arrows up and down, beyond the lifts from
the sounds of crockery and waiters scurrying about was the dining
room.

The hotel was obviously busy, the reception and bar areas were full
of people and most of the chairs were occupied. Everyone looked
smartly dressed in cool looking short sleeved shirts and slacks in sharp
contrast to me dressed in my tropical white linens and sweating, even
in this air-conditioned place. I must have looked out of place yet

nobody gave me a second glance, I vowed there and then to buy a cotton shirt and slacks.

Twitchy was getting agitated at having to wait for attention at the busy reception. I felt giddy seeing all this splendour at first hand, as I had never seen anything like it before, apart from at the pictures, never in real life. I had to sit down my head was hammering now, I felt ill, my vision was distorting, all I wanted was to lay down before I fell down, I couldn't remember if I had, had my tablet today...

"Sign in—" Twitchy was standing over me, he and his voice were fading in and out. "Uhh?" I was trying to concentrate on what he was saying but the noise in the hotel seemed to be getting louder and distorted. I leaned back in my chair feeling very distressed, I knew another attack was coming. "—must go now see you tomorr—"

"Get me to bed—please—feel ill." I said thickly. My voice sounded far away; maybe it wasn't my voice but someone else's. I heard rather than saw Twitchy speaking rapidly with someone, then felt arms lifting me and carrying me towards the lifts.

All the time I heard Twitchy's voice drone in my head telling me that I must register in the morning.

I felt myself being gently laid on to a soft bed voices around me were fading, I was drifting thankfully into nothingness—

When I awoke it was dark. My head was aching like a dull pulse, my mouth felt furry, I needed a drink of water. I knew I was fully clothed and tried to remember what had happened. I remembered being in reception and not feeling well, but nothing more. I put out an exploratory hand feeling the softness of the bed, after so long on an uncomfortable stretcher bed, this was heaven. I just lay there savouring the luxury, the sickness was abating but I was drenched with sweat, the air felt heavy warm and humid.

Fumbling for a light switch, my fingers found a panel with buttons on, pressing one, a radio over my head blared out, I hastily pressed another which switched it off, on my next attempt the bedside lights came on casting a shadowy glow which wasn't hurtful to my eyes.

The curtains billowed with the warm air that came through the open balcony doors, looking up at the ceiling I saw a big motionless fan. The blades were big enough to propel a Spitfire but at this moment couldn't propel air. Searching for a button to activate it, I accidentally found the radio again, turning the volume down to an acceptable level, I managed to find the fan button. With a whirring sound it slowly started to spin, wafting the hot air around the room and groaning, picked up speed, wafting the hot air a little faster. Looking at it, I changed my mind about the Spitfire!

Admitting defeat I just lay there until I felt better enough to go to the bathroom for a glass of water. I drank two or three glasses before my thirst was quenched. It was cooler in the bathroom due too, I suppose, all the tiles, even the floor was tiled and felt cool to my bare feet. I sat on the toilet enjoying the respite from the heat thinking to myself *no more latrines, no more embarrassment when I couldn't control my wind, here I can make as many noises as I want.* To my surprise I heard myself giggling at the thought. Curiosity getting the better of me I wandered into the bedroom, to see what my room was like. I reached over the bed to find the overhead light, which immediately cast all shadows out, and allowed me to inspect! Apart from my bed, which was a double one, there was a bedside table with a drawer, on opening the drawer I found a Gideon's Bible, and of all things, a Readers Digest Magazine! I stood holding this in my hand wondering how it could have got into a bedside drawer, the other side of the world! Putting it back in the drawer I looked around me. In the corner near to the open balcony, sat a rather comfy looking chair with a low table in front of it, rather like the chairs and tables I'd seen in the foyer. On the glass table there was a large glass ashtray with a complimentary book of matches in it. I fumbled in my pockets for cigarettes but found none. A large wardrobe with plenty of coat hangers and a small chest of drawers completed the furnishings.

The floor being tiles didn't need a carpet but alongside on each side of the bed lay a fluffy strip mat.

Walking back into the bathroom I poured myself another glass of water, promising myself to have a shower before I went to bed, having seen the shower unit over the bath.

CHAPTER ELEVEN

Walking out onto the balcony sipping the ice cold water, which tasted so good against my hot parched throat, I thought about Smiler. How she would like this hotel, then with a pang of remorse for having kissed her, thus putting our friendship in jeopardy I wondered if I would see her at the clinic or would she avoid me like she did when I left the hospital.

I was miserable again. Standing on the balcony, hearing the night sounds of Saigon, I felt too weary to appreciate them. Returning to my bed I turned the sheet down, stripped to my underpants not having the energy to have the promised shower, I just lay on the bed staring at the slow moving fan until sleep claimed me.

I awoke with a start. My head hurt, my tongue was sticking to my dry mouth, I tried to swallow but it hurt my throat. Trying to remember if I had taken my Quinine tablets yesterday, I groped for the bottle on the bedside table knocking it to the floor. Groaning I sat up. My head protested by hitting itself with a hammer. Swinging my legs over the bed I tottered to my feet and bent down to pick up the bottle. I almost collapsed with pain. Sliding down the bed I reached for the tablets. Pain stabbed through me making me cry out. I knew I couldn't swallow the tablets without some water, so attempted to stand up, in order to go to the bathroom for a glass of water. Pain shot through me with every movement, stabbing at me like a demented killer, repeatedly stabbing his victim, sweat was pouring from me staining the tiles I was sitting on. I sat still a moment letting the room that was spinning, steady itself.

Again I tried to stand but the effort was too much, I started to half crawl, half push myself to the bathroom just feet away, sweat dripped into my eyes making it difficult to focus. "God. Not another attack please I can't stand anymore." I croaked.

My lips felt tight, my throat so dry I knew the only way I could take my tablets was with water. My heart started to race with the effort of pushing myself across the floor, my head threatened to burst, my stomach threatened to heave, I promised myself not to die.

It was painfully slow inching across the few feet to the bathroom, and I knew I was leaving a damp trail of sweat on the floor. I had to rest often, yet the distance from my bed to the bathroom could only be a few strides. When I reached the bathroom door, to my dismay I found that I hadn't the strength to pull myself up the door frame, my hands were too sweaty to get a firm purchase on the wood and I knew I was defeated. I was by this time crying, not just for the pain but in frustration for being so near yet so far from the tap. I slumped against the doorway eyeing the basin just a matter of feet away, feeling like a child must feel seeing the jar of sweets just out of its reach! I wanted to scream at my useless body for not supporting me, for not giving me that extra bit of strength to get a measly glass of water, I just sat there waiting for the attack to flatten me.

That's when the maid found me. Taking one look at me she rushed out of the room. "Help me don't leave me," I shouted after her. She *had* gone for help, because she returned with two porters who lifted me back into my bed. The maid filled a jug of water placing it within reach on the bedside table. One of the porters held a glass of water to my lips and gave me my tablets, all this time the maid fussed about the room talking in rapid French, my head responded by pounding in unison with her voice. At last they left leaving me alone to fall into a fitful sleep.

Feeling completely drained when I awoke, it took me awhile to realise where I was, my recollection of what had happened since leaving the clinic, although with missing gaps, was frightening. I also realised that what the doctors had been saying about plenty of rest taking regular medication was not just idle talk, no matter how I thought I was getting better and felt better, they, the doctors knew best. I didn't want to go through all that pain again. *So Maurice stop being Jack the lad and heed the doctors, you want to get well again and rejoin your ship, don't you?* I nodded to myself.

I went out on to the balcony it was raining heavily. I remembered Twitchy saying about 'Monsoons' and floods, I remembered also him saying about registering in the hotel, my stomach growled reminding me it had not been fed, so I decided to register and eat at the same time. Turning to go back into the room I had to lean against the wall until the room steadied

With difficulty I managed to reach reception. I was still a little disorientated, the staff were concerned about me, and said that I could have my meals in my room, they had also informed Mr Evans, as to what had happened, he would come later in the day. The thought of Twitchy fussing around very nearly brought another attack on! Thanking them for their kind thoughts and offer, I declined the meals in the room saying, that I needed to exercise and didn't want to be treated as an invalid, if I was to get better quickly, they seemed to understand.

Taking the registration form, and moving along the desk, I started to read it. It was hard to focus on the small print. I kept looking up at my surroundings. The bar was filling up, so I decided to sit in one of the chairs, and over a coffee, fill in the form, finding a chair that was near to the reception desk, in case I needed assistance.

One or two well-dressed people were sitting at the tables chatting and drinking, the barstools were mostly full with, what I call Bar Belles. Low cut blouses, short skirts and plenty of lipstick. One was big busted the buttons on her blouse hardly taking the strain. She noticed me looking at her and pouted her blood red lips at me in what was meant to be a come on smile. I quickly averted me eyes and studiously studied the form cursing under my breath knowing that I was blushing. Covertly I studied them thinking to myself. *Why do all the 'Bar Belles' in all the ports I've been too, always have one or two 'Dolly Parton' look-a-likes? Asian women normally have small or flat chests in fact* I mused. *If a wasp on their chests stung any of them, they would proudly go topless until the swelling went down!* I giggled at my joke, glancing around to see if anyone had heard me. The people on the next table must have, because they quickly looked away.

I started to fill the form in, I wanted a cigarette badly, what did Twitchy say? *Buy what you need and sign a receipt*—Well I need cigarettes so I'll put it to the test! Beckoning a waiter, I ordered white coffee, cigarettes and matches. When he brought them and handed me a pad to sign, I felt like one of the rich guests and signed with a flourish, inwardly congratulating myself on handling it as though I was used to doing it. Book it to my room, sounded good, just rolled of my tongue. *Wait until the lads hear about this* "Room number Sir?" I looked up. The waiter was still standing there with the pad in his hand. He said again. "Room number Sir?"

"Er—"flustered."—I don't know it yet." Coming down to earth with a bump. The waiter smiled and walked over to the desk. *Not such a smart arse as you thought. Eh kid?* The waiter returned still smiling. "Two-O-Eight Sir" placing the chit down in front of me and returning to the bar. *I must not show off—at least until I'm used to it!*

Looking at the form, seeing that so far I had only written my name, began again to fill it in. Place of birth—I wrote. Liverpool. Country of origin—I wrote. England.

Next of Kin—I paused my mind wandering, those words 'Next of Kin' were significant…

CHAPTER TWELVE

Where was it? Oh yes Korea. We were in 'Ulsan Hang' the port was extremely busy with shipping, and there was a heavy presence of military on shore, we were not over the shock yet, Taffy, our ships lawyer with the aid of Sparks, had contacted the British Embassy in our last port India. Demanding that we receive Thirty Shillings, danger money whilst in Vietnam territorial waters or we would not sail. I had voiced the concern of some of us, that suggesting a strike was a little strong. Taffy had replied. It's to show them that we are not bluffing.

It turned out neither was our Government. The reply came back supported by Winston Churchill's cabinet, saying that under article this that and the other of The Merchant Navy Act. We were obliged to sail. Not to do so would constitute an Act of Mutiny on the High Seas. A charge which carries the death penalty.

Hearing this Taffy snorted contemptuously. Death Penalty? This is 1954 not 1754! We couldn't believe it either, but what compounded our disbelief, was when the reply went on to say, that if we were captured or killed, England would disown us for Gunrunning

It wouldn't sink in we were all stunned. What our Prime Minister was in effect saying. Don't sail and face the death penalty—Sail and be captured—Your on your own Jack! All we were asking for was danger money. Through Taffy again, we approached the French Government through their Embassy. Their reply supported by the Mendes-France Government, said that they couldn't over-ride our Governments decision, but ended by saying that if we were captured or killed, £1000 sterling would go to our 'Next of Kin'…

Still in a daze looking at the form Next of Kin—I wrote. Mother!

I was still thinking of what we all believed, as a gross betrayal from our country—

—After mulling over these replies still believing that Churchill wasn't serious about hanging or shooting us, we still put up a show of defiance although we knew we couldn't win. But all we wanted was Thirty Shillings nothing else. It was paid in the Korean War. Which had only just recently finished. All we were getting was death threats and the possibility of our country disowning us.

The final straw for us was when a Royal Navy Frigate was brought alongside our ship, sailors in full strip armed with rifles, lined the deck, and we were given the ultimatum. Sail or be clapped in Irons! We sailed.

It wasn't a happy ship anymore something was missing, Oh we still laughed, we still drank, we still did the things, we always did, but nevertheless something was missing, no one could put their finger on it, only that the ship would never be the same again—

—"Johnny" I was brought out of my reverie startled by a voice. At first I couldn't be sure if I had heard it, or if it was for me.

"Hey Johnny" I looked up in its direction. The Dolly Parton look-a-like-bust, was staring straight at me, her left arm in the air and her right hand clamped over the inside of her elbow giving me the International sign for sex.

"You want Jig Jig?" smiling coyly through her heavily painted lips. "Very cheap!" In a sing song voice. I was irritated by being disturbed from my thoughts and replied testily.

"Fat chance love, I can hardly get my shoes on, let alone a hard on!" Inwardly I giggled again thinking of what Smiler would say when I went to the clinic for my injection and saying to her. *Oh by the way can you give me another one for the clap!*

Stretching, I stood up and walked over to the desk handing my card over to the receptionist and waited, she scribbled something on it turned to the key rack and handed me a key saying.

"We hope you are soon better and enjoy your stay with us Mr Tudor." She pronounced it like Chew-door. I smiled back. "I'm sure I will, Thank you." And returned to the bar. Selecting a chair away from the 'Bar Belles' and smoking a cigarette, I observed my fellow guests, playing a game with myself as to whether they were rich Vietnamese staying here on holiday, business, or diplomats on a war connection. I settled for business or war, because surely no one would come to a war torn city for a holiday?

I saw some Chinese features, although their clothes were similar looking, they were different from the Vietnamese dress. Most of the men wore silk or tropical suits whilst the ladies varied from cool looking bright coloured long dresses or high neck long sleeve blouses with black skirts down to their feet with a split up the side. I had seen this type of dress in Japan. They all looked nice.

The man sitting nearest to me, wore a silk suit, it reminded me of my pride and joy back on the ship, my Sharkskin suit. I'd had it specially made in India, it was pale blue and as smooth as silk, it had also cost me a packet on my wages, but back home in England it would have cost a small fortune, that is if it could be had in England?

Comparing mine with these silk suits, I preferred mine, but decided that I must buy some clothes, for what I was wearing wouldn't last, and would look out of place at night, especially here.

Nodding to my nearest neighbours as I made my way to the desk I deliberately avoided eye contact with Dolly Parton! "Yes sir." said the receptionist, in answer to my query, "We have a 'Boutique' on the first floor, and yes you can sign a receipt to your room." Thanking her I made my way to the first floor using the stairs, I needed the exercise and one floor wouldn't kill me. The stairs were wide and carpeted, pleasant landscaped pictures adorned the walls.

The 'Boutique' sold just about everything from clothes to postcards. It was big and spacious with soft music playing from invisible speakers. A number of people were selecting clothes from racks. Attentive assistants hovering, the whole atmosphere was relaxing. My choice was three short sleeved white cotton shirts, a pair of dark brown slacks, *everyone else wore black* so I would be different, underwear and socks. As an afterthought I added a pair of brown open-toed sandals. On the way to the cash counter I passed a tie rack, choosing one I added it to my pile. After signing for them I made my way back to my room. I had no idea of what they had cost but a lot of zero's were in the total.

My room seemed a lot bigger than yesterday, but then yesterday I wasn't seeing anything clearly. Placing my purchases on the bed conjured up the image of Twitchy popping into my mind, holding the clothing receipt's getting redder and redder in the face spluttering over the total. I collapsed on the bed in a fit of laughter at the thought, and thought to hell with the lot of you.

What life I've got here I'm going to live to the full, no matter what it costs, what happens after I don't give a damn. Feeling better for these brave thoughts and promising myself to try and live up to them, I went onto the balcony throwing my head back gulped the rain washed air deep into my lungs, feeling better than if I had taken my tablets. Leaning on the rail I could see the front approach to the hotel, the clustered rickshaws at the entrance, cars parked neatly, the distant noises carried on the breeze, birds, voices, traffic, general getting on with life noises. Together they gave the impression of normality; the only thing to spoil it was the knowledge of war and the oppressive heat. I stood there with my shirt opened and feeling the sweat trickling down my chest thinking. *what must it be like in the summer?*

I had spent some time in Tropical climates but this heat was somehow different. It was thick cloying, and unpleasant. *Maybe its because I'm sick or even a part of my sickness, perhaps as I get better I won't notice it so much?* Sighing I decided to have a cold bath, if for nothing else just to cool down, then go for something to eat because by now I was extremely hungry. How long ago had I eaten? I couldn't think and my stomach had long ago given up reminding me!

The bathroom was decidedly cooler, *Must be all the tiles and marble that keeps it cool.* I ran the cold tap and slowly stripped my clothes off. I looked for a hook to hang them on, not seeing any I closed the door expecting to see a hook, but instead there was a full length mirror—

I recoiled in shock and horror. A skeletal figure was standing there. I stood rooted to the spot. I was confused, my mind was playing tricks on me, was I about to be claimed by this being, as his prize for me being sick? Is this what you see of yourself before you die? I heard myself whimpering it was like a mewing sound but I couldn't stop. The mirror seemed to undulate, the image swelling then distorting just like the mirrors at the fairgrounds the only difference that at the fairground they were funny this was not. All I wanted to do was scream but could only manage this whimpering mewing sound.

The figure just stood there with its mouth open in a silent scream, it seemed to be moving towards me. I put out a hand to stop it, it did the same, even when I touched the mirror palms flat against the glass to stop it coming out and reaching me, it did the same, putting its hands against mine, was it intending to push me away? Or pull me into the mirror itself?

My head which had started throbbing when I first saw the mirror, was now almost exploding with pain like nails being driven deep into my skull, I knew an attack was starting again and that I was going to faint. The thought flashed through my mind; *will it be the maid again who finds me? This time I will be naked.* I waited leaning on the mirror; head pressed to the glass waiting for whatever it was that was going to happen.

How long I stood there I don't know but gradually I heard the sound of running water. A voice inside my mind said. *The Bath, pull yourself together!* Still with my eyes shut and trembling I turned towards the bath then opened my eyes. The bath was almost overflowing. I stooped and turned the taps off, plunging my arm into the cold water in order to pull the plug out. The shock of the cold water cleared my brain, enough for me to comprehend, that I had just had a massive shock to my system. My mind was taking control again. Sitting on the toilet seat, eyes averted from the mirror, I tried to work it out in my head.

I remembered Smiler telling me that the type of Malaria that I was suffering from, caused rapid body weight loss, but not seeing myself before now in a full mirror only having seen bits of myself I hadn't been prepared for what 'Rapid Body Weight Loss' meant. Plucking up the courage to open my eyes, I approached the mirror to examine myself. What looked back at me was hardly recognisable, a mere shadow of myself, thin body to the extent that I could see my ribs sticking out, my chest bone was very prominent, my arms and legs so thin they looked as though they would snap easy like a dry twig. My face was the worst; gaunt, black hollow circles for eyes sunken cheeks giving a 'Halloween' look. I wept seeing myself like this, this is how other people were seeing me, not the real me. The real me was a healthy lad who only a few years back boxed at Welterweight A-B-A division and trained at 'Snowballs' Gym in Southport, now I couldn't make Flyweight.

Emptying the bath, no more thoughts of a cool dip I went back into the bedroom, flopping on the bed still naked thinking, *No wonder Smiler can't love me, who wants to love a wreck like me?* Then I really did weep.

CHAPTER THIRTEEN

Some time later feeling calmer with my stomach imploring me to feed it, I half-heartedly dressed, after a stand up sponge down. I put on one of my new shirts and my slacks that wanted to slide down over my hips, I made a mental note to purchase a belt in the morning. Glancing at my watch I saw it was almost six o'clock. I almost tripped over at the door because my trousers wanted to join my ankles, hastily using my new tie as a makeshift belt with my shirt out to hide it, I made my way to the dining room or 'saloon' as we called it on board ship.

The dining room was not very busy which suited me. I wasn't ready for general inspection just yet. The few early diners were uninterested at my arrival and carried on talking or eating; waiters were flitting in and out between tables. An appetising aroma of smells came from the kitchen. At the far end, orchestral music played softly, providing the background. The whole room reminded me of the big ocean liners I'd sailed on previously. A waiter came over to me as I stood undecided in the doorway, he ushered me to a table pulling a chair out for me, and opening my napkin with a flourish placing it on my knees whilst seemingly produced the menu in front of me all in one motion. My heart sank looking at the menu. It was all in French. I couldn't read it or even recognise any words. I stared at it miserably thinking I would starve to death or eat soup all the time.

The waiter came to my rescue; "The fish is nice sir." I looked at him gratefully nodding. "Perhaps soup first?" I nodded again; he took my menu and glided away. *I must get Smiler to translate the menu for me; or else I'm going to live on soup and fish!* I ate everything being so hungry and enjoyed it too, asking for my coffee to be served in the bar lounge.

Sitting there smoking a cigarette. I made a promise to myself that I would make a determined effort to fight this sickness and beat it, starting right now by not wallowing in self-pity when things were bad. After all I chided myself, self-pity is not your style is it? But then started to argue back, but I've never been ill before! *There you go again you just said you that would stop it.* My mind said.

I must have been smiling to myself because a hand touched my shoulder, a voice saying. "You look pleased with yourself." Looking up I saw one of the guests I'd noticed before; he was wearing a Tropical silk suit, standing over me with a friendly smile.

"I was just thinking to myself." I replied a little self-consciously. He indicated to the chair next to me. "May I?" he held a drink in his hand. "Yes of course." I was a little flustered. He sat down accepting a cigarette from me saying. My name is Vo Dinh Dah. And laughed at my perplexed expression adding. "You may call me Joe!" He spoke in a lilting accent. I shook his hand saying. "My name is Maurice you may call me Mo! We both laughed at what seemed a joke although I hadn't meant it to sound like one.

I liked Joe instantly. He told me he was here to meet with some French Officials but didn't say why, I didn't ask. He raised an eyebrow and enquired if I would like a drink? I shook my head refusing politely, telling him of my condition and being on medication.

He nodded. "I understand. Malaria is a bad thing I hope you recover completely and quickly." After a few more minutes of idle chitchat he looked at his watch exclaiming. "I must go now Mo, my wife will be ready for dinner." I half rose saying. "I recommend the fish!" I felt pleased saying that, made me feel on his level. Watching him as he walked away I thought how small everyone was.

Hearing a slight commotion at the main entrance. I glanced over to see a group of French officers, smart uniforms, chests full of medals, standing just inside the foyer. Soldiers with rifles were positioned at the doors and the lifts. I had not seen anything like this before and thinking that they must be important to have guards like that.

They moved towards the dining room. Moments later a group of chattering women in evening gowns entered accompanied by yet more armed soldiers. I was glad that I had put my new clothes on, the last time I had seen women dressed like that had been on the big liners, so I knew that a big do was on tonight and glad I'd had early dinner. Seeing all the evening dresses and the pomp took my mind back to the big liner 'The Dominion Monarch' I had sailed on.

I was only just sixteen. My first trip to sea on the flagship of the Shaw Saville Company, sailing from Southampton. She was named ' The Dominion Monarch.' And I was a ' Commis Waiter' learning the trade of Stewardship, which meant working under the supervision of a table steward. We had six tables, one six seater and five four seater's, in two sittings to look after. It was hard work; it was nothing for me to work a sixteen-hour day. But being keen to learn I took it in my stride.

All the passengers that I served on tables; dressed like these people, they were all rich. Some of the more famous that came to mind were Bob Hope the film star. Bobby Lock the South African golfer. Hypnotist named Black, who after almost daily snide remarks, from Lock about his ability to hypnotise, had Lock running around the passenger deck, imitating an aeroplane complete with all the noises and actions, much to the amusement of the other passengers, who by this time, no doubt was as fed up with the taunts, as Black was, Lock talked in a loud voice for all to hear. Someone must have told him about the incident because the taunts stopped. I was starry eyed in those days but loved every minute of my life—Getting up from my chair, I murmured aloud. "Happy Days!"

Back in my room and going to the balcony, I could see more soldiers milling around and cars with the French flag fluttering on their bonnets, yes definitely something big going on!

Next morning after a good breakfast and feeling a lot better than I had in days, I enquired at reception as to how I paid for a rickshaw to the clinic? She handed me some blank receipts telling me to give one to the rickshaw driver and telling him to call at the desk for payment. "Then it will go on your bill sir," she said politely.

Outside I looked at the rickshaws, remembering Twitchy saying, *The pedal ones are dearer, don't overspend.* Spotting one whose driver looked the poorest of the bunch by the way he was dressed, I decided to hire him. He was small even by Vietnamese standards with a cloth wrapped around his middle, rather like a babies nappy, on his feet he wore the makeshift sandals from car tyres if Twitchy was right, he was poor all right. His head was bobbing up and down as I showed him the paper with the clinic address, beaming at me as though I'd just offered to buy his rickshaw. His face was squatter than others I'd seen his nose much flatter, it made me think he would have difficulties with glasses!

I smiled at the thought; he smiled back showing that all his top teeth were missing. With his light brown skin and babies nappy! He looked more like a Chimpanzee than Vietnamese. So I decided to call him Chimp.

On the way to the clinic, I was surprised how effortlessly he pulled the rickshaw, but my mind was more preoccupied with what sort of reception Smiler would give me. I was apprehensive. She hadn't seen me off when I had left the hospital. I agonised over whether I had overplayed my hand in kissing her and telling her that I loved her. The thought of that kiss made my pulse race, I willed Chimp to go faster, every detail of Smiler was etched in my mind as if with a red-hot poker, never to be erased.

On arrival at the clinic I indicated to Chimp, by pointing to the ground and my watch that he wait for me, he nodded understandingly, promptly jumped into the rickshaw legs draped over the shafts hat drawn over his face feigning sleep with a loud snore, then beamed at me. Entering the clinic, I resolved to act cool and sophisticated where Smiler was concerned, be a man I told myself but deep down knowing that I wouldn't. A young Vietnamese nurse ushered me into a waiting room saying. "Doctor come soon." It was the same doctor who had talked to me over a coffee in front of the clinic all that time ago Doctor Jean—? something I couldn't remember.

"Bon jour Mr Tudor." Pronouncing it as ' Shoo-door,' "How do you feel?"

"Not so good Doctor, some days better than others." I went on to tell him about the attack I'd had in the hotel and the shock of seeing myself for the first time in the mirror. He listened, all the time writing on my chart, then when I had finished, explained at some length that it was normal for the severity of the malaria strain for extreme weight loss due to the heavy sweating and loss of appetite.

"How much weight have I lost?" I asked.

"I don't know what weight you were before your sickness so cannot tell you." He replied.

"Eleven stone six pounds." I told him. He put me on the scales and said. "You have gained two pounds since you were last weighed which is good but you must eat as much as you can and have plenty of rest."

"Two pounds? Two pounds to what? What do I weigh now? Almost pleading.

"Eight stones." He replied giving me my injection. I quickly calculated that in about a month I had lost about three and a half stone? I couldn't believe it and told him so.

"Which would you prefer Eight stone alive or Eleven and a half stone dead?" He asked. I just stared at him lost for words.

"There all finished we will see you again in two days, I will give you some salt tablets to help with the sweat loss, eat sleep and take your medication, these attacks can strike you without warning, you will begin to recognise the signs of an attack in time." He added. "The excitement the other day plus not eating, almost certainly triggered your attack at the hotel." I nodded and thanked him, asking if it would be possible to sit outside, perhaps with a coffee before returning to the hotel. He said he would ask a nurse to fetch me a cup and handed me my quinine and salt tablets.

CHAPTER FOURTEEN

Outside I made my way to the table. As before it was still strewn around with cigarette butts. *Not a very good advertisement for a clinic* I thought. A shadow crossed me.

"'Allo, Moor-ise." She stood there looking hesitant, a tray of coffee in her hands. She sat down and started to pour the coffee whilst I lit two cigarettes from the packet she had placed on the table, and handing her one which she accepted avoiding my eyes. A faint tremulous smile traced her lips. For a while we said nothing, I glanced at her, a hollow feeling within me and thinking. *Here it comes, once and for all, Bye Bye Maurice, well if it is I must find out why?* Clearing my throat, perhaps a little too noisily I asked. "Why didn't you see me off the other day?" Adding quickly as I saw she was about to speak. "I have thought of nothing else since, is it something that I have done, or said that has upset you? "My hands trembled on the tabletop; I desperately wanted to hear her reply but at the same time dreaded it. It seemed an eternity, but was probably only seconds before she spoke. Reaching across the table she took one of my trembling hands in hers at the same looking searchingly into my eyes, then speaking very softly that I had to strain to hear said.

"I wanted to Cheri, but I told you I was confused, that is why I didn't say Au revoir, I was too upset my mind was, and still is confused. I feel something Moor-ise here—" Patting her chest. "—But I don't know what? I know I have missed you, but why?" She looked forlorn. I was so happy; the birds singing were in my head! Raising her hand to my lips, savouring the clean hospital smell of her, I kissed it looking into her tear glistening eyes saying softly.

"I don't just love my nurse, I love you!" My eyes were also filling up with tears, there was so much I wanted to say to her to quell her doubts, but I didn't know how too. She pulled her hand away lighting another cigarette with a shaky hand. She didn't say anything just stared into my eyes, giving me that beautiful Smiler smile. I wanted to say I love you so much I would die for you, but instead said "Smiler would you come to the hotel one night and have dinner with me? I would like that very much."

She looked at me a very long time before saying. "I don't know Cheri."

"Where do you go on your nights off?" I queried. "To Saigon, to a dance? Or dinner maybe? You must go somewhere away from here." No answer. "Well do you?"

"Yes sometimes."

"Well then come and have dinner with me at the hotel, call it a thank you for looking after me if you like." Inwardly I was cursing myself for not taking much notice of my teachers at school on how to express myself. I wanted her to understand how much she meant to me and was getting so frustrated with myself that I burst out.

"Smiler I won't always be sick and thin like this, if you could see me as I used to be maybe you could love me too!" I was determined to get across to her that it wasn't a sick mind talking to her, but thought that I was losing the battle and may never get another chance again so not letting her speak I spluttered on.

"I will fight harder than your soldiers to make you believe me—"

"Yes all right."

"—So please say you will—"

"Yes Moor-ise…come to dinner."

I stopped, staring at her dumbfounded, she was laughing.

"Yes. I will come to dinner with you Moor-ise, you wouldn't let me get a word in." I slowly let this sink into my stupid brain, relief washed over me I wanted to shout out to the whole world that she had said yes! I grinned sheepishly at her. "When?"

"My night off is not for another three days yet, I will come to your hotel about seven o'clock is that all right?"

"All right? Of course its all right, but I will see you again before then as I have to come back here in two days." Remembering the menu I handed it to her asking for help in the translation or that my diet would be soup and fish! She laughed taking the menu promising to translate it. "I must go now Cheri, I will give this back to you when you come back." I got up with her and kissed her on both cheeks the French way whispering in her ear. "Do you remember telling me that all sick men fall in love with their nurses?" She nodded. "Well maybe its the other way round. French nurses fall in love with their sick Englishmen!" Smiling she went into the clinic.

The rickshaw was still waiting. "Hey Chimp. I'm in love you know!" He just beamed nodding his head. "You don't understand a word I'm saying do you pal?" Putting my arm around his shoulder, he nodded and beamed.

Back at the hotel I took Chimp to the desk and told them I wanted him every two days to take me to the clinic and to put a tip on the chit for waiting. When this was translated to him he pumped my hand up and down giving me his toothless grin.

The next day whilst having a coffee in the bar, my new friend Joe joined me. On my enquiry about all the top brass in the hotel the other night, he told me that it was the prelude to serious talks that were now being put in process, because the commies were having a lot of success in the Hanoi area of North Vietnam. Fierce fighting was going on in both, major and minor areas, with the French taking heavy losses. Joe seemed worried, telling me he wanted to clear up his business here quickly and return to Cambodia. He also said that terrible atrocities were being afflicted on the civilian population and captured soldiers, as the Ho Chi Minh forces gained new ground. When I asked him to explain, I was horrified to learn that the men were forced to watch their women being raped then shot, children too, he said sadly.

"But that's far away from here, we are well protected here aren't we?" I asked worriedly.

"Yes—for now but its getting closer all the time, I'm sending my wife back to Cambodia to be safe—" I could see he was disturbed so to change the subject I told him about inviting my lady friend to dinner later in the week. He seemed pleased when I said that I would like him to meet her.

Later Twitchy came to the hotel I voiced my fears concerning the stories I'd heard. "Saigon is heavily defended." He said. "Besides we will have you out of here soon."

"But I have to complete my medication first." Thinking of Smiler and hoping it wouldn't be before our dinner date.

"You can have medication in other countries you know, our priority is to get you out of Vietnam as quickly as possible." The thought of being separated from Smiler made me feel sick to my stomach. "How soon is quickly?" I demanded. "A day, two days, a week, when?"

"I don't know, the airport is under constant attack we will have to wait and see." He replied starting to twitch.

"But I need to know." I said a little too quickly.

"Why?" He countered.

"Because I've invited my nurse to have dinner with me here in the hotel, the one who saved my life that's why!" I was trembling and almost shouting.

He must have seen how agitated I was becoming, because he took my arm and in a soothing voice said. "It will take more than a day or two, so you enjoy your dinner." Glancing over his shoulder, as if he didn't want anyone to see or overhear him being almost kind. If he had mentioned the cost I would have knocked his teeth out sick or no sick, but he didn't.

When he had gone I went to my room to have a rest on the bed. I was still upset over the prospect of having to leave Smiler.

As always after an injection, the following day made me feel drowsy, sometimes it was for all day, other times just a few hours, over this period I always felt disorientated. Lying on my bed, my mind wandered back to 'Churchill's' Governments threat of disowning us—I could see images—

—*Rafts loaded with bombs being towed alongside the ship. American stevedores supervising the loading, as they were swung aboard in rope slings.*

Taffy scornfully remarked. If there is a fight somewhere you can bet the Yanks are involved.

We were to learn a lot from the Americans in the next few days; they told us that they were supplying arms to the French.

Behind the scenes so to speak. Said one American. Can't be seen to be actively involved can we? He drawled winking his eye, then went on to say proudly, that America had financed Ho Chi Minh back in 1945 to promote the Commies, is how he put it.

Oh yeah that sure was one big Shee-Bang, a honey it was. He said. They all seemed to chew gum incessantly at a furious pace as if to outdo each other in how many packets a day they could chew through. I could imagine one saying to the other. Hey Mack how many packets today? To the reply of. Twenty how you doin'? Then both chewing frantically, I could almost hear music to it!

The American was still talking.—Now we are financing the 'Frogs' for more dollars I guess. Munching rapidly. There were plenty of dollars then if our cargo was anything to go by.

Bombs in the number one hold. Detonators in the number two hold, both forward of the ship with only a steel bulkhead between separating them. Ammunition and shells in the rear deck holds and trucks lashed on deck. Yes plenty of dollars on our ship but they can't spare a few quid danger money!

I took photographs of the rafts of bombs and the trucks on deck I don't know why, maybe as future evidence?—

My mind kept dwelling on the words *We disown you*. In my present situation those words haunted me. In my locker on the ship I had photographs of the bombs and trucks, one taken of me in one of the trucks, I was actually smiling! Thinking of my shipmates, I realised that I had a serious problem. It all boiled down to my ship and career, or Smiler? I didn't relish the day when I would have to make a decision or even what that decision would be!

The day before our dinner date, as I was about to leave for the clinic, I met Joe in the foyer. He told me that his wife had flown home that morning and he was hoping to do the same in a day or so.

He then asked me what wine would I like tomorrow for my dinner with my lady friend? I was taken aback with his generosity and truthfully told him that I didn't know much about wines.

He said. "Leave it to me I will send to your table a bottle to fit the occasion." Putting his finger to his lips making a kissing action laughing he said. "I look forward to meeting your lady." Thanking him, saying I would meet him later in the bar, I left the hotel to find Chimp.

Staring at the back of 'Chimps' head on the way to the clinic I thought of what Joe had said. *He must think that things are coming to a head or he wouldn't have sent his wife home this quick.* I felt uneasy, I was beginning to think more clearly these days, in fact I was now recognising the onset of an attack and was more prepared, even so, they were violent and painful. I wondered if they would be with me for the rest of my life, for I had heard of some people, who never really got over Malaria completely, I hoped I wasn't one of them.

On arrival at the clinic Chimp did his pretend sleep act; I nodded and went into the clinic. Smiler was there so was another nurse and a doctor; I asked the doctor why I felt drowsy the day after the injection. He replied. "It is not uncommon, the Quinine is fighting for you, the injection is a bigger dose than the tablets and can make you tired. Rest and eat."

I thought, did he tell all his patients no matter what they suffered with, rest and eat? The magic cure! Instantly I regretted these thoughts, I was immensely full of gratitude and admiration for all the doctors and nurses, who sincerely thought more of the care for their patients, than they did for their own care and safety.

Smiler gave me my injection whispering in my ear for me to meet her outside before I went back to the hotel. After more tests, blood pressure and weighing, the doctor said. "You are maintaining your weight, that is good, are you taking the salt tablets?" I nodded pulling a face because they were terrible, I wanted to vomit after taking one, we had them on the ship, hardly anyone took them they were so vile.

"Good come back in two days." He said attending to something else.

Outside I waited for Smiler wondering what all the secrecy was for. When she arrived with the inevitable tray of coffee, I couldn't resist saying rather flippantly. "More medicine for the sick man?" Smiling she pulled me down into the chair next to her saying. "Yes if it's me giving it to you!" Whilst she poured the coffee, I lit two cigarettes thinking, *this is becoming a ritual, just like as if we were married!* It gave me a warm feeling of contentment.

She held my hand in her lap. I could feel the heat rising from her, like a well-stoked furnace, seeping through the thin fabric of her uniform. She smelt clean, of scented soap, I must have smelt the opposite. What with the heat and the long rickshaw ride. I pressed my hands harder into her lap; she released them with a laugh saying.

"You are getting better Moor-ise!"

I blushed and said nothing but pulled hard on my cigarette, blowing smoke out of the corner of my mouth, just like she did and said thickly. "Umph—What's the big mystery? Why did you ask me to wait?" She again took my hand, this time on the tabletop.

"Moor-ise I can't come tomorrow night."

CHAPTER FIFTEEN

I started to speak. Putting her hand to my lips to stop me saying anything, she went on. "I have to evacuate the wounded again and was only told a few hours ago, I did tell you that I was on call for this." "When will you be back?" I had Twitchy whispering in my ear. *Any day now! will save the company money! Ha Ha!*

"Probably Saturday I will come to your hotel as soon as I get back." She squeezed my hand. "I'm so sorry Moor-ise, Cheri."

"So am I Cheri." Kissing her swiftly on the cheek. "So am I." We sat quietly holding hands, I was content at this moment, at least we were together nothing else mattered.

A shadow flitted across us. Looking into the sun, I saw one of the Vietnamese nurses holding a box camera smiling shyly, she spoke to Smiler then started to giggle, Smiler laughed then replied to her in French.

"What are you saying?" I asked, laughing too.

"She wants to take our picture, she says we are like two people in love!" Smiler was still laughing. I put my arm around her shoulders drawing her closer to me. Cheek to cheek we smiled at the camera. The Vietnamese nurse still giggling said something again to Smiler who I'm sure blushed under her tan.

"What did she say this time?" I wanted to know.

"She wants one with me kissing you." She *was* blushing now.

"Well let's oblige her then." I said. Bending and kissing her full on the lips. I felt her responding, returning my kiss; the click of the camera brought us apart. Then still giggling the Vietnamese nurse hurried away speaking over her shoulder. "She says she will give you a copy when she has them developed as a souvenir." Smiler said. Gripping my hand tightly. "And I want one too."

On the way back to the hotel I lay back in the cushions mulling over the events of the day and felt happy and contented despite our dinner date being put back.

The following day which should have been the *big dinner date.* I was sitting in the foyer, idly drinking coffee, hoping to see Joe to tell him of the change of plan for tonight but there was no sign of him. I was bored, and began to wonder if I had done the right thing in demanding Twitchy to move me from the hospital, at least there I could move about and talk to the wounded or the nurses, and of course there was always Smiler! Since I had been here I'd only been out of the hotel to go to the clinic, and I was beginning to feel a little bit claustrophobic.

Looking around the almost empty foyer. I didn't relish the thought of spending the rest of the day in complete boredom, just on the off chance of meeting someone to talk to. So decided to hire Chimp and go on a bit of a sightseeing tour for a couple of hours.

Maybe if its not too far away I could visit the docks, perhaps an English ship would be in, it would be nice to mix with my own kind for a few hours. My mind made up I went outside to find Chimp.

He came over to me with an enquiring look in his eyes the beaming smile as though it had been permanently etched on his face never to be erased. I marvelled at these people even in the adversity of war they always smiled, or in Chimp's case beamed.

"The docks." I said. about to get in the rickshaw.

"Clinic?" he enquired.

"No Docks." His face had a blank look. "Ships?" Making a sailing motion. Still blank look. I tried a rowing action saying at the same time

"Ships?" Nothing but a beam. Getting a little exasperated and noticing a waiter passing by, I called him over asking him to explain to Chimp that I wanted to go to the docks. He did so; a dawning expression crossed Chimp's face, nodding he said.

"Oh Dooks! Ok." Thanking the waiter, I climbed in and we set off for the Dooks!

We went in a different direction than to the clinic, it appeared as if we were crossing the city of Saigon. Large buildings, better dressed people milling about. A lot of the buildings were flying the French Tricolour. I thought it must be market day because all along the shop fronts were rows of pedal rickshaws, some even motorised, from what I could see, their drivers standing alongside as if on parade. Some were dressed in shirts and long loose skirt-like material down to their ankles, whilst others in more conventional dress which I'd seen before, but all wore trilby hats not the coolie hat.

On the other side of the street more into the road itself, women with large coolie hats were squatting, or standing by large wicker baskets pilled high with French stick bread, fruit, vegetables, and sandals made from all sorts of materials including car tyres. The whole atmosphere was market day, cars hooting, bicycle bells ringing, people shouting, and a general hive of activity. Chimp was forced to a walking pace as he weaved in and out of all the traffic, and people, but once we had left the bustle behind us and getting into more open country, the roads once again became rock strewn tracks.

I pitied Chimps feet. I now knew why they wore the sandals made from car tyres!

The jungle seemed as though it was trying to reach itself across the tracks. Dwellings were becoming fewer. I began to wonder if it was a good idea after all, going to the docks? Remembering Twitchy's advice—*keep to the hotel*—*very dangerous*—

Attracting Chimp's attention by tapping the shafts with my feet we stopped. I indicated for him to sit down and rest, which he dutifully did.

Lighting two cigarettes I handed him one, at the same time pointing to my watch saying. "Dooks" widening and shortening my arms like a fisherman boasting over his catch. He understood and put up five fingers beaming with the cigarette dangling from his lip, I just hoped he meant minutes not hours! After our rest we again set off.

It was with relief when I saw the unmistakable signs of the docks, the high cranes, the shrieking of gulls, but most of all the smell of the sea. I took deep breaths of it relishing it, without a doubt this was my life, without it I would be like a fish out of water. I knew I could never give it up. But what about Smiler? The rational part of my mind whispered. *When you come home from your voyages, you can visit her like you do now with your family, if your relationship develops who knows? Smiler might come to England or you could go to France! Worry about that when the time comes.* This time I listened to my mind because I needed too.

Noticeably as we neared the docks was the military presence. Groups of soldiers in lines of threes and fours were marching in and out of the dock, officers at their side. The sounds of boots on concrete drowned the cries of the seagulls. Everywhere as far as the eye could see sandbagged posts were set up, guns pointed up at the skies manned by two or more soldiers. I noticed that the majority of the soldiers were of mixed nationalities. Vietnamese, blacks, whites, legionnaire's, and French. All wearing uniforms of different colours and shades, but all marching under the French flag.

Once on the dock I scanned the ships eagerly looking for a British flag. From my position in the rickshaw they all looked huge. Many were loading or unloading cargo's, the quay hoists groaning and screeching under the heavy weights, shouts and curses of men labouring in the fierce heat, winches grinding, tugs in the river hooting their horns, all added up to a deafening noise. To me, it was music to my ears.

I stopped Chimp, getting out of the rickshaw to stretch my legs, and slowly walked along the quayside, Chimp trotted happily behind me. I was so engrossed in looking at the ships that at first the voice didn't register with me.

"—you lost?" Looking back thinking, *Christ Chimp can speak English!* I saw a large man; dark tanned wearing just shorts and a Stetson type hat grinning at me. He was carrying a bag, which chinked as he moved, his teeth were startling white against his tan. He spoke again. "I said are you lost cobber?"

"Er yes and no." I replied. "I was looking for a British ship."

"Oh you want to stowaway do you?" He was laughing now.

I laughed back and told him a little of why I was looking for an English speaking ship.

"No problem Limey, come aboard ours and have a drink, we have plenty of booze on board and more here, holding out the bag.

I asked about the rickshaw with me, saying that I couldn't be long but would like to come aboard for a short while.

"Oh don't sweat about that cobber; send him off we can get you another one later, plenty about." Turning to Chimp I indicated for him to go, offering him a chit, taking it he trotted over to the other side of the quay.

"My names Tommy by the way." Aussie said putting out his hand.

"Maurice" I said, shaking it.

"Come on Maurice have a beer with the lads." Ushering me up the gangway.

CHAPTER SIXTEEN

"Cheers Limey." A beer was thrust into my hand. We were in the mess room, not unlike ours on my ship. They looked a cheerful crowd, possibly eight with myself I couldn't be sure because they were coming and going. The cabin was thick with cigarette smoke. After the initial coughing my lungs accepted the conditions. I raised my bottle to my lips letting the cold beer run down my parched throat, it was heavenly, I hadn't had a beer for god knows when, it tasted like nectar or 'Amber' as the Aussies called it. "Cheers." I replied.

They all wanted to know why I was here and my ship wasn't, apart from passing beers about they listened, to some extent sympathetically to my story. When I had finished. Tommy handed me a whisky saying. "Get that down your belly cobber." I refused with a wave of my hand slurring. "God no, I'm a bit pissed now, that would really kill me off." They roared with laughter, I felt a little sheepish, to them I must look a sight, a skinny Englishman who couldn't hold his beer! I'd heard the Aussies were big drinkers, judging by this lot that was true.

Tommy told me that they were due to sail home in a day or so, my tongue felt swollen, I knew I was talking funny, finding it difficult to get my words out, no one else seemed to notice which I thought odd.

"Wha—is your cargo Tommy—Aussie? I heard myself giggling, finding it amusing that Tommy Aussie rymned, and tried to sing,

"Tom-my the Aus-sie went to sea, in a lit-tle yel-low basket—" Laughter drowned me so I joined in.

"Beans mostly amongst other things." Said Tommy.

"Beans?" I said giggling louder. "Beans? You could save fuel going home couldn't you?"

"How come?" Came the chorus.

"Well—You eat your cargo—Bare your arses—squat over the side and fart together, its not combustion—its Bumbustion!" The cabin exploded with laughter and yells of "Good on yer cobber." I sat there beaming at them bleary eyed, but feeling quite pleased with myself.

Tommy knew the hotel where I was staying so it was natural for me to invite them all to come to the hotel later to finish the party off.

"My treat." I yelled happily waving a bunch of chits in the air. "My Company will pay." Twitchy's face swam in front of me disapprovingly. "I don't care Mr-bloody-Evans. These are my mates." I mumbled collapsing in my seat. Tommy agreed to come later to the hotel and helped me down the gangway.

The sun was still high in the sky; I had to shut my eyes from the glare. Tommy put a couple of beers in my pocket saying.

"Get your head down mate when you get back, I'll see you later about eight." I was swaying that much, I had to clutch the gangway ropes for support, and for a moment I thought we were under way the quay felt like it was moving.

A rickshaw appeared and a voice said. "Hotel?" Squinting at him I said incredulously. "Chimp?" Seeing that beaming face floating in front of me, I thrust a bottle of beer in his hand saying.

"Here you are my old mate, put some fuel in the tank!" And climbed in tilting my bottle to my lips spilling most of it, Chimp did the same except he didn't spill any. On the way back, I sang lustily into the sky "Oh Maggie-Maggie-May, they've taken her away—" Over and over again, even Chimp after a while, was joining in on the Oh's and May's, much to the amusement of people we passed.

I must have dozed off because the next thing I knew was Chimp pulling my arm and pointing to the hotel. We went in together, Chimp to the desk, me to my room flopping onto my bed and falling instantly asleep.

It was dark when I awoke something had aroused me, I couldn't think what. Putting my hand to my mouth, meaning to pull out the sponge that was threatening to choke me, only to find it was my tongue, my head was arguing with my stomach telling it not to hold any more drink, stomachs reply was to heave! Groaning I raised myself slowly of the bed glancing at my watch as I did so. "Christ almighty its eight o'clock." I was wide-awake now.

Stumbling to the bathroom, I filled the basin with cold water and taking a deep breath plunged my head in, gasping as the cold water numbed my brain. Towelling myself rapidly thinking of Tommy and his mates down in the foyer, and wishing that I had not invited them, as all I wanted now was to go back to bed. Inwardly cursing myself for having all those drinks after all this time and on medication too! What would the doctors say if they found out?

I said aloud. "Oh God I've messed it up again, I won't have another drink again until I'm better." My head didn't agree with me, it knew me better that's why!

On the way downstairs I convinced myself that they wouldn't come, after all they had been drinking longer than I had, there is a limit after all as to how much one could drink wasn't there? If they aren't there I'll have a coffee then go back to bed. Having settled that I entered the foyer.

"What kept you Limey?" My stomach dropped; there they were sprawled out at all the tables, bottles of beer everywhere.

"My names 'Mo'" I said testily. Instantly they all in chorus shouted "Mo-Mo-Mo them all down." And clapped loudly. I didn't know where to put my face; people at other tables were casting disapproving looks at us. A glass of beer was thrust in my hand.

"Have a drink Mo." Tommy said.

"Thanks" I replied, thankfully sitting down away from all the stares, and taking a deep swallow. "Cheers." *Didn't take you long to break your promise,* sneered head.

I knew it would be useless to ask them to modify the noise it would only make it worse, so thinking to myself. *Fuck it we all could be dead tomorrow! So if you can't beat 'em join 'em.* went to the bar and ordered drinks all round.

As the night progressed I was signing chitty after chitty as if there was no tomorrow, refusing all offers from the Aussies to pay their corner. Leaning on the table with my elbows, I motioned Tommy to lean over, almost nose to nose. With some difficulty I focused my eyes to his and said in a voice I didn't recognise.

Giggling in yet another voice as another, Tommy head joined Tommy. Shaking my finger at him I said with a smirk. "I didn't know you had a twin?" He made a brave effort to be serious saying. "Mo you must let us pay sometime." Seeing me shake my head, he went on. "Well if the bar runs dry we can go back to the ship Eh." clapping me on the back so hard my face very nearly dented the table.

I took a deep breath and wished I hadn't, because the room began to revolve, for a moment I thought the fan had stopped and the room was doing its job. Noses now touching I whispered conspiratorially.

"You don't pay. My Company pays." Tommy looked at me nose still pressed to mine, making him cross eyed, said. "What?" I went into another fit of giggles, all the others were watching us even the bar staff, everything had gone quiet. Talking stopped; expectation hung heavy in the air. I re-focused my eyes to Tommy's, stared long and hard at him and whispered again, Tommy's lips moving silently with mine.

"My-Company-Pays-My-Company!" His face slowly broke into a wide grin as it dawned on him; some of the others had already got it

"I've got it. The Chits!" He said belching loudly. It was then I realised how quiet it was I nodded triumphantly at Tommy and belched loudly too.

"Get the drinks in." Bellowed Tommy I winced, these Aussies sure could drink! Tommy broke wind loudly.

I mumbled "Have you farted?"

"I hope so," he replied amidst howls of laughter, "'cos if its my beer that smells like this I'm not bloody drinking it!"

We progressed steadily downhill from there until we were the only people left in the bar. The lights had been dimmed, some of the lads were snoring, heads on tables. *Looks like a battlefield.* I thought as I put my head down and joined them.

On awakening I was alone. The bar was closed; the dim light cast shadows like an accusing finger pointing out that a serious binge had taken place. My bleary eyes surveyed the half-empty glasses and overfull ashtrays, the slightest movement of my head sent shock waves through my body. My mouth was dry; I needed a drink of water badly to quench the thirst that was threatening to engulf me completely, like a man under the midday sun in the desert dying from lack of water.

Carefully moving my head I searched the glasses around me to see if any contained liquid that wasn't beer, seeing a glass of orange juice I inched myself towards it ignoring the pain signals my head was pumping out, my only concern was to drink the orange juice. Reaching my goal I put it to my lips ready to swallow it in one go. A wave of nausea swept over me as I smelt gin! Hand over my mouth I rushed up to my room and kneeling down in the bathroom, head draped over the toilet retched until my stomach ached. I gulped water from the tap then slumped on my bed closed my eyes and went into a drunken slumber.

CHAPTER SEVENTEEN

The busy bustling sounds of daily life drifted through the open window bringing me reluctantly awake. I lay there trying to remember last night; a thumping hangover made me feel extremely fragile. Slowly the events of the party came back, then the awful thoughts of the recriminations.

What would the hotel have to say about the shindig? Worse still. What would Twitchy say about all the chits I signed? Remorse set in I cursed myself for being so stupid trying to out drink the Aussies, when they were renowned for their beer drinking capacity. Even if I was fit and healthy, I couldn't begin, and wouldn't take them on in a drinking contest, yet last night me, Jack the lad did so, now laying on my bed suffering.

Aloud I reproached myself. "Your bloody stupid. You'll never learn, you deserve everything your going to get from the hotel, Twitchy, and Smiler if she finds out." I sat up with a jerk; my head punished me for the sudden movement. *God! What if Twitchy tells the clinic!* I was wide-awake now. Swinging my legs off the bed, to my further consternation I realised that I was still fully dressed. In dismay I looked at my crumpled new slacks. Stripping off I tried carefully to straighten them putting them under the mattress hoping that a crease would miraculously appear. Tottering unhappily into the bathroom, I stood under the cold shower. The icy spray did a lot to bring me round, and I was further uplifted when towelling myself, I noticed in the mirror my ribs were not so prominent as before, my face still looked gaunt, but then last night hadn't helped!

I silently promised the mirror not to do it again. This time I meant it. I felt better after the shower but felt hungry, I couldn't remember when I last ate. Going to the bed I lifted the mattress my slacks were still all rumpled. It dawned on me as though as part of my punishment that Saturday was only two days away and Smiler was coming to dinner the slacks were meant for that, what could I do?

I could always buy another pair! No. I couldn't face the wrath of Twitchy. Sleeping on them might do the trick! No. that's no guarantee. A light bulb flashed in my head, ask the maid to press them for me, but how do I ask, not speaking the language? I'll ask Joe to ask her. Feeling satisfied with these arrangements I dressed in my shirt and shorts and went downstairs to eat.

The first person I saw was Twitchy with his back to me talking earnestly to the reception. Not wanting to meet him just yet, I sidled into the dining room. The waiter appeared at my side before I had settled in my seat.

"Just soup and coffee please." I said before he could thrust the menu under my nose. He gave me a knowing look as he went away, I knew he knew about last night, all the hotel would know, that's what Twitchy is doing here they are telling all the tasty bits to him now.

On the ships we all knew what the passengers got up to, par for the course, the hotel was no different. Whilst waiting for my soup I fumbled through my pockets to make sure that I had at least one cigarette to have with my coffee, that's when I found the note—! It was from Tommy. He must have pushed it in my cigarettes knowing I would be certain to find it, I opened it out and read.

'Thank Your Company, for Your Company!
Cheers 'T'.

I started to smile. A shadow crossed the table, looking up expecting to see the waiter my smile faded, standing opposite me clutching a batch of chits and grim faced was Twitchy. *Oh no* I groaned inwardly, *not before my soup*. He sat down pushing the chits towards me glancing over his shoulder at the same time; I glanced also expecting to see the receptionist watching me get my comeuppance. Clearing his throat several times and glaring at me like an overbearing schoolmaster. He started very quietly to dress me down. "I told you over and over again not to overspend as your Company will only pay the bare essentials." He was getting very agitated. So was I because those in the dining room were listening and the waiters had joined the audience.

"What do you—" His finger was trembling as he pointed to the chits. I didn't say anything, I was afraid to say anything, because I would have lost my temper with this jumped up little twerp, so just sat there silently. He probably took my silence as a sign of guilt for he went on. "I am responsible for you, I have to justify everything you spend but this amount of drinks? What were you thinking of?" He went on and on over the same ground glancing continuously over his shoulder. I stopped looking at him because to keep up with his rapid twitching made my head start to ache again, it was like watching a table tennis ball in full flight one end of the table to the other end. I tried to shut out his voice and was just about succeeding when the waiter put down my soup and coffee, looking at the waiter, who gave me a sympathetic look, I couldn't resist snarling at Twitchy.

"Is this overspending?" and started to eat my soup blotting out his voice until some words made me stop eating, spoon in mid air I glared at him. "What did you say?

"When?" He looked flustered.

"Just now, what did you say about dinner on Saturday night?"

"I just said it is irresponsible of you to invite someone to dinner at the Companies expense!"

I let the spoon fall, it caught the side of the bowl and fell to the floor, and in the silence of the dining room it sounded very loud. I sensed that all eyes were on me but didn't care, I was seething with anger. Leaning forward staring straight into his eye's hands clenched into fists under the table. I hissed at him through clenched teeth.

"Someone? Someone? That someone you bastard, is the nurse who saved my life! Do you understand? S.A.V.E.D M.Y L.I.F.E." I stood up glaring down at him in undisguised anger, struggling to keep myself under control. Then in a voice that I found hard to believe was mine. "You call inviting her to dinner as a token of my gratitude. Irre— bloody—sponsible?" My voice was getting louder, I was seeing red. What made me worse was that Twitchy had stopped twitching, instead he was looking at me with frightened eyes.

"Irresponsible?—Fucking—Irresponsible?" I now was on the edge of uncontrollable rage almost to the point of going berserk. Half standing over him, swaying on my feet I yelled for all to hear.

"Fuck you Mr fucking Evans and Fuck your Mr Bastard Churchill as well!" picking up the chits and throwing them at him like so many pieces of confetti. He scrambled out of his chair knocking it over in the process, gathered up the chits looking very flustered and nervous, hurried out of the dining room. I stayed where I was taking deep breaths to try and calm myself shaking my head like a shaggy dog.

I looked around me; the diners were studiously eating their meals as if nothing had happened. I left the dining room and headed for the bar, ordering a whisky, my head warned me to be careful. "But I need it." I said aloud. I stood with the drink in my hand. My mind was in a whirl I had perhaps over reacted to Twitchy. He may have just unfortunately used the wrong words at the wrong time, God knows I'd done it enough times in the past, perhaps I should apologise to him next time I see him? A soothing voice spoke in my ear a hand on my shoulder. I swung round ready for trouble.

"Hey steady Mo." It was Joe he looked concerned. "Don't be upset my friend." I tried to stop the tears that threatened to overwhelm me and thought of poor Tommy back at the hospital. *Friends eh? My friend!* I was glad to see Joe, I needed friends, I was going crazy here not being able to hold a conversation with many people and Joe would soon be leaving as well. I gulped my drink; it burnt its way down. Joe beckoned to the barman to fill it up and one for himself. Taking my arm he led me to a table. When the drinks arrived I reached for mine; the glow it gave me inside was calming me down. Joe put his hand up to stop me drinking anymore saying. "Lets talk a little first Mo then have your drink." "What about?" I mumbled.

"Well, we couldn't help overhearing what went on in there, I thought you were going to hit that man!"

"That man, as you call him, is from my Embassy and he struck a raw nerve." I replied. Joe nodded sipping his drink. I went on to tell him the whole story, of how I was here, of my sickness, my ship leaving, of my Governments betrayal, of how frightened I was being alone here in this war not knowing if I would survive or finish up dead and my family not knowing, finishing up by saying.

"She saved my life Joe, and I love her, all I want is to have dinner here with her to show my gratitude, I just want her now and always." I looked at him tears were trickling down my cheeks I made no attempt to stop them. Joe picked up my glass putting it in my hand then picked his up, raised it and said. "Cheers to your nurse and all nurses." I echoed his toast. Putting down his glass he looked seriously at me. "Now listen to me Mo. I have not known you very long, but what I have seen of you I like, my wife likes you also, so never mind your tactless Embassy man—" Pausing, he beckoned the waiter for more drinks I refused ordering black coffee. "—So then, what I want to do, no, would like to do, is to pay for your meal myself Saturday night."

When I started to protest he held his hand up. "I have already paid for the wine I promised, thinking it was for last night and I may never see you again Mo, for tonight's entertainment if nothing else, I want to pay. No papers for you to sign, my treat!" He looked at me smiling. I clasped his hand. "Only if you promise me one thing Joe."

"What's that?"

"That you will have drink with us in the bar to meet my Smiler."

"Of course I will, that was going to be my stipulation." He laughed. I wanted to hug him, he was a good man, a man that I was proud to know, but sadly I also knew I wouldn't see him again after this, for a while if ever. Like that Vera Lynn song, We'll *meet again, don't know where, and don't know when*—

Shortly after I had to excuse myself, I needed to go to my room, I could feel an attack coming on, and my body was starting to shake and sweat. I didn't want anyone especially Joe to see me like this. He understood saying he would see me later.

CHAPTER EIGHTEEN

Once in my room I made straight for the bathroom swallowing two Quinine tablets and two salt tablets, which I nearly brought up again. I knew I was in for a severe attack, which I was partly to blame, what with the drink and my run in with Twitchy. I quickly stripped off my clothes and got into bed pulling the sheet tightly around me.

I was shivering violently and sweating profusely, within minutes the sheet was soaking wet, I lay there miserably wishing that Smiler were with me. I knew that I shouldn't have taken all those drinks and obeyed the doctors. But in defence of myself, I also reasoned that being alone, and not being able to converse properly, plus meeting at the docks, my kind of people. Stronger men than me in my situation, would have thrown all caution to the wind and done the same thing.

The rational part of my mind reminded me that I had probably put back my healing process by a day or two at the very least. I knew this to be true but a lot of the time the best part of my mind was irrational to the point of hallucinating. Whilst in this state I wondered whether I was going insane. It seemed a long time before sleep claimed me ending my suffering.

I awoke to a cool breeze blowing through the open window, causing the curtains to billow. Rain was pattering down onto the tiled balcony floor with a monotonous slapping sound. A broken gutter somewhere was making a loud 'Plop' 'Plop' noise, this was the noise which had awakened me, my reaction was to get up and close the windows to shut out the sounds, besides the curtains would be getting wet but I felt too weak. The shivering had stopped but my head ached, and my body was red hot to the touch. *If I went for a cold shower now, steam would come off me I'm that hot!* I heard myself giggling. I was doing a lot of that lately? I must try to stop it I told myself. Eventually I did get out of bed with the intention of closing the windows, but instead I stepped out onto the balcony. The rain washing over me was cold and sharp, but invigorating. I lifted my face upwards letting the pure beads cascade over my nakedness, I was almost in a trance swaying to the rhythm of the pelting rain, hands crossed over my chest, for a moment in time I was idllically frozen.

Starting to feel the cold I went back into my room leaving a wet trail of footprints across the tiled floor, towelling myself vigorously dry and feeling a lot better I dressed and lit a cigarette, again going to the balcony. The rain had eased off; the air was cooler and cleaner. I could hear the sounds of gunfire and see flashes of lights arcing across the sky, was I imagining it or were they getting closer, normally they were background noises but these seemed to be, more foreground noises now! Worriedly I closed the windows and went downstairs in search of soup to replace the uneaten soup earlier.

I ate not only the soup but the fish as well and enjoyed it; the waiter didn't pass any comments. Later in the bar dawdling over my coffee I studied the translated menu that Smiler had done for me thinking of the meal tomorrow. The pianist was softly playing melodies from the Forties. I listened in contentment, a thought flashed through my head, I wonder if he would play something romantic for me tomorrow night. I went over to him, waiting until he had finished playing, then leaning on the piano, I asked him if he would play a request tomorrow night; he shook his head smiling. "No Inglis, parlous vous francaise?"

It was my turn to shake my head. "'Casablanca' film?" He looked blankly at me. In frustration I looked around and saw Joe leaving the lift" Joe." I called. He looked my way and waved his hand and proceeded towards the entrance.

"Joe wait a minute." He paused, then came over.

"What's the problem Mo?" I explained that I would like something romantic played tomorrow night, something to dance too, maybe something from the film 'Casablanca'. Nodding Joe turned to the pianist chuckling, the pianist was nodding and looking at me at the same time then started to play snatches of different songs. I listened trying to think of what my sister would like to dance too with her boyfriend, my taste was 'Frankie Laine' 'Jezebel' being my favourite, hardly the thing to dance romantically to—

'Jezebel' had caused ructions for me in the past. I was on a coastal ship. England to Holland, backwards and forwards every 10 days, I took my wind up gramophone with me and played 'Jezebel' every moment I could, over and over again driving the rest of the crew potty, so much so that someone nicked it, gramophone as well. I searched everywhere, and asked everybody, but no one knew anything about it, or so they said! I really thought I'd lost it forever, until the night before we docked in Liverpool. I heard strains of 'Jezebel' drifting out of the engine room, I was so pleased to get them back that I always played it softly from then on. I had learned my lesson!—

Listening now to the strains of 'As Time goes By' it hit me.

"That's it Joe." I said eagerly. "That's the one, it's from 'Casablanca', ask him to play that one for me tomorrow night."

Again Joe spoke to the pianist who smilingly nodded to me, thanking him I shook his hand, then Joe and I went over to the bar ordering coffee that I insisted on signing a chit for.

We talked about the war I expressed my fears that I may never leave this place, how I felt that the war was coming nearer. Joe tried to allay my fears, but I knew in my heart that something horrible was going to happen to me. Before Joe excused himself, to cheer me up he talked about my dinner date and how much he was looking forward to it.

Before going to my room I weighed myself on the hotel scales and to my delight found I was still putting on weight, nearly nine stone now. With a spring in my step I climbed the stairs singing under my breath. *Tea for Two and Two for Tea*—

Entering my room I saw the maid had pressed my slacks. They were neatly laid out on my bed. I hadn't thought that she had understood me when I had asked her. *Must be getting better at this communicating lark.* I thought. Picking up the slacks and selecting a shirt, I put them both on a hanger; spotting the tie I added it as well. Closing the wardrobe door I stepped out onto the balcony, just as a French Fighter plane went over the hotel low in the sky, screaming off towards the jungle on the outskirts of the city. My ears vibrated with the deafening sound that drowned all other sounds. It was barely out of sight before another thundered by, then another, engines seemingly trying to out scream each other. I could smell the fuel tracks pungent to the nostril, then as quick as they came they were gone, all that was left as a reminder, was the ear popping silence and the smell of fuel. I was overawed never having seen planes that close before.

Shading my eyes against the sun and peering in the direction of the distant jungle. I could see great black palls of smoke billowing high into the sky, hanging there determinedly, until dispersed by the wind that carried the sounds of war, as if as a grim reminder of its futility.

Shuddering I stepped back in the room lying down on my bed, hands behind my head, trying to rid my brain of all the things I'd heard in the past few weeks. About the atrocities the communists were inflicting on the local population, as they swept south at an alarming rate. I'd heard repeatedly, tales of wanton slaughter of innocent peasants. Of rape and torture, looting and burning and even worse, tales of what happens to captured French soldiers, tales of the Vietminh tank caterpillar tracks being clogged with bloody human remains, resulting from prisoners being tied alive to the tank tracks and pulped as the tanks moved through the jungle. Even if some of these stories had been exaggerated in the telling, the horror was still implanted in my mind. No wonder the South Vietnamese were killing their own officers in their panic to desert, what happened to them if caught I'd heard, didn't bear thinking about.

Needing some fresh air to clear my mind, I went outside with the express purpose of having a walk around the hotel area. The first person I encountered was Chimp. He trotted over beaming as usual, with his eyes enquiring Clinic? "No, No, walk." making a walking motion with my fingers. I lit a cigarette offering him one, which he promptly put into a pocket carefully, so I lit another and gave it to him, he put it in his mouth and went back to his rickshaw puffing away. I was becoming fond of him and reminded myself to ask the English-speaking waiter to tell me something about Chimp's background.

CHAPTER NINETEEN

Walking outside the hotel gates I paused to get my bearings. I could see the curve in the road that I had seen on my arrival and decided to go in that direction. Both sides of the road were covered in deep red Hibiscus shrubs, splashing colour against the white background of the hotel walls; it was the first time that I had seen them in their abundant glory, but couldn't rid my mind of the image of blood. Shaking my head I continued to walk towards the curve in the road, I knew it was in the direction of the city centre from my ride to the docks. I walked slowly stopping frequently to rest I hadn't walked any distance before, and my legs knew it.

My determination to beat this Malaria bug grew stronger with every step I took. I thought. *I must ask Smiler for more tablets, I'm low on both Quinine and Salt tablets.* Looking over my shoulder I noticed the hotel was some distance away, and remembered both Smiler and Twitchy warning me not to go far on my own, as it wasn't safe. Glancing warily about me at the dense shrubbery, I saw by my watch that I had been over half an hour. I thought. *I'll rest awhile, have a cigarette then go back.* Seeing a low branch, which afforded some shade from the relentless sun, I sat down and lit a cigarette. As I squinted at the sun, hammering its rays down to earth, reducing us mortals to lethargic sweating beings, I couldn't help thinking, was this some form of punishment for what we were doing to each other? Sighing, I slowly got to my feet and made my way back wishing that I hadn't gone so far.

Entering the hotel with the intention of having a cool shower and a rest. Joe, who wanted to chat about the dinner, stopped me, after about ten minutes tiredness embraced me in a bear hug. Hoping Joe would understand I excused myself and made my way to the stairs. Seeing the lift open, I used it for the first time, for the stairs seemed in my tired mind daunting.

After my shower, wearing only my underpants I lay on my bed letting my thoughts wander in a dream like trance to Smiler—

She looked lovely as she bent over the rug on the grass laughing as she tried to keep the rug flat from the cool breeze which blew over us from the near perfect glass like sea, the breeze was teasingly tugging the corners of the rug.

She looked up at me saying gaily. Moor-ise put the picnic things down or the rug will blow away. For one heart stopping moment I took in the sheer beauty of her kneeling on the rug looking up at me with a radiant smile, her brown hair looking copper brown in the sunlight, gently ruffled by the breeze. Putting down the picnic hamper to act as an anchor to the wayward rug I gently took her in my arms, lowering my face to hers and kissed her lingeringly, she responded and seemed reluctant when I pulled away for air.

We knelt there looking into each other's eyes. For the first time I noticed a thin scar running under her hairline around to the back of her ear, touching it gently with my finger I traced it round to her ear, she clasped my hand turning it over and pressing it to her lips murmuring My Cheri. Pulling her down with me onto the rug, and pushing the hamper out of the way, using it as a backrest. I put my arms tightly around her soft body my chin in her hair and contentedly we both stared out to sea oblivious to any-thing, or anyone around, we were as one.

We had chosen this spot because it was a quiet cove surrounded on two sides by heavy rock hillocks. Grassy banks sloped gradually down to the waters edge, which was breaking with little sloshing sounds against the rocky shore, sending ripples out to sea again. The glinting sun shining on the disturbed water gave a mirage effect of stars glittering and sparkling, like a child's sparkler at a bonfire party. Birds twittered to each other in the nearby trees, faint faraway noises didn't spoil this idyllic scene.

We were sitting on the grassy bank from which large rocks protruded through the lush green grass. Over the years the weather and the sea had pockmarked them into looking like large coral with crevices and hollows, home to the wild flowers which adorned them rather like a bridesmaids headress. From our high position on the bank looking down into the still waters of the cove, the darker green of the under currents stood out in bold relief against the surface blue water, like giant jigsaw pieces.

She stirred in my arms saying that she was hungry and tilting her face to be kissed, then laughing gaily she jumped up pushing me over. I attempted to grab her but she easily avoided me running away shrieking like a young child being chased. I ran after her, not wanting this game to end, so just kept behind her just out of reach—

Suddenly everything changed. Out of the bushes ahead of her came Vietminh soldier's charging with rifles at the ready. I screamed in a silent voice for her to stop, and come back, but she thought it was part of the game, unaware of the danger she was running into. When she did realise, she turned towards me, her face an ugly mask of terror and with arms outstretched, came running back, her mouth a wide Oh! I ran madly towards her but the gap seemed to get wider—not shorter.

The grinning soldiers were catching up to he. I threw my head back screaming—"No, Oh No"—

Drenched in sweat heart pounding, I sat up in bed, it had seemed so real I couldn't believe it had been a dream, I tried to recapture it to grab Smiler to safety. My head started to pound signalling another attack. Putting my head into my hands in abject misery, I sobbed loudly, the thought wouldn't go out of my head. *I'm going to lose her—I'm going to lose her*—People say that seamen are superstitious! Which made it worse. For I was very *superstitious*.

Going to the bathroom I swallowed two tablets and swilled my face with cold water. After a short time I calmed down. Although I wasn't religious in the sense that I attended church regularly, I had been, as a schoolboy, in the choir at my local church. Opening the bedside drawer I clasped the bible in my hand and prayed to God to keep my Smiler safe. This seemed to calm my fears, walking to the balcony and looking up into the pale blue sky searchingly, whispered "Please."

I needed company. Even Bar Belles. I could not bear to be alone. So I went down to the foyer. The piano was playing softly, a young Vietnamese girl in a low cut evening gown, was crooning a French song with her elbow on the piano, a wistful smile on her face. She had an almost childlike look about her and her voice reminded me of someone, but I couldn't put my finger on it. The bar was full; almost all eyes on the singer, voices were low, muted. I looked around the bar hoping to see Joe but he wasn't there. The Bar Belles were one or two smiled at me I didn't smile back.

A burst of clapping brought me back from drifting off again into this sense of unreality. The singer was bowing to the audience she had a pretty smile showing her white teeth. She walked to the bar amidst more polite clapping, and joined a group at a table. The pianist started playing again.

Walking over to the bar and taking an empty stool in the corner, I ordered a sandwich and a coffee. When asked by the barman what kind of sandwich? I just replied any kind because although I was hungry, I knew I would not taste it. I could not get the dream completely out of my mind.

Surprisingly when the sandwich did arrive, I enjoyed it and ordered another, it was some kind of spicy ham. I also asked the barman for some notepaper and a pen, my mind was arranging words in my head whilst he fetched them.

At school I'd often doodled with words in verse, I found it kept my mind busy whilst at the same time stopped me thinking of things I would rather forget. My mind at this moment had been on food and of course the war.

I believed that all wars should not be allowed to happen and if there was a God above he must not let it happen. Thinking these thoughts I started to formulate a poem in my head, when satisfied with it I pulled the paper towards me and munching my sandwich I wrote—

Stop all war! Feed the poor. End the sorrow.

Show that love's not just a thing that one can just borrow.

Fix my doubts and then I'll pray. Give me proof here today.

Then, and only then, will I follow!

When I read the written words, I knew my mind was tortured, I tried to tell myself that it was the sickness that was making me think in this way, but I couldn't help but wonder! Joe still hadn't appeared so I ordered an orange juice to be sent to my room and made my way there using the lift.

I felt cooler after a cold swill at the basin. Taking my orange juice, which had arrived whilst I was in the bathroom, out to the balcony, I sat holding the cold glass against my hot clammy face just staring out into the darkening night sky wishing for a good nights sleep for a change. When it began to get a little chilly I went inside and getting undressed I lay on my bed my mind full of troubled thoughts waiting for sleep to claim me.

Early in the morning sitting on the balcony smoking a cigarette, feeling only slightly better after a restless night. *The dream had tortured me for most of the night and I had wakened often moaning.* I was deep in thought about our dinner date tonight. The sun hadn't reached its torturous best yet. I saw by my watch that it was only 9-30am I had already showered and been down to breakfast. No sign of Joe at breakfast. I was beginning to think that he had gone back to Cambodia after all. But no, he would have said good bye, we had become good friends not to say farewell to each other, and he was going to have a drink with us tonight.

Stretching I decided to ask the barman, they knew everything that was going on. My usual barman was on duty; he raised his eyebrows in greeting saying. "Drink?"

"Er, yes lemonade, plenty of ice please." I replied rather distractedly. When he returned with my drink I asked.

"Have you seen the gentleman who is usually with me?"

"Oh, you mean Mr Vo Din Dah?" He replied.

"Well I call him Joe, he sits with me most times." I seemed to remember that he had introduced himself by that name.

"Mr Din Dah go early to French Embassy, important meeting."

"Will he be coming back here soon?" pointing to my watch.

"Oh yes Mr Din Dah very important man he come back here maybe two hours." Holding up two fingers.

Thanking him I took my drink over to a table going over what the barman had said. So my Joe was an important man! But how important? Important enough to get me out of here?

"Mr Shoo-dor" the barman called. Looking up I saw he was holding a bottle of wine. Winking at me he said. "Mr Din Dah leave you this for lady tonight." I smiled at him then looked away not so sure of where this conversation could lead to.

I wandered over to reception asking her yet again if my table for eight thirty was still all right? She nodded smiling; assuring me that everything was in order. I smiled back sheepishly for I must have asked the same question a dozen times. I was fidgety and was willing the hours away until I could see her. Looking at my watch, ten forty-five, another eight or nine hours to go. I went into the dining room. The waiter seeing me, put his thumb up I thought, *I'm doing it again I'm making a fool of myself they all can see, it must be written all over my face, anyway what am I doing here its too early for lunch.* I turned and left the dining room.

I sat on the balcony it was too hot. I ran a warm bath and let it go cold. I tried napping but that only brought memories of the dream flooding back, giving me a deep sense of foreboding. I rearranged my clothes for the night, how many times? Three? Four times? If my watch could speak it would have said. Not again. Because of the number of times I'd looked at it. I desperately wanted to see Smiler.

Picking up the copy of the Readers Digest and flicking through it not really seeing or registering the words, my thoughts wandering to things I'd heard and seen. The night out with the Aussies. But all the time my thoughts were being constantly interrupted with other thoughts of Smiler and tonight. *That's funny,* my mind said. *How can thoughts be interrupted by more thoughts?*

I must have dozed off because long shadows were draped over the balcony; the pale blue sky was being etched with pink clouds as the sun went down, reminiscent of an artist's palate with all his various paints. I didn't remember when I had come out to the balcony or how long I had been there. I looked at the sky admiringly for this was my favourite time of night, sunset, this sunset was like one big canvas with invisible artists splashing colours with complete freedom, I was enraptured. Idly glancing at my watch and seeing that it was six thirty pm made me jump up. Rushing to the bathroom I turned the bathtaps on, whilst I went to my wardrobe laying my clothes on my bed. *Hold it. Hold it. It's only six thirty she won't be here until at least eight to eight thirty. Don't panic!* I stood still a moment feeling like a school kid and a bit stupid. *Calm down lad,* I told myself, *Get agitated and you'll bring on another attack, you don't want that, do you? Tonight of all nights!* "You can bet your bottom dollar I don't." I said aloud.

Going to the bathroom and stripping off my clothes, I stepped into the bath letting the warm water soothe and relax me. Once dressed checking myself in the mirror making sure that I was looking my best, I thought that my windsor knot in my tie was too big, so undid it and making it smaller. Satisfied I went down to the bar.

Sam, as I now thought of him from the film 'Casablanca', was playing the piano. One or two couples were dancing. The foyer and the bar was filling up. Saturday nights were the same the world over I thought, going over to the bar. "Yes sir?" The barman enquired.

"Orange juice plenty of ice." Looking around I could see that the hotel was going to be packed out, and hoped that we could have a table later. Standing on tiptoe to look over the milling people I tried to catch a glimpse of either Smiler or Joe but couldn't see either of them. I hadn't seen the bar so full before, the piano was being drowned out with the chattering of the drinkers at the bar. The whole place was buzzing and a little was rubbing off on me!

"Your drink sir." Turning back to the bar I signed a chit and thanked him, sipping the drink and leaning on the bar, watching everything that was going on around me through the large mirror behind the bar. But didn't notice Smiler until her voice, in that unmistakable accent. "Bonjour Moor-ise."

CHAPTER TWENTY

Turning slowly heart beating happily, I looked at her, she was smiling at me. Taking her hands and stepping back at full arms stretch, I carefully etched in my mind every inch of her, this was the first time that I had seen her out of uniform other than in my dreams.

She was sheathed in a Chinese type dress that went almost to her feet, with a split in the side that opened almost to her tiny waist when she moved. The dress was white, edged with gold sequins, which both contrasted and complimented her lightly tanned bare arms. The tight bodice accentuated her breasts, on her feet she wore white open toed shoes, no stockings. I stared at her she looked wonderful. Her lovely deep brown eyes stared back at me shyly, a crinkle starting to appear in the corners as she smilingly released her hands saying.

"Are you going to stare at me all night? Or buy me a drink?" Tossing her head as she spoke. Her brown hair almost to her shoulders swirled with the movement, the light picking out the sheen as she did so.

"Oh—Er—Yes of course, what would you like?" Furious with myself because I knew I was blushing. She asked for a red wine. Armed with our drinks I ushered her to a table, which fortuitously had just been vacated. We found it difficult to talk without shouting so gave up. Lighting cigarettes for both of us, I said loudly in her ear.

"We will have dinner after this drink, too noisy here." She laughed nodding her head in agreement. I sipped my drink watching her with pride feeling so happy I could have burst. Our drinks finished I took her hand and led her into the dining room.

The waiter ushered us to a table and after seating us presented the menus with the usual flourish. He smiled at me as Smiler bent to smell the single red rose in a slender vase in the centre of the table. I could see that he had arranged for the rose, as all the other tables had little posies, no roses. I made a mental note to show my gratitude later. Also on the table was an ice bucket with the wine Joe had promised days ago.

The waiter opened the bottle and poured a tiny drop in my glass standing back with an expectant look on his face. I looked at Smiler then at my glass wondering. *What's this? Hardly worth dirtying the glass.* Smiler leaned over whispering. "You must try it first, before he pours mine to see if you like it."

"Oh." I whispered back taking the glass and draining it, nodding to the waiter who poured Smiler a glass then mine, then putting the bottle back in the ice bucket with yet another flourish. He smiled at us before walking away, accompanied by a tinkling laugh from Smiler, an embarrassed grin from me.

"Well I've never done this before, I'm not used to it." Then seeing her trying to stifle her laughter with her hand over her mouth. I said. "What? What have I said?" She spluttered in between laughing.

"Your face Moor-ise." I started to laugh too.

"You looked—" more laughter "—so forlorn." My reply, in my best stern voice was. "I'll have the last laugh, you see if I don't my girl." Then picking up the menu pretended to read it.

Smiler chose to have the Entrecote with butter and parsley sauce, with side salad, starting with Consommé soup. I ordered the same but with chips not salad. The waiter with an over exaggerated action accompanied by a wink whisked the menu away placing a basket of crusty French bread on the table.

We spoke little during the first course, I hadn't realised just how hungry I was, and the soup was delicious. Smiler laughed when I broke the bread over my soup allowing the crisp crumbs to fall into the soup, scooping up the crumbs from the cloth and adding them to the soup.

"I'm a slob aren't I?" I looked about sheepishly.

"You are you, Cheri." she replied. When our plates had been cleared away I raised my glass saying.

"To us." She raised hers in answer. "To us." The steaks arrived and looked magnificent, butter melting over rich brown meat emitting a rich savoury aroma which made my taste buds salivate in anticipation of devouring the morsel in front of me. A separate dish was placed near me on the table no matter what he called them; they looked like chips to me! The salad Smiler had, looked oily with green and red bits in it. "Peppers." She said seeing my puzzled look.

The meal was every bit as good as it looked. As we ate I decided to tell her about the stupid thing I'd done in her absence, drinking with the Aussies, and how ill I'd been. She listened in silence, at times nodding her head not interrupting me. When I had finished, she reached across the table, taking hold of my hand said softly in an understanding voice.

"You must not do anything like that again Mon Cheri, you are not well enough yet, you're body has to fight the sickness, medicine alone will not do it."

"I know but I missed you Smiler, I missed talking to people in my own language, you have no idea how much I care for you I was so lonely."

"You don't know anything about me Moor-ise, nor do I of you."

"It doesn't matter my love, what matters is, we have all the time in the world to learn about each other—together." In the back of my mind the niggling doubt was digging away about the dream!

"Anyway what do you want to know about me?" I said as brightly as I could releasing her hand.

"Well—about your family? Where you live in England, things like that, so I can feel that I know something about you!"

I smiled at her. "Nothing much to know about me really, just an ordinary family background nothing exceptional—" Pausing whilst the waiter cleared the empty plates enquiring if would like dessert? Glancing at Smiler who shook her head I ordered two white coffees. Smiling he cleared the table, then with the bottle of wine, refilled our glasses upending the empty bottle into the ice bucket, from his trolley he put cups and saucers before us, then pouring coffee placed the pot on the table together with an ashtray, half bowed and moved away.

"Go on." She murmured lighting cigarettes for both of us.

"Well, like I said, my life has been uneventful until now!" I then proceeded to give her a quick run down on my life so far, how I was from a family of five, and as a child I was restless but didn't know why, that I wasn't very close to my family only my Mother and elder sister. After leaving school, still restless, I cajoled my local vicar to help me raise the money for my fare to London to join the Merchant Navy without telling my parents, in effect ran away to sea.

"Do you see your parents Cheri?" she enquired.

"Oh yes, I love my parents and spend a lot of time with them when I am on leave, you must visit them in Southport when you get a chance, in fact I will give you my address you could write to me there and you must give me yours as you promised so that I can both write and visit you." She nodded. "I will, I promise, before you leave." Stubbing out our cigarettes we arose from the table, whilst doing so I remembered the photographs taken at the clinic.

"How did the `photo's turn out?" Taking her arm and leading the way to the bar. "Oh they should be ready when you next come to the clinic. She replied.

The bar was not so crowded as before some of the tables were empty. As we made our way to one, I spotted Joe; he was speaking with two men and hadn't noticed us. When Smiler sat down her split dress opened revealing a shapely tanned leg, quickly she adjusted it but not before I noticed a few heads admiring her, going to the bar for our drinks I felt elated that other men admired my lady too.

As I edged my way back to the table, our drinks held high. I saw that she was watching me with a look in her eyes that I hadn't seen before. Whilst bending down to place the drinks onto the table, a voice shouted. "Mo!" Looking up, it was Joe waving to me. I acknowledged indicating for him to join us, he nodded then resumed talking to his companions.

"Who is that man?" Enquired Smiler.

"He is staying here and we have become friends, or I should say he befriended me!" I went on to explain, then told her about my fight with Twitchy over the chits and Joe paying for the dinner, she glanced over at Joe. I regretted telling her about the dinner for fear that she might think that I was a cheapskate this worried me until she said. "How sweet of him, I would like to meet him." I looked into her eyes to see if she meant it or was just saying it to please me.

"He will be joining us shortly." I said.

"How many friends have you made since I've been away? She teased. "Not them I hope?" pointing to the Bar Belles sitting at the corner of the bar.

I was blushing again and was thankful that Joe came to my rescue, by choosing that moment to come to our table saying.

"May I?" indicating his intention to sit down. I introduced Smiler to him, he held her hand to his lips kissing it and saying

"Mo has never stopped talking about you, I feel that I know you already." He sat down grinning at me. I didn't know where to put my face it was red-hot. Under the table Smiler clasped my hand.

"Well." said Joe. "I would like to celebrate my finishing of my business here, so why not you join me in a bottle of wine then I will leave you two lovebirds together to enjoy yourselves—Eh?"

I could only nod I did not dare to speak just yet or else I was sure to stammer and make a bigger fool of myself.

"Good what should we have?" Looking at Smiler. She smiled at him. "We had a lovely bottle of Burgundy with our dinner, should we have the same Moor-ise?" I nodded beckoning the waiter over saying. "I'm paying this time!" Looking pointedly at him.

"Of course my friend, of course." He replied. Then leaning towards Smiler began to speak in French. I was just about to interrupt when the waiter arrived with the wine and three glasses. I asked for a chit, when he produced one, using his pen I signed it with a show of 'I've done this before many times!' Smiler leaned over picking up the chit saying.

"Its the first time I've seen your signature, it's very—Chic—how do you say in English?" I didn't know. Joe did. "Stylish or Elegant." He said. "Yes that's it, Elegant." She leaned her head on my shoulder handing the chit back to the waiter. Joe poured the wine, I felt good, Smiler on my shoulder and Joe across from us. Raising my glass to Joe I toasted him by saying, "To my friend." Joe looking pleased replied. "To all friends." We all touched glasses and repeated the toast.

"Joe. I was getting worried that you had returned to Cambodia not seeing you for over twenty four hours and thought that I was not going to have the chance to say goodbye to you." I said. Looking at him affectionately.

"Oh no Mo, I wouldn't do that, I had very urgent business to attend too, now that is done I should be returning home within the week but I promise you we will have a farewell drink before I leave." I would be sorry to see Joe go, 'Important' or not, I valued his friendship. Smiler was dreamily listening to the singer her head swaying to the music. It was a French song which I couldn't understand, the only word I did know which was repeated over and over was 'amour. Suddenly Smiler stood up arms outstretched saying impishly.

"Let's dance Cheri."

"I don't know how to." I said getting up and glancing at Joe. He nodded his head knowingly.

"I will teach you." She said, almost dragging me to a gap between tables. She snuggled into my arms her head on my shoulder; I could smell her perfume it was making me quite heady.

Gripping her more firmly feeling her soft body pressed to mine, I bent and kissed the top of her head. We swayed there in time to the music; I was oblivious to all around me. The music stopped to a ripple of polite applause. Over Smiler's head I saw Joe earnestly talking to Sam the pianist, the singer was looking in my direction. Don't look up Smiler I silently pleaded.

The music started again and to my relief other couples had stayed on the floor. The singer started to sing. *'A kiss is just a kiss—'*

Smiler looking radiant smiled at me then put her head back on my shoulder—*A sigh is just a sigh*—I was almost swooning not dancing, my heart was bursting with sheer happiness, here in my arms was the women I loved, wining and dancing on a night that I would never forget—*As time goes by*—I mentally prayed to god to extend this night just a few more hours.

We swayed together, I crooned badly out of tune in her ear, following the singer, and I could visualise Bogey staring at the piano hearing him say. *Play it again Sam!*—*'A kiss is just a kiss*—I tilted her face to mine and kissed her softly but firmly on the lips, she returned my kiss with eyes closed. How long we stayed locked together I don't know but was brought back to reality by the noise of clapping. The music had stopped. I gave a little bow to the singer who acknowledged with a smile. Arms around each other's waists we returned to our table, I groaned when I saw that Joe had ordered another bottle I was a little tipsy already.

He must have noticed my expression seeing the bottle and said.

"Well it's a special night for all of us isn't it?"

I smiled ruefully. "Yes mate it is, but only if my nurse says its all right." I looked at her; she was a little flushed too.

"Only if you don't get drunk on me Cheri." She laughingly replied.

I asked the waiter for two more glasses, filling them I went over to the piano placing them carefully down on top, the singer nodded her head in thanks, leaning over the pianist I whispered conspiritually in his ear.

"Play it again Sam!" He looked blankly at me I winked at him saying. "It's just my idea of a joke."

Returning to the table I saw that Joe was dancing with Smiler, I was able to observe her better she glided in Joe's arms, as she moved, her leg tantalising flashed, the lights casting a sheen over the tanned skin giving it a sculptured bronze effect. Joe saw me watching, smiled, and twirled her around to see me she put her hand to her lips and blew me a kiss. When they returned to the table and were seated Joe asked. "I hope you didn't mind my asking your lady to dance?" I told him I didn't adding in a jocular way. "What are friends for?" We all laughed it was a night for laughing and being happy. In my mind and I'm sure in theirs too, it was a case of take all the happiness you can today for tomorrow—who knows?

We chatted relaxed, the music washing over us; Joe and Smiler danced again then Joe glancing at his watch exclaimed.

"It's eleven thirty, where does the time go? I must leave you two love-birds, big day ahead of me tomorrow." With that he drained his glass and rising to his feet said something to Smiler in French, she giggled putting her hand to her mouth. Turning to me and clasping my shoulder said. "Thank you Mo, for sharing your special night with me, I only wish that we could do this more often." The latter a little wistfully. When he had gone I asked Smiler what he had said to her. She pretended to be a shy little girl and just giggled.

"Go on what did he say?" I pressed her. She rested her head on my shoulder saying. "I have to look after you, because you are a good man." "Well?" I said teasingly. "Will you?" I felt her head moving on my shoulder "Yes." She whispered.

Tugging me by the hand forcing me to get up she led me to the gap between tables and seemed to melt into my arms. As we shuffled to the music I knew we were both tipsy. Suddenly she raised her face to mine and kissed me fiercely, then whispered. "Show me your bedroom Cheri."

CHAPTER TWENTY-ONE

My heart ached with love for her I gripped her tightly. She disentangled herself from my embrace, her flushed face grinning at me. "You will break my bones Cheri, for a sick man you don't know your own strength!" Going back to the table picking up the bottle and two glasses I led her to the lift.

Once in the room, she went into every nook and cranny with the curiosity that only women seem to possess much to my amusement. Whilst she was doing this I poured the wine, going out on the balcony and placing the glasses on the wide ledge of the railings then stood there with outstretched arms on the rail looking out over Saigon. She joined me ducking under my arms snuggling her back against my chest, she kicked her shoes off, I encircled her with my arms and nuzzled her hair, which tickled my nostrils, she wriggled about and despite myself I felt aroused.

We stood for a long time just soaking in the lights and sounds of Saigon city carried on the wind, content not to talk, content with the messages passing to each other through the closeness and warmth of our bodies. She stirred sighing murmured. "Cheri, I don't have to go back on duty until tomorrow afternoon would you like me to stay with you tonight?" I turned her to face me. "Sweetheart is that what you want to do? "Yes." She breathed huskily.

Returning to the bedroom I fiddled with the radio until I found a station with music and we danced around the room laughing gaily.

When the music stopped she suggested that she go to her car for her uniform then she could go straight to the hospital the next day.

"I will come with you a breath of fresh air will do us both good." She laughed pointing to the balcony, raised her eyes. "Fresh air?" "You know what I mean." I replied.

We held hands in the lift not letting go when the doors opened on the ground floor. Outside, whilst Smiler went to her car, I picked one of the deep red flowers which were climbing the hotel walls, one of the staff had told me it was called 'Hibiscus' I loved the rich colour. When she returned I hid it behind my back until we were back in the lift, then I tried to lodge it in her hair but it kept falling out so instead I put it between my lips and leered at her.

Back in the room she hung up her uniform in the wardrobe, then still with her back to me said. "Help me with my buttons Cheri." I was all thumbs as I undid the buttons, each button was held by a criss cross gold thread that exposed a little of her skin, as more buttons were undone. I ran my fingers down the bumps of her spine she shivered, turning she shook the gown loose letting it slip down her body to her feet then stepped out of it looking at me a small smile playing around her mouth. Standing before me her tanned skin startling in contrast with her white underwear. Staring at her, my eyes lingered taking in her small but firm breasts then down past her flat stomach to her hips, then her shapely legs. My breath caught in the back of my throat, she was a vision of loveliness to which I had never seen before.

I caught her in my arms and kissed her as though I could breath my love directly into her heart, she clung to me for several moments then pushing me away said breathlessly.

"A glass—of wine please—Moor-ise." She bent down and picking up her dress hung it in the wardrobe. I thought. *She has dressed especially for me tonight, to please me!* The thought rolled around in my mind. I was thrilled that anyone would do that for me, but she wasn't just anyone, she was my Smiler.

I had taken my shirt off Smiler picked it up and put it on, it came almost to her knees she had only buttoned it in the middle. Twirling around she said coyly "How do I look?"

"Better on you than me." I replied. Downing her drink she pushed me down on the bed sitting astride me laughing gaily, then slowly, tantalisingly, she leant over me her hair falling across my face and tickled my lips with her tongue, jerking her head back as I tried to catch it with my mouth. She breathed softly in my ear. "Lets have a shower together."

In the bathroom after turning the shower on and adjusting the curtain, I turned her around and undid her bra', cupping her breasts in my hands, she shimmied out of her briefs and turning to me she undid my slacks allowing them to fall to my feet, I stopped her hand when she tried to do the same with my underpants. I was almost going crazy. Quickly snapping of the overhead light, leaving just the small light on over the basin, I tugged off my underpants and we both stepped under the shower. The water was a refreshing cool cascade; we soaped each other kissing and whispering each other's name.

I was the first to get out of the shower. Grabbing a towel I walked a little unsteadily towards the balcony vigorously towelling myself. Seeing a full glass of wine on the rail I drank it swiftly, turning back into the room to see Smiler standing in the bathroom doorway a bath-towel wrapped around her, towelling her hair.

Going past her into the bathroom I pulled her in with me closing the door with a back flip of the foot exposing the full length mirror, turning her to face it both of us laughing happily I whipped the towels away from both of us saying. "Behold the man with the woman he loves". She turned in my arms her face uplifted eyes closed, I gently kissed her nose then her lips, she pressed her body fiercely against me making little moaning sounds. I buried my head into her damp hair smelling the fragrance of her mingled with soap. I was content to stand there forever just having her in my arms. I was feeling a little more than tipsy and knew Smiler was as well.

The music was still softly playing from the radio, we seemed to glide rather than walk towards the bed, earlier I had turned of the overhead light leaving just the bedside light on, it cast a glow over us as we lay on the bed with the sheet cast casually over us. She lay with her head on my shoulder, teasing me, by nibbling my ear and caressing me. Her breathing became more rapid, her hot breath on my neck made me wild with desire, rolling over to face her I kissed her breasts feeling her nipples hardening, her breathing quickened and she was softly whispering my name. Clutching each other tightly we made love together.

Later as we lay spent still in each other's arms; I turned both the radio and the light off and stared at the ceiling. Muted music from downstairs could faintly be heard, in a few hours it would be dawn already it was that twilight time neither dark nor light. I could feel her breath on my chest as she slept, looking at her I silently thanked God for granting half my prayer of earlier, by extending my night.

I must have dozed off because I came fully awake feeling agitated and frantic. The dream had invaded my mind again it frightened me, what did it mean? I'd had dreams before but on waking could remember little or nothing of them, yet this dream kept reoccurring why? As if it was trying to warn me of something yet to happen, a sense of doom troubled me. I felt Smiler stir murmuring in her sleep, her head was still tucked in the crock of my arm that was now protesting by sending cramp pains to my brain. I gently tried to reposition my arm without disturbing her. Seeing her there sleeping peacefully, her arm across my chest, tugged at my heartstrings, I thought *oh my darling how I do love you.*

Parts of the dream still lingered in my mind naggingly—The scar!

I froze—*The scar.* I looked at her, gently, carefully, so as not to wake her, I raised her hair to look for a scar—nothing—Maybe *its the other side.* My mind said. Moving her head gently I felt the other side nothing—Disengaging myself from her I sat up swinging my legs over the side of the bed and put my head in my hands sitting there not understanding.

In my dreams I remembered quite clearly tracing the scar with my finger around the back of her ear!

She stirred, and then kneeling behind me on the bed clasped her arms around my chest her chin on my shoulder. "You are so tense Moor-ise, why? She nibbled my ear. "Come back to bed." The dreams were so vivid each time they occurred, was it a premonition of impending disaster for Smiler, or me?

I lay down again beside her deeply disturbed. She had kicked the sheet off the bed; it was very warm in the room even though the balcony windows were wide open. Very little air was coming through; her body had a slight sheen of perspiration, which I thought alluring.

"What is troubling you Cheri? She murmured, tracing her fingers up and down my body. Saying nothing I rolled over facing her and pulling her close, feeling our bodies pressing against each other I kissed her urgently, feeling a deep sense off loss. I bent over her and kissed her breasts feeling the hardening of her nipples. Hearing her sighing was too much for me in my despair, the hot tears came gushing out, silent sobs shook me. This feeling of doom was about to overwhelm me. She rolled me onto my back then bending, kissed my salty tears, kissed my mouth, then sliding on top of me started to make love to me, it was intense and urgent until with a cry she sank down on me our bodies soaked with sweat with our lovemaking.

After a while we both went and had a shower then with just the towels around us sat on the balcony smoking cigarettes. She urged me to tell her what was troubling me thinking that it was something to do with her.

"Oh no." I reassured her. "You have done nothing wrong, far from it, its this awful dream I keep having, it won't go away."

"Tell me about it Mon cheri." Holding her hands I told her about the dream, about the picnic, she smiled when I described how I had held her in my arms, how we were teasing each other, but frowned when I mentioned the scar. Then I told her about the dream ending with her running towards me, but not getting any closer.

"But what does it mean? I don't have a scar!"

"I don't know sweetheart." I replied with troubled thoughts.

"But I'm very superstitious as all seamen are, I won't walk under ladders, or cross knifes on the table that sort of thing. Seaman won't harm Albatross's for fear of harm befalling us—" I was worried.

"—Yes I'm very superstitious, that's why this dream is troubling me. Its trying to tell me something and I don't want to know, if it means we are to lose each other."

She didn't say anything, just looked at me then her watch, and said. "Its four-thirty lets go back to bed!" As she snuggled up close to me she whispered. "Please don't worry cheri, nothing will happen to us you'll see." I hugged her tightly.

When I knew that she was asleep by her rhythmic breathing, I drew the sheets up to her chin, turning the bedside light off watched the dawn stealthily creep in, I thought of her words—*nothing will happen to us*—Settling down to sleep I thought. *I hope you are right my darling.*

The sounds of a new day brought me out of my sleep fully alert. The sun was already casting shafts of light through the open window, promising another warm and sultry day. Feeling hungry I decided to go down and order some breakfast to be sent to my room, seeing that Smiler was still sleeping, and not wanting to disturb her I inched my way out of bed and made for the bathroom.

After a quick shower and a change of clothes I went downstairs to order croissants and coffee for two to be sent to my room. The waiter didn't even raise an eyebrow as I thought he would. *Probably seen it all before.* I thought smiling to myself; I certainly had on the big liners.

Returning to the room I ran a warm bath for Smiler, who was still soundly asleep. When the discreet knock sounded at the door I quickly opened it with my finger to my lips in a shushing motion and signed the chit. Taking the tray to the bed I said loudly.

"Bon jour Madame, breakfast." She opened her eyes blearily squinting in the light saying. "Put it down Monsieur and join me in bed." Lifting the sheet.

I replied in my best waiter's voice. "But Madame what if your 'usband walks in?"

"Oh he is at work Cheri, Come to me." Throwing off the sheet. I attempted to grab her but she ducked under my arms giggling and dashed into the bathroom closing the door after her shrieking with laughter. Sitting on the bed with a cup of coffee in my hand listening to her singing and splashing in the bath, I resolved to myself that nothing or anybody would separate us. When she re-emerged from the bathroom she had my shirt on unbuttoned, hiding nothing. With a towel wrapped around her head she joined me on the bed sitting cross-legged and ate some breakfast. I was mesmerised by her; she was the most beautiful woman I had ever seen.

When we had eaten we decided to go for a walk. Smiler said she had to be at the hospital for one o'clock this gave us about three hours. I was already dressed so just sat and watched her dressing. Seeing her dressed in her nurses uniform brought me back to earth again. Last night was something to cherish, today was the harsh reality that a war was going on and that we were part of it.

Outside the hotel Smiler went to her car, placing her dress and shoes in the boot compartment. Then holding hands we walked out into the road, passing Chimp who beamed his toothless smile, I nodded to him returning his smile.

Instead of turning right towards the curve in the road, we turned left into what was a tree lined road which sheltered us from the strong rays of the sun, although it did penetrate in some parts where the branches were bare of leaves or were broken through shell damage. It reminded me of our main street at home, but without the shops. After a short distance we came to a clearing in the trees, the masses of fallen leaves made a soft cushion for us to sit down on. Choosing a spot near a fallen tree to act as a backrest we lit cigarettes, smoking contentedly listening to the sounds of the birds and small animals that inhabit the semi jungle areas. I asked Smiler what she had been doing whilst away the past few days evacuating the wounded.

She told me how difficult it was for the Red Cross planes to take off and land due to the constant fire of the Vietminh guerrillas. When I asked her if she ever became afraid in those circumstances, she nodded yes, I begged her to promise me that if she ever felt threatened enough to fear for her life that she would go with the wounded on the 'plane to safety. She grasped my hand and promised, this made me feel better

Standing up and brushing leaves of each other, I gently put my hand to her cheek "Smiler. Last night, I will never forget how happy you made me—" She put her hand over my mouth saying.

"I was happy too, and still am happy, please Moor-ise be patient with me, I told you at the clinic that I am confused, if we were in France or England who knows? But we are not, we do not know what is going to happen here, so we must live one day at a time and just enjoy each other." As we walked back to the road I said. "What are you confused about? You know I love you. I will always love you, so what confuses you, were you confused last night?" She stopped and turned to face me looking a little sad. "Oh cheri, you love me now, but when you leave here and meet girls of your own age, you will forget me—I am almost twelve years older than you, what will you feel in ten years time when you are in your prime—and I will have past mine?" I felt angry; she must have seen the anger in my eyes for she stepped back. I gripped her shoulders hard, my fingers digging in. She said fearfully. "Moor-ise, you are hurting me!" I released her panting to control myself, taking a deep breath feeling calmer. I said.

"You silly girl, can't you see—age makes no difference to me, I love you, for who you are, for what you are, not for how old you are, now, or ten or twenty years from now. In fact if I thought that we would still be holding hands in twenty years from now I would be still as happy as I am now, can't you see that? I wanted so desperately to make her understand that it was not a casual affair on my part, but didn't know how too.

"My sweet love, believe me when I say it's not last night or what we did that makes me love you, oh sure sex plays a part, but only a small part, that's not what I mean about love. To me love is not just looking into each other's eyes. It's looking in the same direction. Its looking into our future—" I just looked at her helplessly I couldn't say any more. I knew if I was mature like Sparks I would be able to use fewer words more eloquently, rather than the dozens of words I had been saying.

I could feel a headache coming on. I felt sick, the dream was festering in my mind like a canker, and the thought of losing her was surely driving me mad. She was saying something, I couldn't comprehend my ears were buzzing and the ground was tilting alarmingly. "—do care— Quinine—" Slowly the pounding in my head receded, I was sweating and shaking, I felt her pushing me down onto the ground, she held me in her arms rocking me saying something in French. I felt her prising my clenched teeth apart and pushing a tablet in my mouth, I couldn't swallow it. "Chew it Moor-ise." she urged. I tried but the taste was awful, I very near vomited. She held my mouth shut until I managed to get it down, her face looking down at me, was full of concern, she wiped my brow and then said sternly.

"You almost brought on a severe Malaria attack, you silly man." She looked at me angrily. "You are going back to the hotel right now and going to bed." I expected her to stamp her foot she looked so angry.

"Give me a smile." I asked feebly.

"I'll give you a smack if you ever do that to me again." she replied. But then she smiled; leaning down kissed me on the forehead. "Can't you see that I care for you a lot, I don't make a practice of going to bed with all my patients, you make me cross Moor-ise."

She helped me to my feet and arms around each others waists we made our way back to the hotel, we didn't speak, she had said that she cared for me—*a lot!* To me that was French for I Love You!

CHAPTER TWENTY-TWO

Feeling much better when we arrived back at the hotel, I asked her to have a coffee with me. Looking at her watch she said she had enough time before returning to the hospital. Once seated with our coffee's she asked me how many Quinine tablets I had left? I didn't know I told her, probably six or eight why?

"Well you are due at the clinic on Tuesday for your injection, so space them out three more today, the rest tomorrow. On Tuesday I will give you a big bottle, you must not forget to take them regularly do you understand cheri?

"Yes." I replied. "Smiler I won't be able to sleep tonight without you." She blushed and hurriedly lit us both a cigarette.

"Will you come again soon?" I asked. She didn't reply.

"Twitchy may fly me out any day, please say yes." She looked sadly at me "I wish I could Moor-ise, but I can be called anytime to evacuate the wounded."

"But you came last night, so they can't call you all the time." I reasoned.

"Last night cheri, I told them not to call me, I wanted to be with you." This said quietly.

I walked her to the car, opening the door she turned and kissed me fiercely then getting in she started the engine, winding down the window she said. "See you at the clinic, Au revoir cheri." Then drove away. I waved until the car was out of sight, then walked back into the hotel, was I mistaken, or where their tears in her eyes as she drove off?

My room was just as we had left it; the maid hadn't been yet. Everywhere I looked I could see Smiler, on the balcony with a glass in her hand, leaning on the bathroom door wrapped in a towel, standing by the wardrobe with her gown around her feet just looking at me. I undressed and lay on the still rumpled bed smelling her perfume on the sheet and pillows, drawing the sheet up to my neck I thought back to all what happened last night until sleep overcame me.

It was early evening when I wakened the long shadows creeping over the balcony as the sun went down made me realise just how long I had been asleep and that I was hungry despite still feeling queasy! Going to the bathroom to swill my face, I glanced in the mirror noting my red rimmed eyes and haggard features, my headache was still with me but bearable, I put this down to the excitement of last night and the fact that I was hungry. I glanced at the bath half expecting to see Smiler there, but it was empty, dry and hiding its secrets.

Smiling ruefully I went downstairs; the strains of…'Slow boat to China'—could be heard. As I walked to the dining room I thought. *It's a fast boat to England I want!*

Not trusting my stomach I ordered soup and omelette, promising myself an early night. After I had eaten I strolled to the bar ordering coffee. Sitting on a barstool I looked around for Joe but he wasn't to be seen, finishing my coffee I went back to my room for my early night I had promised myself.

At breakfast the following morning, even after a good full night's sleep I still felt unwell. I had taken two Quinine tablets on awakening leaving me only two tablets to last me until tomorrow when I was due at the clinic. I thought about what was in store for me without tablets if another attack should happen, so decided to go now today, the thought of seeing Smiler a day earlier convinced me it was the right thing to do, anyway I convinced myself I need more tablets don't I.

Outside the hotel I looked for Chimp, but he wasn't there so I picked another rickshaw showing him the paper with the clinic's address and settling down for the ride. All around me I could see the tension on the faces of the peasants and the evidence of destruction from stray shells, *or were they stray shells?* Trees with long strips of bark torn off or hanging loose; branches broken hanging by a sliver to the parent tree reluctant to let go.

We passed shattered carts with dead oxen still in the shafts and the cargo strewn across the road. My rickshaw man just weaved amongst the obstacles as though it was an every day occurrence. I remembered the aircraft screaming over the hotel, maybe the Vietminh were closer than we thought, I shuddered at the thought. The hotel was very near to the jungle from an aircraft's point of view, what if a stray shell hit the hotel. ?

Arriving at the clinic, I gave my driver a chit indicating that the hotel would pay, he seemed to understand and trotted off. I didn't want him to stay for selfish reasons. I wanted to spend more time with Smiler and perhaps persuade her to drive me back to the hotel.

I was greeted with smiles from the nurses on entering the clinic, they were dashing about a little more than I remembered, and their normally clean uniforms were rumpled as though they had slept in them and one or two were bloodstained. I sat in the waiting room idly flicking through a French magazine not really seeing it, feeling uneasy, when the nurse returned, she beckoned me into the room that I normally had my injections then left me alone. I was by now very uneasy and kept glancing at the door hoping to spot Smiler.

Eventually a tired and harassed looking doctor came bustling in holding my chart, at first I didn't recognise him and was shocked that when I did, how changed he was. It was the young doctor who had sat with me outside the clinic some time ago, I couldn't remember his name, or when it was. "You are a day early." He grumbled. I told him that I was unwell and had run out of tablets. As he gave me my injection he explained that if I was in hospital in France or England I would have been in intensive care and would be treated with different drugs. But shrugging his shoulders, said that in a war zone drugs were in short supply, all medication was limited, he seemed angry when he said this, patting me on the shoulder he said. "You must give yourself intensive care, I keep telling you, eat and rest, do not exert yourself." He offered me a glass of a whitish grey liquid that tasted awful; I gagged but managed to swallow it. He smiled. "Nasty things often do more good." I didn't believe him.

"You may feel drowsy in a little while, but don't worry go outside in the air, I will send a nurse with your Quinine tablets, then we will see you Thursday." With that he strode away. I walked the long way through the clinic so I could pass the office where I had seen Smiler all those days ago, I wondered why I couldn't remember simple little things like what happened and with whom only a few days ago? The office was empty so I retraced my way back to the front of the clinic and gratefully sat down at the table in the shrubs.

When the nurse came with my tablets, she was the one who had taken our photograph, I asked her by gestures of camera and kissing and cuddling, where Smiler was? She nodded pointing to an ambulance saying Airport. I thanked her as she went back into the clinic.

Putting the bottle of tablets in my shirt pocket I walked around the clinic towards the hospital wards, there were more trucks with red crosses on them than I'd seen before, outside each doorway were large baskets on wheels overflowing with bloodstained sheets. Over towards the perimeter I saw two tanks. I'd never seen tanks before at the hospital? More soldiers were milling about; and stretchers were being loaded into waiting ambulances—*I can be called anytime to evacuate the wounded*— her voice echoed in my mind. Looking around me at all the frenetic activity, I thought to myself. *Please Smiler, get on the plane with them.*

I had intended to speak with some of the wounded but what I had seen sickened me. Now all I wanted was to get back to the hotel. I was in a confused state and feeling drowsy as the doctor had predicted and got into the first rickshaw I came across, mumbling the hotel name, I vaguely registered in my mind that this was a pedal rickshaw, hadn't someone told me not to use pedal rickshaws? I settled back in the cushions closing my eyes being lulled by the motion of the rickshaw.

I opened my eyes to see that we were on a different road, I didn't worry to much just thought maybe this was a better route for pedal rickshaws, until later glancing at my watch realised that this was no short cut, we had been out too long. I thought about all the warnings I had been given of straying to far, about guerrilla sniper attacks. Becoming increasingly alarmed I called for the driver to stop. I tried to explain that this was the wrong road to my hotel, I could see by his sullen expression that I wasn't getting through to him, he kept muttering Airport.

My head was aching again, had I said Airport by mistake. After all my hotel and the airports name did sound alike, if so it was my fault, I just couldn't remember. At last he seemed to get the message and with a lot head shaking and muttering, turned the cart around viciously and pedalled furiously back the way we had just come. When I started to recognise where we were, I directed him to the hotel, venting a sigh of relief when we at last arrived. When I presented him with a chit he became very agitated waving his arms about shouting Piastre—Piastre I pointed to the hotel indicating for him to follow me saying. "Hotel will pay Piastre" and turned away, my head was pounding madly now.

I felt a push in my back, which made me stagger forward. My legs wobbled, I sank to my knees supporting myself by my arms on the ground. My head, no matter how I struggled to keep it up, slowly sank to the ground. Dimly I heard voices shouting and running feet, then just before everything went black I felt arms around me—

Chapter Twenty-Three

The bright light hurt my eyes; the swishing sounds were heard again, muted voices in the background. Shutting my eyes against the glare of the light; my mind screamed at me. *It's starting all over again; you've been here before.* Opening my eyes again I moved my arm, to see that I had a long white gown on and a tube went from my arm up to a plastic pouch suspended on a stand, the mere movement of my arm sent shock waves of pain through my back. I tried to remember what had happened to me, something in my mind was saying—*Guerrilla snipers—Oh Christ I've been shot,* snatches of my dream came back—*Soldiers with rifles running towards Smiler—*

With relief, I now knew that my dream had been warning me, not Smiler that something was about to happen. I called out her name. A face appeared over me, not Smiler's, I felt a prick in my arm, the nurses face distorted then faded as my eyelids became heavy then nothing—

When I opened my eyes again the room was darker. I felt someone holding my hand. Turning my head I saw Smiler sitting there, she looked tired and drawn. Seeing I was awake she gave me a wan smile squeezing my hand tightly.

"Oh my Cheri, I 'ave been so worried about you." Tears glistened in her eyes. I tried to sit up but gasped as searing pain tore through me, laying still I could see that my upper body was heavily bandaged. She leaned over me and kissed me gently. Lifting my arm slowly to brush away her tears I asked.

"How long have you been here?"`

"Most of the night." she replied.

"Oh my darling you must sleep—What happened to me? Have I been shot?" It all came out in a rush.

"You were stabbed Moor-ise." She went on to tell me what she had heard, that the rickshaw man had argued with me then stabbed me in the back. How the other drivers had rushed to help me, the hotel ringing the clinic for an ambulance. It started to come back to me.

"But why stab me? I was going to pay him."

"He didn't understand your chits Cheri, and thought you were not going to pay him."

"How do you know this?" I asked.

"Your regular man saw it happen and called the police. The man who stabbed you told the police that he was afraid that you were not going to pay him, he has a large family to feed and panicked." She explained.

"But I'm all right aren't I? I'm not going to die am I?" I asked her anxiously.

"You were stabbed near your kidney, so the doctor had to operate to make sure that your kidney wasn't damaged, but you have lost a lot of blood, and I was afraid that I would lose you cheri." She was silently crying and looked so sad.

"So that means you do love me then." I teased her feebly.

"Oui." She said simply. Laying her head on my chest

"It will take more than this for you to lose me, when I put back on all my weight again, you will see a big difference, a different me! In fact I'm told that I'm quite handsome!" She lifted her head smiling again.

"Don't 'vantardise' cheri."

"What does that mean?" I demanded.

"Big Head!" She replied. I lay silent for a moment or two, then reaching for her hand I looked at her; she looked so tired and unhappy.

"Darling please don't be sad, I know the reason now why I'm still alive after all the things that have happened to me, I honestly believe that the reason is you." She smiled through glistening eyes, bent and kissed me tenderly whispering. "I will come back soon." and left the room.

Before she returned, I had been looking around the room. I saw it had two cot beds, one was empty, and I was in the other. Asking Smiler why I was here and not in the main ward with the other wounded as before? She explained that this room was in the clinic, used only for emergencies like mine, when not in use it doubled for a rest room for the night staff to snatch what sleep they could get.

"You mean I'm taking up space you and the other nurses need?" Pointing to the other bed. "Someone could be sleeping there but not with me here. I felt humble that they would give up sleeping comfortably just for me. She assured me that the staff would still catch some sleep, on couches and office chairs as they often did, reminding me that after all there were only two beds and twelve staff, this modified me a little.

As she adjusted my pillows she told me I would be in bed for at least two days for my wound and stitches to settle.

"I can keep my eye on you, now you are completely in my hands." She smiled, kissing me lightly on the forehead.

"Sleep now Moor-ise, I will come back later after I have had some sleep myself." I tried to stop her by saying.

"Give me a proper Goodnight kiss." but she laughing went out of the door with the parting shot of. "Think about your stitches!"

I gingerly felt at my body and encountered a soft pad in the small of my back tightly bound by the bandages; a dull aching pulse was plaguing me in my hips. The thought crossed my mind of how it would feel after the painkillers wore off. Smiler had turned the overhead light off when she left, leaving just a small night light on but light spilled through the open door from the corridor casting shadows on the walls competing with the pale moonlight coming through the window. For a while I watched the shadows as they changed, making pictures, much like I did as a child, making animal pictures with my fingers on the wall from shadow light.

"Bon jour Moor-ise." I opened my eyes, Smiler was holding a glass of juice, she put her cool hand on my face. "Drink this with your tablets." She handed me the glass, and supported me as I sat up; I drank some juice and swallowed the tablets. The effort of sitting up sent the dull pulse in my back into a raging agonising pain, reaching spider web like into my groin, stifling the scream which leapt into my throat, I groaned instead.

"What is Cheri?" she was concerned.

"The pain." I gasped. "Give me something for the pain—Ple..ase." I arched my back with a shout as another spasm ripped through me, my spine seemed to lock so I was rigid, I couldn't hold back the scream as pure white hot agony engulfed me, I was drenched in sweat.

"Please help me." was all I could manage. I had bitten my tongue and could taste the salty blood, I was almost out of my mind with the pain, I knew my bandage was wet I could feel it. Someone gripped my arm and I felt rather than saw a needle going in my arm, strong but gentle hands were pushing on my chest, I was resisting because I needed to keep my back up off the bed away from the pain. Gradually the pain ebbed away and I let the hands win pushing me down. I saw through glazing eyes the doctor bending over me and Smiler with her hand over her mouth, a shocked expression on her face, I also saw a lot of blood through my bandages before I passed out.

When I came round, I was laying on my side facing the wall, with the entrance door just within my vision. My movements seemed restricted, on exploration with my free arm I felt pillows behind my back, wide straps across my body prevented my moving, the dull ache in my back was a reminder of my injury but that was acceptable to me after the excruciating pain of when—? Last night? It must have been because I could feel the warmth of the sun on my back and the room was filled with natural light. A movement behind me caused me to try and roll my eyes to see who or what had caused it, but that only hurt my eyeballs so I gave up and instead I said "Hello?" Coming out in a croak. My throat was dry, I felt miserable and afraid. I desperately wanted to hear my ship mates voices, for them to tell me that this wasn't real, tears of frustration and self pity dripped onto the pillow.

Smiler came into my vision looking haggard and strained her eyes were red rimmed and her uniform looked rumpled like she had slept in it. She sat by me and stroked my damp hair. A lot of tubes seemed to be going into me, one even in my hand, I looked at her, exhaustion showed in her face, my thoughts were that she surely was an Angel of Mercy. "Smiler I'm thirsty." I croaked. She raised my head slightly and spoon-fed me with water, most of which ran down my chin onto my pillow but enough went down my throat to ease the parched feeling.

"What happened last night? Why all that pain?" I whispered. I was feeling sleepy again but managed to stay awake as she explained that I had Haemorrhaged due to a small vein rupturing. This had caused the pain and that in my struggles I had burst my stitches and lost a lot of blood. She added that the doctor had been worried in case it had ruptured my bladder, but it hadn't, and that if I rested like this, in a couple of days I could get up. The straps were so I didn't roll over on my back and burst the stitches again; also I was sedated to help ease the pain. I stopped her by saying. "Have you had any sleep yet?" She nodded. "Yes I had an hour or two throughout the night." "In a chair I suppose not a proper bed." I mumbled.

"No Mon cheri, I stayed here with you in the other bed, I needed to be near you." Her eyes were bright with tears. "Oh Moor-ise Cheri, you have nearly died twice in four weeks." The tears ran down her cheeks, I wanted to hold her and kiss her tears away, instead I could only hold her hand. "Darling it would need a bullet through my head to keep me from you." She gripped my hand tightly. "Anyway it's a good job I didn't know you were in the bed behind me last night, or I would have dragged myself over there tubes and all!" I quipped. Trying to cheer us both up.

She started to fuss with the bed, checking drips, reading the chart notes, when she reached for my wrist to check my pulse, I grabbed her hand pulling her down to me and kissing her firmly on the lips, loosening my grip but not releasing her, I whispered. "Sweetheart I'm going to be all right. With a nurse like you, I can't fail, so stop fussing about, sit down and tell me what all these drips are for."

With a faint smile on her face she sat down and told me that the tube in my hand was a painkiller, one was glucose to keep my sugar level up, and the other was Plasma to help combat shock through blood loss. It was all very technical to me but I knew they would not have done all this if it wasn't necessary and Smiler wouldn't be so upset if it weren't serious. So being serious myself I asked her. "How long do you think I will need these tubes, and how long will I have to stay here?"

"Tomorrow, Doctor may take out some or all of the tubes. It depends on your body strength, you are so weak, what with the Malaria and now this, maybe he will decide one more day, but you will be here for a few days yet, then I will take you back to your Hotel." She smiled. "But only as a patient!"

I pretended to be shocked. "Whatever do you mean nurse?" She laughed almost her old self again. "You know Cheri!" She left promising to return after she had rested.

I lay there thinking of what had happened, if I hadn't been so stupid going to the clinic a day earlier I would have had Chimp who was always available on clinic days, then this wouldn't have happened. I shuddered thinking, *what if the knife had pierced my kidney or a little higher, gone through my heart? Could it have gone through my heart from the back?* I didn't want to dwell on it any longer because it frightened me, in order to put it out of my mind I tried to think of other things, but sleep came to my rescue and I drifted off.

"—how's the patient?. " Someone was talking as though through a funnel "Are you awake?" I struggled to clear the ringing noises in my ears, and felt something on my arm. "—He is awake now—" Opening my eyes I saw the young doctor unclipping the tubes. Seeing that I was awake he smiled down at me. "Monsieur Tudor, you `ave started your own war with the local people Oui?"

"But it was soon over—I lost!" I weakly replied.

He laughed, and for one horrible moment I thought he was going to slap me on the back. I flinched, but he reached over me still chuckling, to reach another tube.

"Doctor! How long must I stay here for?"

"Oh one or two days yet, why?"

"Well you must need all the beds you have, I could rest up at the hotel." He looked at the chart, then slipping his glasses down his nose, peered over them at me frowning. I couldn't help laughing although it hurt to do so, he reminded me of Will Hay! The way he looked at me down his glasses. "You want to leave us eh? Don't you like your nurse?" He emphasised nurse, grinning at me. *So he knows, what the hell I don't care who knows.*

"No, if I can have my *nurse* I'll stay forever." Putting emphasise on nurse as he had. We both grinned at each other. Lifting the cotton padding on my back he seemed satisfied with what he saw, he pressed gently around the area asking if it hurt. I nodded. He said.

"I will give you another injection for the pain you will still be sore but it will be bearable, if not ask the nurse for some more." I asked him if I could have the straps off so I could lie on my back, and that I needed a bedpan! But could I have an another nurse for that please! He smiled raising an eyebrow and left the room.

The giggling nurse came with the bedpan, the one who had taken our photographs. She undid the straps and propping me up with pillows helped me sit up. My back twinged in protest but with the extra pillows, I half sat, half laid and felt fairly comfortable, the nurse started to loosen my pyjama's, I stopped her quickly and grabbed the bedpan off her waving her away, she just stood there giggling. I pushed my pyjama legs down and slid the bedpan underneath me holding the sheet up with one hand to act as a screen, the sun was hot, and I could feel my face burning!

When I had finished she handed me some small damp towels; I couldn't manage the pan, the towels, and the sheet all at once so let the sheet drop, avoiding her eyes. I gave her the bedpan back with a mumbled thank you and pulled up the sheet to my chin quickly. I felt so embarrassed; I wanted to pull the sheet over my head. I could hear her still giggling as she went down the corridor.

I tried to pull my pyjama legs up again but the effort was too much making my back hurt so I gave up. From this position in bed I could see out of the window, I hadn't seen this part of the field before. What I saw made me more unsettled, a large number of tanks were lined up with what appeared to be light armoured cars, lines and lines of them; some of the cars had gun carriages hooked to the back of them, lots of jeeps were tracking all over the field. But what caught my eye the most, was the soldiers. There must have been hundreds of them all in full kit; it was like something I'd seen on Pathe News. I watched this activity for a long time and was so engrossed that I never heard Smiler come in until she spoke.

CHAPTER TWENTY-FOUR

"Are you hungry Moor-ise?" She looked refreshed and had changed into a fresh uniform; but she still had tired eyes. She placed a bed table over the bed putting down the inevitable hospital soup and a crusty French roll I was hungry. Picking up the bread roll I began to break it letting the crispy bits fall in the soup. I stopped hearing her tinkling laugh. "What—? Why are you laughing?" I asked bemused. Infected by her laughter I started to smile. "What's so funny?" She pointed to my soup. "You did that at the hotel."

I looked at my soup to see all the breadcrumbs floating on top.

"I know, I'm a slob aren't I?" I said laughing.

"What is slob?" she asked.

"It means I'm not a gentleman." Then I began to eat my soup. When I had finished she cleared the dish away and began to tidy my bed, I told her I couldn't pull my pyjamas up and why, she whipped the sheet down and adjusted my clothing, tut tutting as she did so then said. "You should have let the nurse do it, she has seen more than that! She looked stern but a little smile played around her mouth. I said nothing; I didn't know what to say!"

Once I was settled and the bed was to her liking, she reached into her pocket pulling out some photographs and handing them to me silently. They were the photographs that the giggling nurse had taken of us. There we were, cheek to cheek smiling at the camera, she looked lovely the camera had captured her perfectly, smiling that smile of hers, I

146

looked awful! The other one was of us kissing but most of it was the back of my head although I could make out Smiler.

"What do you think cheri?" I showed her the first one saying.

"This is the best. Can I have it?"

"They are for you." She said. "Souvenirs of Vietnam." Turning them over I saw she had written her name and address in Lyon and across the bottom she had written `Cher ami'

"What does that mean in English?" I asked, although I was pretty sure what it meant, I wanted to hear it from her.

"Sweetheart." She replied. I placed the photograph to my heart and repeated. "Sweetheart! Have you got copies of these?"

She produced two more from her pocket, I took them from her and asking for her pen, I wrote my address on the copy of the one she had written for me, adding across the bottom, `Cher ami'. and giving them back to her. She looked pleased at what I had written. I whispered "I love you Smiler." She laid her head on my chest and mumbled "I love you also." Stroking her hair I thought it's almost worth getting stabbed to hear her say those words. Raising her head she said that she must go but would return soon, picking up the dishes she made for the door. I stopped her by saying. "The doctor knows about us." Blowing me a kiss she replied. "The whole Clinic knows!"

Later in the day the doctor accompanied by Smiler, came to see me to ask if I wanted to press charges for attempted murder; against the rickshaw driver, the police were here for my statement. They both urged me to do so, but I wasn't so sure, after all he had a big family they had already told me, what would happen to them? Also I had been partly to blame in not giving clear instructions in the first place.

I asked if they knew anything of his background. What little they knew was that, he had a large family and was very poor, that recently one of his children had been killed by a land mine whilst trying to steal rice in order to help the family.

I thought of me on the golf course as a child earning what little I could to help my mother.

"Where is he now?" I wanted to know.

"He is at the police station, but his wife has sat outside the clinic for hours praying that you wouldn't die." Replied the doctor I then asked what would happen if I didn't make a charge.

"He will be fined, then freed." The doctor said.

"I must think about it, can I let you know later? I asked him. Frowning he agreed, but said that I must be quick as the police would not be very happy about it, then left me and Smiler alone We talked of what was the best thing for me to do; she thought he should be punished. I argued that since I was going to recover without any permanent damage and reminding her that with this war and the Vietminh getting closer, none of us could be sure of any tomorrow's. If I had this man jailed he may never see his family again; they could starve, or worse be killed by guerrilla's. Also I argued to myself, I could be out of here in a week or so, but they have to stay, his wife has sat outside praying for me that must mean something. Smiler is it possible to see this woman if she is still here?

"I don't know, I will have to ask the doctor."

"Tell him it will help me to decide what to do." I implored her as she left in a serious mood.

She returned with a wretched looking Vietnamese women, whose bare feet looked swollen to me, her clothes were rags, she stood there hands clasped together staring at the floor. I looked beseechingly at Smiler, she just stared at me, her eyes seemed to bore into mine unblinking, no help forthcoming from her.

"Tell her I won't be pressing charges, but it is because of her and her children not her husband." I told Smiler. She rapidly translated this to the still eyes downcast women, who immediately broke into a weary smile, bowing to me repeatedly as she backed out of the door.

I felt awful that I had the power of virtual life or death of another human being because of this futile war. A war that could have no winners, but plenty of losers, I didn't feel happy about the whole thing and spent some time feeling miserable. When Smiler returned she remarked that it must have been hard for me to forgive someone who had caused me such pain and suffering. I reasoned that it would have been unforgivable of me to cause pain and suffering to an innocent family, purely as an act of revenge that to me would have been a hollow victory, nevertheless the turmoil persisted in my mind. Smiler understood what I was feeling and said so. If I had not known about his family nor seen his wife, I would have probably seen that he got his just desserts.

The following day the doctor said I could get out of bed for short periods, but with walking sticks. I was eager to go outside for some fresh air and a cigarette and waited impatiently for a nurse to help me out of bed. Once on my feet and leaning heavily on my sticks, I made my way to the front of the clinic to my usual table taking deep breaths before sitting down, I had to do this very carefully because of my stitches which I could feel pulling when I moved, my whole lower back felt tender and bruised.

I lit a cigarette and inhaled with pleasure; doing Smiler's action of blowing smoke from the side of my mouth, deeply in thought of all the military build up I had seen from my bed. It could only mean that the French were expecting a battle in this area, this made me more agitated for Smiler's safety. I told her this when she brought a tray of orange juice to the table, she again reassured me that she would think of her safety, but I still worried.

Feeling stronger the next day and with the help of pain killer tablets and my sticks, I ventured into the hospital grounds hoping to see some of the soldiers I knew for a chat. I came to the hut that I had been in; the door was open and not many people were about so I went in. It had changed, the smell seemed stronger, the floor which was swilled twice a day when I was there, looked like it had not been washed for days dried blood was evident, just inside the doorway soiled and blood stained sheets were piled high awaiting collection. The flies buzzed around them making them look more obscene and sickening making my stomach lurch. Further down the ward I paused at the spot where I had sat and talked to Tommy, I felt a pang of grief. It was now occupied by another young soldier who in the dim light appeared to be sleeping, his legs were heavily bandaged, the thought crossed my mind if every bandage and dressing used daily in Vietnam were piled high they would make a formidable mountain.

I said brief hello's to one or two patients as I walked around the ward but didn't linger with any of them, it was so distressing to see how horribly they were wounded it made my own sickness seem like no more than the common cold. I also kept a watchful eye open for Padre garlic breath! with me on two sticks he could easily take me prisoner! The disinfectant was still valiantly striving to combat the smell of the sick and dying. With a heavy heart I left the ward and went into the clinic to my bed.

I didn't see Smiler for the rest of the day; I just rested and dozed on my bed. When she did come, it was with my supper, as she fussed with my bed I tried to grab her but she nimbly avoided me telling me to stop and let her get on with her job, she did stay whilst I ate my supper. We talked about me returning to the hotel, she told me that she or another nurse would come each day to the hotel to give me an injection and change my dressing. I told her I only wanted her not any other nurse to change my dressing. She said that she would do her best, as she didn't want other nurses to see my body, her face was deadpan when she said this, but then she burst out laughing, I laughed with her saying. "It's a body I don't wish to advertise at the moment!" We idly talked until looking at her watch she jumped up exclaiming how the time had gone and she had other work to do picking up the dishes she kissed me and left the room.

I lay watching the sunset through the window, marvelling at the changes in the sky. It was a different artist this time he was bolder with his colours; large streaks of red with splashes of purple, cotton wool tufts of clouds hurrying across the sky as if they needed to get home before it got dark. A wind was getting up the air felt cooler. Shivering in the sudden change of temperature I pulled the sheet up to my neck wondering whether we would have a monsoon tomorrow.

We did. I awoke to the sound of water beating against the glass of the window; it sounded like waves pounding against my ship. For a moment I thought I was in my bunk out in an Atlantic storm. The wind was hurling the rain at the glass then retreating, allowing the water to run rapidly down the glass creating a smearing effect, then blowing again with renewed fury making vision through the window impossible. Small pools of water crept through the cracks in the window frame gathering on the sill then dripping off, slowly at first then gathering momentum to appear as a transparent cord of water beads splashing in miniature explosions on the tile floor.

I'd heard of what Monsoon's could do and wondered that if this kept up the clinic could be flooded, the hospital surely by now must be, because it was ground level, no steps. I watched as the pool widened, inching its way across the floor like an incoming tide. Having a mental bet with myself as to how long it would take to reach my bed, I was winning when a nurse came in with an armful of towels laying them on the floor to soak up the water, and rolling some to place in the cracks, making faces at the window as she did so, or was it at the unrelenting lashing rain?

Turning to me she made a despairing gesture at the window, I nodded in agreement assuming she meant the weather. Before she left she straightened my sheet and shook my pillows, making a sound of approval as she examined my bandages then left the room.

A little later I carefully got out of bed and holding on to it went to the window. I peered through a spot I'd rubbed clear in the misted up glass.

The rain pounded the glass as if to chastise me for spoiling its uniform misting. I couldn't see much anyway through the driving rain only the huddled figures near the trucks, the field seemed like a quagmire with miniature lakes. I visualised the soldiers in the trenches up to their waists in water and pitied them.

Hearing the door open and turning, I saw Smiler with a tray of bottles and a glass of orange juice. She smiled as she put the tray down then walked over to me. I took her in my arms pressing her head to my chest, she stayed like that for a moment then raising her face to mine kissed me, I had to lean against the window to support myself and her weight. "You have to take your tablets now." She said.

"Just look at that rain, pity those in the hospital." I replied adding. "How long will it go on for?"

"Oh, at least another hour then it will dry quickly, its the time of year for Monsoon's, most of the roads will be flooded and un-passable, you will be here for another day or two then I or someone else will drive you back to your hotel, Ok Cheri?" Helping me to my bed she handed me my tablets, I drank all the juice before the tablets went down much to her amusement?" I grinned at her sheepishly; tablets were a nightmare with me.

She unbuttoned my pyjama top and slipped it off, pushing my hands away when I tried to unbutton hers saying.

"Stop it Moor-ise, someone may come in." Rolling me onto my stomach she examined my wound.

"Very good, the stitches are clean, you should heal very quickly now." Giggling she slapped my buttocks then jumped back out of my reach.

"Wait until I'm better my girl you won't be able to get away from me then so easily." I leered.

Placing two tablets on the table before leaving the room, she said.

"Take these if you have any more pain. I will come back later. I eyed the tablets as I gingerly felt my back, although the wound area felt tender it was bearable, so crossing to my clothes I wrapped the tablets in some tissue and carefully stowed them in my trouser pocket. Afterwards I wondered why I had done this; after all if I needed tablets all I had to do is ask! Shrugging my shoulders I returned to my bed thinking, *You're like a squirrel hoarding his nuts for a rainy day!* Smiler was right, as sudden as the rain had started it stopped. The heavy clouds moved on allowing the sun to do its drying bit on the sodden land. I first became aware that the rain had stopped when, as though a light had been switched on in a darkened room, the sun burst through the misted windows chasing the shadows away that tried to lurk in the corners. Going to the window and peering out, I could see steam was rising from the ground and the wet clothes of the soldiers, giving the impression of a ground mist on a cold winter's morning. I watched for a few minutes enjoying the warmth of the sun on my bare chest, then turning I picked up my sticks and slowly walked out of my room into the clinic corridor for some exercise.

Later when Smiler brought my meal, she informed that she would be taking me back to my hotel the next morning, commenting that she was amazed but pleased that I was recovering so quickly from my wound considering my weak condition. My reply to this was. We British are a tough lot!

CHAPTER TWENTY-FIVE

The next morning after breakfast, she helped me to dress as I couldn't bend without causing myself pain in my back, she told me that I would have to rest in bed at the hotel for a day or two. The thought of being cooped up in my room without seeing her caused me some dismay, but I brightened up a little, when she said that she had arranged for herself to come to hotel to give me my injections until I was well enough to come back to the clinic under my own steam.

Her car was mud splattered from the heavy rains, in patches the colour blue vainly made the effort of showing itself. I couldn't make out the make and didn't ask her as she led me to it. To me a car is a car.

On the long drive to the hotel although I was heavily padded with pillows every rut in the road had me gritting my teeth as the shock waves pounded my back. Occasionally the road became fairly even which allowed Smiler to drive with only one hand on the wheel, then she would flop her other hand down between us allowing me to clasp it in mine, for most of the journey we said very little, she concentrating on the road, me gritting my teeth and hoping the hotel would come to meet us!

When we arrived at the hotel I had difficulty in getting out of the car being so cramped. To my relief Chimp with his usual beam came over and helped Smiler to extract me from it. I gave him a brief hug as he handed me my sticks; he hovered at my side until we reached the main entrance jabbering away in rapid Vietnamese. Smiler had gone ahead saying that she wanted to give the hotel instructions and for me to take my time. Before entering I shook hands with Chimp thanking him for everything he had done for me, he just bobbed his head up and down beaming.

The foyer was almost deserted for which I was thankful. I didn't relish the thought of having to steer my way through crowds of people, walking with my sticks was bad enough, the strain on my arms just made my body cry out to lay down and rest. I did pause briefly, looking around for Joe but didn't see him, so continued towards the lift that Smiler was holding the doors open for me. On the way up she put her arm around my shoulders.

Once in the room she helped me to undress and get into bed. It felt good. I knew that I must obey orders and rest, the short walk from the car had taken its toll I felt giddy and exhausted. I noticed a vase of fresh flowers; amongst them was some Hibiscus. Looking questionably at Smiler, she explained that she had phoned the hotel the previous day, they suggested putting flowers in my room and she had remembered me trying to put a Hibiscus flower in her hair, so had asked the hotel to add some for me. She said this in a simple matter of fact manner, but I knew in my heart that she had arranged this with the hotel, not the other way round and loved her more for it.

She opened the balcony doors. Picking up the flowers she smelt them before putting them down on my bedside table. She laughed when I asked her were the grapes were. Placing my tablets within reach and telling me to take my Quinine three times a day for two days and the salt tablets at least two or three times a day.

I grimaced at the thought of the salt tablets because they always made me want to be sick. Lastly she showed me a bottle with six small pills in it explaining that I must be careful with them as they were Morphine and I should only take one as a last resort if the pain became unbearable. I said I understood but asked that she put them in the drawer so I couldn't mix them with the others. I had a sudden need to hold her and opened my arms to her; she sat on the edge of the bed and folded into them, I hugged her tight whispering her name over and over.

After releasing her she looked searchingly into my eyes and kissed me tenderly. As she was putting my clothes away I asked for the photograph. Propping it against the flowers—a cold chill engulfed me causing me to shudder and gasp, a feeling of extreme sorrow swept over me, a feeling of loss so strong that I felt tears pricking my eyes.

"What is it Moor-ise?" She was leaning over me concern in her eyes. "Are you in pain?" *Pain!* Yes I was in pain, not from my wound, not from my sickness, but from deep within my heart. I was bewildered and the tears flowed. I couldn't understand the crushing feeling of deep loss that threatened to blow my mind. "Please hold me." I gasped; my chest was gulping air in with loud sucking noises.

She turned to the door and locking it. Then quickly came to the bed undoing her uniform and shrugging out of it. Lifting the sheet she lay facing me, arms clasping me to her whispering soothing words in my ear. We lay there until I had calmed down. I was thinking that if these feelings I keep getting, mean that I was to die then I wanted to die now in her arms.

When I was calmer Smiler gently disengaged herself and picking up her uniform got dressed. I never took my eyes off her. She said that she had arranged for my meals to be brought to my room and that she would try to come the next day to give me my injection. If she couldn't another nurse would come. When I protested that she had said she would come and no one else, she reminded me of her being on call to evacuate the wounded made nothing certain, but she would do her best. I nodded, I knew that I was being selfish, that she had her job to do and personal feelings shouldn't come into it, her priorities were with the wounded not with me. But I wasn't listening to rational mind; I was listening to selfish mind.

Before she left she put a fresh glass of water besides my bed and kissed me. I lay there amidst jumbled thoughts and helpless frustration in not being able to put them into perspective, these now almost constant headaches and nausea were a daily reminder that I was sick or going mad.

The noise of distant gunfire and the nearer noise of shrieking aircraft overhead culminating in a big Whomph sound as a shell landed. I tried to shut out the sounds by pulling the pillow over my head to no avail until sheer exhaustion overcame me and I fell into an uneasy sleep.

Someone was shaking me. I clung on to sleep not wanting to awake. More shaking and a voice. I reluctantly opened my eyes. The waiter was placing a wheeled trolley over my bed, taking a lid of a plate that emitted tantalising smells. He helped me to sit up placing a napkin in my hand. Thanking him and signing a chit, he left closing the door softly. I had to eat my meal by forcing myself, it was tasty enough, soup and omelette, but I had no appetite.

I kept glancing at our photograph whilst I ate; seeing Smiler in my minds eye remembering—our dinner date—my dreams—my fears. Pushing the half-eaten omelette away and turning the tray outwards I climbed out of bed going into the bathroom. After swilling myself and using the toilet I felt a little better.

Going out on the balcony and lighting a cigarette, I doubled up with coughing. I groped for the chair and sat down. The sounds of gunfire and rumblings of bombs were everywhere. The sky lighting up with sudden flashes casting for seconds an eirie glow over the jungle.

I thought of all those wretched soldiers dying out there on both sides, and at one time thought of saying a prayer for them to stop all this killing but didn't, because if all the professional vicars, priests and padre's, who spend all their waking moments praying and never get them answered, why would God single me out and answer mine?

Stubbing out my cigarette, I returned to my bed to settle down for the night with the photograph on my pillow.

It was the maid who awakened me the next morning by her cheerful bon jour, throwing back the curtains letting the sun sweep the room. I didn't remember drawing the curtains, but seeing the tray from last night had gone assumed that the waiter had closed them when clearing away the dishes. Her cheerfulness rubbed off on me for when she put my breakfast in front of me I heartily got stuck in and enjoyed it. After breakfast and a good wash down, I went downstairs to sit in the bar to await the arrival of Smiler; perhaps I would see Joe?

The foyer was busy with cleaners, a few people sat at tables drinking coffee, and some acknowledged me with a nod of the head. I gingerly sat down at the table the three of us had sat last Saturday night lighting a cigarette declining the waiters offer of coffee, placing my sticks on the table. I chained smoked, lighting cigarettes from the previous ones, trying to keep the spirit going in me that the bouncy maid had implanted.

I began to get bored just sitting there and my back was starting to ache, so with an effort I stood up picking up my sticks and hobbled to the lifts. In the lift my back was so stiff that I had to press myself hard against the side to alleviate my discomfort.

Entering my room I went straight to the bathroom for a glass of water, and with some difficulty swallowed another tablet. I then went out onto the balcony, the sun hadn't reached its peak yet and the air was a few degree's cooler, in an hour or so it would be its unbearable best.

For about an hour I sat half dozing until a car door slamming brought me wide awake. Leaning over the rail I saw the familiar mud splattered blue car and a nurse in white uniform, back to me locking its door. I leaned over further, excitement building up ready to wave if she looked up, excitement turned to disappointment when she turned, it was the nurse who had taken our photograph, not Smiler. She leant into the back of the car and withdrew a small medical bag then locking the rear door, turned and going out of my sight as she entered the hotel.

Slowly I went back into the room and sat on the bed waiting for her knock, my head buzzing with whys. When the knock came I opened the door standing aside as she breezed past me with a cheery Bon jour. I closed the door leaning my back on it watching her place the bag on the foot of the bed, opening it and producing a paper and holding it out to me. Walking over to her I took the paper from her, it was a note from Smiler and read.

[Cheri, I have been called to evacuate the wounded at the airport, if I get back in time I will come to the hotel. G M]

My hopes soared I read it again and hoped she would get back in time. The nurse helped me take my shirt off and checked my back; she then gave me my injection and took my pulse, writing something in a little book. I smiled to myself thinking that if it were Smiler taking my pulse, it would blow the watch out of her hand! The nurse thought I was smiling at her and smiled back, she rattled the bottle of tablets with raised eyebrows, I nodded holding two fingers up, satisfied she closed her bag saying Au revoir and left.

Glancing at my watch and seeing that it was almost one thirty, I wondered if Joe would be in the bar now, so went down to have a coffee and soup. The bar was unusually quiet I wondered if everyone was in the dining room, if so maybe Joe was there and I would see him later on. I ate my snack with relish being hungry but not hungry enough for a full meal, I chuckled to myself thinking Twitchy would be pleased with all the meals I'd missed, not so many chits. *Making up for the Aussie binge you old fart!* I laughed aloud at the thought.

"Share the joke Mo." I looked up with delight to see Joe standing there with an amused grin on his face.

"It must be a good one to make you laugh like that?" he said sitting down. I wanted to hug him but instead shook his hand. I told him what I'd just been thinking about Twitchy making him smile.

"Where have you been Joe? I was worried about you and missed you." I blurted. He held his hand up.

"I was worried about you when I heard you were in trouble again, how long are you going to keep this one man war going? How are you feeling now?" I shrugged my shoulders and said in my best 'John Wayne' voice. "Oh it's nothing, just a scratch." We both burst out laughing.

Joe ordering a glass of wine raised his eyes at me enquiringly, I shook my head. "Orange Juice, please." When we had our drinks in our hands, Joe looked at me.

"A scratch Eh? That's not what I heard." We both burst out laughing again. For a minute or so we were silent. Joe was drumming his fingers on the table top deep in thought, then sighing he told me that he had been to Hanoi, explaining that the fighting in the North was intensifying, that both sides were massing for a big showdown soon.

He didn't think the French had the manpower, and in his opinion the odds against them was about ten-to-one maybe more in some areas. "Giap, has one of the biggest armies in the world at the moment." He said. "Three quarters of them without uniforms, even children now are carrying small arms and shooting the French in the streets." I shook my head in disbelief.

"Oh yes Mo, they are, in fact the night before last here in Saigon, near to this hotel. A French legionnaire was caught in a crowd and a young child shot him dead with his own gun, he was then stripped and his body left naked in the street, it was all over in minutes. By the time the authorities arrived the crowd had gone."

I listened to his story in horror, my mind conjuring up a scene of Smiler being ambushed on her way here to the hotel, being pulled out of her car by a screaming mob, raped then shot. I broke out in a sweat and started to tremble. Joe looked at me with concern putting his hand on my arm. "Are you Ok Mo." I looked him and expressed my fears for the safety of Smiler.

He didn't say anything for a moment then as if making his mind up pulled a notebook out of his pocket saying. "I have some contacts in the French Embassy I will see what I can do to ensure her safety."

"Can you do that Joe?" I was almost pleading. "How can you do that?" He looked me in the eye for a moment.

"Well Mo, I may as well tell you as I will be leaving here in a day or two, sooner if I can manage it. I am a senior diplomat in my Embassy in Cambodia. I am here on behalf of my Government to assist the French Embassy to try and reach a settlement with Ho Chi Minh. We fear this war cannot go on much longer, France has promised to conscript more soldiers, but they won't be trained for this type of war and they will be to late to be effective." He stopped then went on. "So Mo, I promise to do what I can for your lady."

With tears of gratitude in my eyes I thanked him and showed the picture, and the note Smiler had sent me, telling him of the promise she had made me concerning her safety. Joe handed the note back, looked at the photo again before handing it back saying. "When I was your age I too loved my sweetheart just like you. I married my sweetheart; you met her here in this hotel. I hope you marry yours, I could see the way you looked at each other at your dinner party that you were both in love. These are troubled times make the most of what you have, now!"

He glanced at his watch and rising said. "I have to go to a meeting now, maybe I will see you here later." He gave a little wave of his hand and walked away. I gazed after him until he was out of the door, at that moment I loved two people. Him and Smiler.

I returned to my room and made for the bathroom. Stripping of my shirt I twisted myself to the mirror, trying to see my back, the pad seemed huge and with the bandages I couldn't see much, but did notice bruising below the pad. Touching the pad I gently pressed around it, a nerve twitched, but it was bearable, under the pad I itched, *that's a good sign* I thought putting my shirt back on.

Going to the balcony I idly watched the night draw in, remembering Joe's story of the shooting of that poor soldier, every dark patch I saw I visualised blood, shuddering at the thought I went to my bed stripping of my shirt and lying down. The sun although going down still generated an oppressive heat. My head was beginning to ache again as I strived to go to sleep.

I sensed movement near my bed I had only been half-asleep. It was the maid with my supper I could only drink the juice and the soup. Taking the coffee to the balcony to have a cigarette. I was still there when the maid came to collect the supper dishes; she looked at my bare chest swathed in bandages, crossed herself picked up the tray and hurriedly left the room. I stayed on the balcony smoking cigarette after cigarette, gluing my eyes to the hotel gateway, and willing Smiler to drive through. At ten thirty I gave up and going to the bathroom sponged myself down being careful not to wet the bandages, then going to the door I left it on the latch just in case.

Taking a tablet before climbing into bed I pulled the sheet halfway up in case a member of staff came in the night, I didn't want them to see me naked! Turning off the light I lay on my side thinking of Smiler as I drifted off to sleep.

I could feel her body against mine, her flesh was cool against my hot body, hands were stroking me, soothing me, It felt so real, I murmured her name and rolled over...

I opened my eyes. It was real! She was in bed with me. The pale moonlight shone through the open curtains enough for me to see that she was naked.

"Tell me this is not a dream." I whispered. She moved her head closer to mine kissing me deeply. "If it is a dream then I'm having the same one." I returned her kiss; cupping her breasts in my hands I felt the rapid rise and fall of her chest. Putting my head on her breast I could hear her heartbeat. I kissed her neck, her breasts, going down her body. Her breathing became more rapid in panting gasps, then she grabbed my hair pulling me up and dragging me on top of her, we made love to each other gently but urgently until finally I collapsed beside her, both our bodies shining with perspiration.

I ran my fingers through her damp hair, nuzzling my mouth in the concave of her neck; she ran her fingers up and down my back causing me to shiver with pleasure. I reached over her to switch the bedside light on. She screwed her eyes shut to the sudden light, half raised I just looked at her sheer beauty.

Later as we smoked a cigarette, her head on my chest she attempted to pull the sheet up to cover us. I kicked it down again saying. "I want to look at you, not cover you up."

"But what if someone comes in?" She teased. I looked at my watch, two-thirty am.

"If anyone comes in at this time of the morning, it's a burglar!" I quipped. She snuggled up to me pulling the sheet up as she did so. I didn't stop her. "How did you manage to come here, and so late?"

"Well." She replied. "I was with one of the doctors in the clinic car and he decided to stay at the airport. So I came back alone and thought I'd stop here first."

"I'm glad you did." I said hugging her.

"Your door was unlocked," said accusingly. I just hugged her tighter.

"Anyone could have come in and you wouldn't have heard them, you were snoring your head off." "I was not!" I said indignantly. "I don't snore."

She laughed gaily. "You didn't hear me nor feel me creeping into your bed did you?" I pouted blaming the tablets. She pulled a face at me. "I thought about us all day and needed to see you."

"Well, need to see me again!" I said, starting to pull the sheet down and reaching for her. She pulled away rising from the bed.

"No cheri, I must go back to the clinic, the car will be needed and I must get a few hours sleep." As I watched her dressing I admired the firm lines of her body.

"When will I see you again." I asked.

"Later today I hope, if not tomorrow." I had to be content with that but knew I wouldn't be. At the door we clung to each other for a moment. I asked her to thank the Vietnamese nurse for the photographs as I had forgotten too when she came to the hotel. She said she would then slipped out of the room.

Going to the balcony I watched until her car lights disappeared then returned to my bed thinking of her and what had occurred before lapsing into a deep sleep.

CHAPTER TWENTY-SIX

It was late morning when I awoke. The maid had left my breakfast without disturbing me. Touching the coffeepot and finding it stone cold, I leapt out of bed going to the bathroom and had a good sponge down. My back still felt tender to the touch and I decided to ask Smiler to remove the bandages and if possible the stitches too so I could bathe properly.

I felt better after such a restful sleep, after straightening the rumpled sheets I poured a cup of cold coffee. Lighting a cigarette I sat on the balcony reflecting fondly about last night and wondering what I could do with myself for the rest of the day?

For much of the day I just wandered around the hotel restlessly, I couldn't settle. I had a light lunch, sat in the bar over a long drawn out coffee, went outside for some air and to have a smoke with Chimp, he wasn't there, I was bored out of my skull and my watch remorselessly, slowly, ticked on. I didn't know what to do with myself. Going to my room I ran a warm bath sitting on the side sponging myself so as not to wet my bandages. Feeling slightly better I examined myself in the mirror, my face still looked haggard but I was definitely putting weight back on I was pleased to see. After shaving I lay on the bed and took a tablet noticing that I was nearly out again. *Must ask Smiler for more, I'm going through them at an alarming rate, wonder if one can overdose on them? I often take two or three when I should only take one?* As I relaxed I tried to get my thoughts in some kind of priority, but all I could come up with was what the doctor kept saying. Eat and Rest.

He was right of course the body can heal itself quicker without hindrance, and I'd done a lot of that lately! I fitfully dozed off into the early evening. It was the knock on the door that roused me. Making sure that I was covered and decent before calling Come in, I sat up in bed expectantly, it was the waiter with my evening meal, he seemed preoccupied not his normal self, as he waited for me to sign the chit.

When he left I wondered about this for a moment then shrugging my shoulders and putting it out of my mind I began to eat my meal. Glancing at my watch and seeing it was almost eight o'clock I began to worry. Having no nurse in the day I wondered if Smiler intended to come later, thinking of her made me excitable in anticipation. Later, still no Smiler, feeling tired almost to the point of exhaustion I quickly fell asleep.

Something had disturbed me I couldn't think what, not being fully awake I started to drift of to sleep again. WHOOMP. There it was again. My watch read six thirty. Climbing out of bed and grabbing my sticks, I went to the balcony. I could hear the crackle of gunfire and over the dawn sky, large black plumes of smoke drifted ominously towards the hotel area, followed intermittently by the loud WHOOMP noises. I listened for the sounds of aircraft but couldn't hear anything.

Down below activity seemed more frantic, people scurrying about, some loading suitcases on cars. The rickshaws had gone? The space that usually had eight to ten rickshaws was empty; it was as though they had never been there?

Feeling very uneasy to the point of alarm I quickly dressed and went downstairs in the lift. The foyer was milling with people, staff and guests, laden trolleys with luggage everywhere. I looked for Joe but couldn't see him so went over to the reception desk to ask what all the fuss was about? She smiled a strained tired smile, saying that some guests were leaving early, nothing to be alarmed about sir, turning she produced a note from slot 208. It was from Twitchy saying that he would be coming to the hotel around noon. I asked if there were any messages from the clinic for me. She shook her head, when I asked if she could ring the clinic for me, she again shook her head saying that the telephone was out of order, then turned to another guest.

What did all this mean? I wondered as I went over to the bar and absently ordered a coffee. Was it all the gunfire that was causing all this seemingly panic? Twitchy had said that Saigon was heavily defended hadn't he? I couldn't remember; memory lapses were becoming quite common now. I lit a cigarette surprised to see that my hand was shaking. Did the guests think that Saigon was going to be attacked? If so, How? Is that what this mass exit was. Saigon is attacked? Twitchy has some explaining to do when he arrives.

After a while things became almost normal again, the foyer was almost deserted but I noticed that very few Vietnamese staff were visible. Even the barman had gone; waiters and cleaning staff normally going about their duties were conspicuous in their absence. *This is the beginning of the end.* I thought uneasily. *Twitchy must be coming to tell me that I'm leaving!* This thought uplifted me, then I thought of Smiler. The telephones being out of order I couldn't contact her, nor her me. I was very uneasy by this time.

A light bulb lit up in my head. *After Twitchy has gone I'll get Chimp to run me to the clinic!* The bulb went out. There were no rickshaws. Drinking my now cold coffee, I became increasingly worried about Smiler. Seeing a waiter going by, I drew his attention and ordered a pot of coffee and two cups, any moment now Twitchy could come through the door. Talking of, or in my case thinking of the devil, he came in. I waved my arm to attract his attention. Seeing me he hurried over. He didn't look his normal pompous self; there was a grim look about his strained face. He sat down mopping his face with a large handkerchief and glancing over his shoulder. Before anything was said the waiter brought the tray of coffee. Twitchy didn't say anything as I signed the chit he was preoccupied drumming his fingers nervously on the table.

"Would you like a cup of coffee?" I asked.

He looked at me with tired eyes. "Oh...Er...Yes please no sugar." As I poured the coffee I watched him agitatedly glancing over his shoulder, I didn't find it amusing anymore, I was feeling nervous myself and wouldn't have been surprised if I started twitching as well.

A headache was lurking at the back of my head, a shiver swept over me causing goose bumps on my arms. I handed him a cup. He murmured thanks and spooned sugar in his cup spilling coffee in the saucer, he didn't seem aware of what he was doing, he had declined sugar and now was filling his cup! He was nervous all right. I waited silently whilst he composed himself. With a deep sigh he started to talk. The war was intensifying. He said. The Embassy was starting to evacuate so I was to be prepared to be moved at a moments notice day or night. I asked, would it be today or tomorrow?

"Tomorrow or the day after, as soon as we can safely arrange to go to the airport." He replied. I asked if he could take me to the clinic or find out if they were still there and all right. He shook his head saying he had too much to do at the embassy. Draining his coffee he stood up to go, his parting words were to be ready for his call.

I sat there confused. Did it mean that the French were pulling out of Saigon? I had heard tales that the communist's guerrilla factions had overthrown parts of Saigon before, but the French had always thrown them out again. About three times over the last twelve months this had happened; I had been told, but the alarming thing about it was, that until the enemy were trounced they did a lot of damage and killings. The last time that they were in control it was some weeks before the French resumed control apparently! I looked around for Joe but couldn't see him anywhere, I hoped he had gone home as he had indicated he was doing.

Walking to the dining room I sat at my usual table ordering toast and coffee, there were only two waiters on duty, both French. I longed for a cup of tea but the tea in the hotel was awful, tasteless and weak. After eating I went outside for some air. It was strangely quiet after all the earlier noises, even the air seemed still as if waiting with bated breath for something to happen. The whole atmosphere was affecting me. I was feeling tense; my nerves were as taut as a fiddle string, making my eyes hurt, shielding them from the already hot sun I went back into the hotel and directly to my room. The bed was still unmade so the maid hadn't reached my floor yet. I sat on the bed in a daze rubbing my temples trying to ease the throbbing pain. Groping for my tablets I popped two in my mouth and with what was left in my glass of water I tried to swallow them ending up crunching them, gritting my teeth I went to the bathroom to refill my glass and swill my mouth from the gritty acid taste.

I had to lie on the bed before I fell down, clenching my teeth as my back protested by shooting pain through it. I closed my eyes, I felt weak and my body was burning. Smiler had warned me that the fever could strike without warning, especially if I got over stressed. Just thinking of her made me take out the photograph, seeing her smiling face brought a terrible premonition over me that something was about to happen to one or both of us.

Memories of the dream flooded back, Smiler being chased by soldiers, running towards me her mouth open in a silent cry for help, me running towards her but the gap widening not narrowing. Tears pricked my eyes I pressed the photograph to my chest. With a sudden pang of grief I threw back my head against the headboard and cried out in anguish. Drawing my legs up to my chest and clasping them in my arms I rocked back and forth in time to my moaning.

The rest of the day I alternated between grief and sorrow with a mixture of anger, it was a deadly cocktail. I was on the edge of madness but didn't care. I was like a man in a drunken rage yet I was sober, I pleaded, I cursed, and I bloodied my knuckles punching the walls and all the time my sickness crept up on me. I could hear voices in my head but refused to listen just sat abjectly on the floor. I crawled to the bed, opening the bedside drawer and reached for the bible. For a few moments whilst I gazed at it my mind became lucid enough for me to open it and put Smiler's photo between the pages, whispering for him to look after her then replacing it in the drawer.

I half laid on the floor and the bed; shivering and sweating at the same time, drifting in and out of consciousness until I pulled myself into bed curling up my knees to my chin and pulling the sheet over me.

Chapter Twenty-Eight

The sudden noise of my door crashing open and a loud jabbering voice brought me half way out of my sleep I opened my eyes and stared at the intrusion to my room. I was still groggy and wanted to go back to the security of sleep; so closed my eyes again; the voice got louder and shrill hurting my ears. I felt something sharp pricking my feet, mumbling to myself I opened my eyes again, then came completely awake.

A soldier stood at the foot of my bed pointing a rifle at me shouting and gesturing for me to get up. I was in shock not daring to believe my eyes. I thought I was hallucinating, that I was awake, but at the same time in my dream that was always haunting me.

The soldier was covered in dried mud, his eyes and teeth showed white against his mudcaked face. His uniform looked as though he had crawled through mud, everything about him was mud, and he stank of stagnant mud. I still thought I was in my nightmare until he prodded me painfully with his rifle then I knew that this was real and was the start of all my worst fears.

He shouted again indicating with his rifle for me to leave the room and follow him; he was small and squat featured, with the high cheekbones of the Vietnamese. When I reached for one of my sticks, he shouted loudly and with his rifle flicked it out of my hand then roughly pushed me back onto the bed. Picking up my stick, he broke it across his knee like a piece of firewood, laughing at me as he threw it across the room.

Prodding me again, he made me go into the corridor, I couldn't walk fast having to hold onto the wall for support which made him shout louder and pushing me. I stopped at the lift but more shouting and prodding made me go to the stairs.

The noise from downstairs was a mixture of shouts and breaking of glass growing louder as I stumbled down the stairs, hanging on to the banister rail to stop myself from falling. I was feeling very disorientated, the soldier sounding very angry now, almost pushed me down the stairs. The scene that met my eyes was directly out of a nightmare. The foyer was teeming with both soldiers and civilians, people were gathered in small clusters some still in night attire, some bleeding quite freely from cuts to the head, some looking very dishevelled in rumpled clothes, all looking very frightened.

Soldiers were everywhere, all alike in stature and mudcaked uniforms; some drinking from bottles from the wrecked bar. The long mirror which I had often surveyed the foyer through, smashed; some long shards of glass clinging stubbornly to the gilt frame reluctant to join the smashed glass which littered the floor. My dazed uncomprehending eyes took this unbelievable carnage in and immediately wanted to shut it out as a bad dream.

I was pushed into a small group of hotel staff who were ashen faced and cowed, looking about me trying to see Joe or anyone that I knew, but all I could see were frightened people and jubilant drunken soldiers. I thought I recognised one of the reception girls looking terrified with her hands crossed over her bared breasts, amongst a group of soldiers. Her blouse was torn off her, hanging in shreds around her waist; I tried to see clearer by standing on tiptoe but the movement of the milling crowd hid her from me.

I felt faint and wanted to be sick, the thought of Smiler being surrounded by soldiers like the poor receptionist and the fate that awaited her made me sick. I retched until my stomach ached, the nearby soldiers sneering and saying things that I could only imagine. I was truly unashamedly frightened. We were shuffled slowly towards the dining room, cowed, dejected, like sheep to the slaughter. G

Glancing over the reception desk as I passed, I saw the manager lying on his back eyes closed, to all intent and purpose asleep, then I saw the blood on the front of his shirt. I wanted to be sick again, holding my hand to my mouth I averted my eyes and moved on my feet crunching on broken glass getting ever nearer to the dining room, to what? My eyes were sore through sweat dripping in them and tears spilling out.

We were halted at the dining room door, looking around again shutting my ears to the wailing and shouting I saw the grand piano. It was badly damaged, the lid; only last night majestic in its triumph of the music it contained, was hanging off, broken glass and cigarette ends adorning its once silvery keys. Nearby chairs slashed.

Loud laughter from the group of soldiers around the reception girl made me look in that direction, the group had parted slightly and in plain view was the girl naked now sitting on the floor still with her arms across her breasts just staring at the floor. The jeering soldiers looked drunk to me, I shuddered at the thought of what was going to happen to the women later. The tiled floor was strewn with debris; the potted plants pulled from their tubs and scattered about, nothing but wanton destruction belying the fact that only a few hours ago this was a hotel of opulence.

The dining room door opened and one of the waiters was pushed out his nose was swollen and one eye was puffed closed. His shirt was stained with blood, I wondered if he had tried to help the receptionist as they had been very friendly with each other.

The soldier who had bullied me upstairs was strutting up and down our line smirking. I studied him covertly, I guessed he weighed about nine stone, being small made him look muscular no more than five two or three, couldn't guess his age, I thought to myself. *If I weren't so sick you bastard I would have battered you up in my room.* My mind sneered. *Oh very good Maurice, then you would have been shot!* The thought of being shot frightened me, my short-lived bravado vanished I was shaking, I didn't know if it was with the fever or fright, at that moment I was very scared. We moved a little nearer to the dining room door. It opened again members of the staff came out, some were putting different armbands on, some black, some white and others red.

The laughter became louder as the beer flowed; one soldier staggered to the entrance door, stopping to unbutton his trousers, and urinated against the doorframe laughing loudly. Others started to do the same, the stench of urine filled the air. I needed to sit down my legs felt weak and my head was pounding I had to have a tablet before the attack hit me proper, I held grimly to the wall afraid that I might collapse and not knowing what this drunken lot would do to me if I did. When my turn came to go into the room, as I went through the door two soldiers grabbed me and marched me to the centre of the dining room where some tables had been pushed together. I was glad that they were holding me because I would not have made it on my own.

Three Vietminh officers sat behind the table. The one in the middle seemed older than the other two, and appeared to be in charge. The tables were bare of cloths only having a large jug of water and some glasses; a side table had the armbands. I stood swaying barely able to focus my eyes. A voice was jabbering away getting louder then fading away. I couldn't understand a word, and to stop myself pitching forward, I put my hands on the table, by this time I was sweating profusely and shaking. Slowly I raised my head to look at the one doing the talking, he was pointing to something in front of him, I couldn't focus on him only the jug of water. I croaked. Water…Malaria…More jabbering then a chair was pushed under my legs and I was roughly forced onto it, I was grateful, for the room was swimming before my eyes, my head lolled on my chest. I mumbled. "English." Arms lifted me still in the chair and I felt a cool draught on my sticky body, it revived me a little, enough to notice that I was near an open window.

The officer was still jabbering away and getting angry; the veins in his neck were standing out, he was banging the table and pointing to me, the other officers were writing on a pad; in front of one of them was the hotel register which they kept referring too.

More people from the queue were now in the room. As each one stood at the table the officer with the register checked them against it then handed them an armband, the staff seemed to get a white one. I was lifted again in the chair and placed near the end of the table that the officer with the register was sitting; he turned it towards me saying in English. "Name." I flicked the pages until I saw my name pointing to it and turning the book round to him said. "Tudor, I'm English." He wrote on his pad without looking at me or saying a word. The officer said something then slid something down the table towards me, to my dismay I saw it was Tommy's shirt, I could hear Twitchy warning me not to keep it as I could be mistaken for a soldier and be shot at. I stared at it with a sinking feeling and wishing that I had heeded Twitchy instead of being such a stubborn fool, now they think I'm a legionnaire! I hastily tried to explain how the shirt was in my possession. How I had no change of clothes when I was brought to the hospital and the shirt had been leant to me whilst mine was being washed, and I had forgotten to give it back, I was sick and couldn't remember much. I was so scared I would have told them anything as long as it pleased them I didn't want them to hurt me, I was hurting enough.

One of the officers gave me a glass of water, which I drank gratefully and thanked him; he spoke good English and seemed more

sympathetic than the other two, so I concentrated on him. Writing on the pad hardly looking at me. He asked me questions so quickly that I hardly had time to answer before he asked another, I started to get worried again.

CHAPTER TWENTY-NINE

"Why are you in Vietnam? Where is your ship? How long do mean to stay in Vietnam? What is your position in this war? Why did you keep an army issue shirt? What did you intend to do with it?" I was so scared that I told him my story from being taken ill with Malaria on the ship and waking up out of a coma in a French hospital. My ship leaving, that I was waiting for the Embassy to fly me out of Vietnam to rejoin my ship, that I was still sick and needed regular medication.

I looked at him helplessly not knowing if he understood or even believed me. At that moment I desperately needed a friend, but most of all I needed my bed, I felt so sick and knew I was going to have my worst attack ever. He looked up at me saying nothing just stared. I spoke pleadingly in a last desperate effort to get out of here and lay down on my bed.

"I'm not your enemy, please don't be mine...Mr Evans from the British Embassy is trying to arrange for me to fly out of here—" He stopped me, saying something to a soldier who promptly left the room, then turning to me said.

"We will contact your Embassy in the meantime tell me what your ship cargo was?" I was flustered, I didn't dare tell him that it was bombs and guns or that my Government had forced us to sail here and now they disowned us for gun running. My mind was in turmoil, what would Twitchy tell them? Did they already know? I asked for more water to gain time to think.

Well?" He asked, pen poised over the pad.

"I don't know." I lied. "I think it was grain or something like that." He wrote on his pad, then looking at me said not unkindly.

"You will remain in your room, you must not leave it for any reason and wear this armband at all times, when we have checked your story we will talk again." He handed me a white armband. "Do you understand?" I nodded. He went on. "You will have a guard at your door and only if he says, do you leave your room, it is that or a prison, have you any questions?" "Yes." I said, feeling a little braver. I need injections three times a week and daily tablets, will I still be able to go to the clinic for my treatment?"

He replied. "We will do what we can but medicine is in short supply so I make no promise." Producing a bottle of tablets out of his pocket he said. "Are these yours?" Reaching for them I said. "Yes without them I go into a fever attack, I am having one now." He let me take them saying. "Use them sparingly I don't know when you will get anymore." He nodded at a soldier who grasped my arm and led me away.

Back to my room I was pushed in then the door slammed shut. I heard the key turn in the lock. The room was a shamble. Horrified I saw my clothes scattered about, the mattress was on the floor the bedside cabinet was on its side the drawer on the floor spilling out the bible and the readers digest dry muddied footprints on them. The bathroom was the same my toilet gear thrown onto the floor. I sat on the toilet seat to numb with shock to comprehend my desperate situation, all I could think about was what happens next?

I swallowed a tablet and went back to the bedroom to survey the mess. *I must have a rest before I attempt to clear this mess up.* I thought. Turning to the bed I tried to put the mattress back but every time I lifted one end onto the bed then lifted the other end it slipped back on the floor, I didn't have the strength to lift it so gave up and flopped on it on the floor. I lay there trying to get my breathing under control, thinking of what I had just witnessed, the naked terrified receptionist, the frightened hotel staff, the manager? The wilful destruction and the drunken soldiers.

I hoped it was only the hotel the Vietminh had captured and soon the French would re-capture it like they had before. But if Saigon had been captured then so will the clinic as well.

If the clinic was taken...Smiler...? I jerked upright, scrambling on the floor for the bible! Where is it? I know I've seen it. I found the readers digest but not the bible. I sat on the floor wondering why my room had been vandalised; I had nothing to steal? Yet they had taken Tommy's shirt and my tablets. I was lucky about the shirt! They could have mistaken me for a spy or something; a drunken soldier could have easily shot me...I shuddered at the thought. Closing my eyes I tried to sleep but how could I sleep when I was in a living nightmare?

I must have slept because the loud noise of my door slamming against the wall brought me to full consciousness, a tray slithered across the floor making a nerve grating eeehhh sound, coming to rest against the edge of the mattress the door slammed shut. On examination I saw a revolting dish of rice and fish, the fish looked half cooked and not very fresh from the smell of it, no knife or fork and nothing to drink. I tentatively picked a piece of fish and putting it in my mouth spat it out in disgust, my stomach heaved, it was raw and tasted off. I tried another bit that looked cooked, it was almost as bad but I swallowed it with difficulty, pushing the fish aside I ate the rice. *You must eat or you will waste away and die and they won't care.* My mind said. After eating what I could and hold it down, I pushed the tray away nearer to the door and going to the bathroom filled a glass of water from the basin, it didn't taste as nice as the drinking water but it was better than nothing. *Don't drink too much of it or you will get dysentery.* My mind warned me. *That's the only thing I haven't had yet!* I thought. I managed to lift the mattress back onto the bed, and there was the bible. It had been under the mattress all the time. I opened it and frantically flipped through the pages and to my relief found the photograph. Putting it to my lips I kissed it and then carefully put it back in the bible and stowing it in the comparatively safety of the drawer.

My eye caught sight of the tray with the uneaten food and swept over it in disgust, then back again. Something was nagging me in the back of my mind about uneaten food in prisons, what was it? This is a prison now isn't it? So what is it? Then it hit me, if any food was left they thought you had to much in the first place so gave you less next time. I needed all the food I could get if I was to build my strength up and get well again. Getting up I flushed the uneaten food down the toilet

I took it easy putting the room back in order, when I felt groggy I sat down. Once the room was almost to my liking I started on the bathroom waving to the ghost in the mirror who waved back. My spare soap was gone so was the bottle of painkillers. I sat on the side of the bath thinking of this. My painkillers were my only hope of coping with the pain that I knew lay ahead, when my Quinine ran out I was going to be in deep trouble. I giggled to myself, how deep is that? I would have thought I couldn't get any deeper.

It had crossed my mind earlier, after seeing that poor naked girl looking in resignation at the floor, knowing what her fate would be, that if things got too bad for me, if more pain was threatened then I would end it all with the painkillers. Now they were gone, I'd even been denied that. Part of my mind was still working the other part was trying to build barricades to block everything out. I knew that I must keep the lucid part working or I would be lost forever. *Make a plan, a daily plan and stick to it.* Lucid mind suggested.

"Like what? Sleep, eat, sleep and eat that's all I can look forward too." I cried out. *Count how many tablets you have left and split them, you have double then.*

"How do I do that?" *You've got a razor blade haven't you?*

"Yes" *Use that and split your matches too* I looked on the basin ledge, a razorblade looked back at me.

Going back into the bedroom I emptied my pockets on the bed, six cigarettes, a few matches, eight Quinine tablets. I looked at my meagre collection then crossing to the wardrobe checked my pockets finding in my trousers a screw of paper containing two painkiller tablets. I remembered Smiler leaving them for me at the clinic that monsoon day. Looking at them and remembering that day, I could feel my heart breaking. Fighting back tears I put them back in my trouser pocket returning to my bed grief-stricken knowing that the pain of grief was bad enough but the real pain was yet to come, when grief explodes and the flying fragments hit you, that's when the pain really begins. I went to the bathroom and unscrewed my razor and taking the blade back to the bed. I carefully cut the tablets and cigarettes in half, then split the matches down their length then put everything in the drawer placing the bible on top. Keeping one half of a cigarette I lit it and went onto the balcony to smoke it. I kept away from the rail to avoid being seen from below and sidled up to the end wall of the balcony and cautiously peered over ready to jump back if spotted. The forecourt was crowded with soldiers in drab brown uniforms, trucks everywhere. The French flag had been torn down, in its place fluttered a blood red flag with a large yellow star in the centre. Sporadic gunfire could be heard but also normal city noises as well, the city noises didn't seem any different than usual, I supposed the locals didn't care who ruled as long as they could lead their dreary lives and get their rice without too much trouble.

I turned and went back to my bed lying down thinking of what things to do on a daily basis to keep me occupied, but mostly to keep what bit of rational mind I had left, intact. Taking the bible out I tore a blank page out from the back and reaching for my pen began to write.

One...   •Stay in bed as long as possible
Two...   •Exercise to keep fit (press ups)
Three...   •Eat as much as possible (even rotten food)
Four...   •Keep check of the days

Five...   •Only take tablets when absolutely necessary
Six...   •Shave every other day to conserve blades
Seven...   •Read at least two pages of the Digest daily
Eight...   •Try to keep clean, wash clothes
Nine...   •Take afternoon nap
Ten...   •Don't Upset the Guards

I thought about item Four, my pen was almost finished, then I had a brain wave. Each day starting at page one of the bible, turn the corner down, then at a glance I could see how many days had passed. I was pleased with myself for having such a good idea. Looking at item ten thinking.

No Way! *You have written your version of the Ten Commandments!* Lucid part of mind said. I didn't know what to say to that so just giggled. Jiggling with the radio buttons all I could get was excited jabbering voices so I switched it off vowing to try every day in case music was played.

CHAPTER THIRTY

I wasn't prepared for the door to be opened and it startled me hearing the lock being turned. In apprehension I looked at the door wondering what he, or I would do if it were the first bully guard who came. It was a different guard he looked older but wore the same brown uniform, but his was more loose fitting than the ones I'd seen downstairs, maybe his wasn't a fighting uniform and I would be treated a little better? He pushed the tray with his foot which I noticed was clad in a kind of slipper shoe not boots, he looked at me and nodded at the tray before closing and locking the door. The meal was rice with bits of meat in it and a greasy looking liquid in a glass. Trying the drink first I found it bland but palatable, the rice was tasteless but warm and quelled my hunger pains.

After eating I automatically went to the door meaning to go down to the bar for a coffee with Joe but it was locked. Why? I had to think very hard; my mind came up with the answer. *Because you are a prisoner that's why.* I tried to hold on to this thought and analyse it. It was replaced almost instantly by thoughts of Smiler. Was she all right? Was she out of Saigon and safe? Her words of assurance that she would fly out with the wounded if things got bad were going through my mind, the torment of not knowing for sure if she was safe and well made me bang my head on the wall crying out her name over and over again. The image of the receptionist naked surrounded by jeering soldiers was strong in my mind, but now it was Smiler on the floor not the receptionist…

"Oh God please keep me sane." I heard myself wailing. As though far off a voice was talking to me, it was very near, I looked round in wonder, who could it be? I was alone wasn't I? I answered back asking it to slow done, as I couldn't understand all it was saying. I went to the bathroom it was empty. I went to the balcony it too was empty. I sat on the floor sobbing clasping my knees to my chin, my Mum whispered in my ear. *Little men in white coats will take you away if you talk to yourself like that.* I was both laughing and crying. "Your wrong Mum its not white coats its brown uniforms.

I awoke still huddled on the floor. I was hot and sweating badly. The sun was shining through the open balcony windows. Even when I moved sluggishly away from it, it seemed to follow me. Wearily moving into the bathroom and pressing my head against the cool tile floor in an attempt to revive myself. I looked at my watch eleven thirty, a meal must be due. Swilling myself in cold water helped to clear my head but my headache was still niggling me. Craning my neck to look in the mirror, I could see my back was a mess. My skin was tinged with yellow. The wound looked as though it was healing but was still a livid blue black bruise almost to my hips; I touched it gently, it still felt tender but was itching, the itching pleased me for it was meant to mean that nature was healing it. But all my body was itching why wasn't nature healing all of me?

I went to the bedside drawer for a tablet and stared at the bottle, my mind in a whirl, It was empty? I tried to remember when I last had one but couldn't! It was only yesterday when the commies came wasn't it? How come my tablets are gone? I suddenly remembered I was turning the pages down in the bible to keep track of the days and opened the drawer and reached for it.

Four corners were turned down? Had I been cooped up in here for four days? Was it more had I forgotten to turn any pages? I couldn't remember so turned another page down just in case.

I looked at Smiler's photo and with tears in my eyes whispered. "Good morning darling." I no longer cared about tears, I had been having weepy moods often, when least expected tears just flowed, I was talking to myself a lot as well but was past caring.

The door opened, thinking that it was food time I looked expectantly for the tray but the guard beckoned me to follow him. I hesitated, was this part of a cruel game? If I followed him where would he take me? I was confused, this was totally out of the blue, no warning, I followed him anyway, stretching my legs felt good but the walk down to the foyer was the longest I had walked in days and my legs knew it, they protested as though I'd been on a route march.

The foyer, although an attempt had been made to clear it up, was still a mess. I was led into the dining room and the English speaking officer was there still with his paperwork. I made my mind up to ask for medical attention if I got the chance. He indicated for me to sit down in the chair opposite him, feeling apprehensive I did so not saying anything waiting for him to speak. He, still bent over his papers, suddenly said without raising his head. "Are you being looked after?" I didn't know what to say in case it was the wrong thing.

"Yes sir." I mumbled.

"Good." He looked up and stared at me hard. "I have spoken to your Mr Evans and he confirms your story about trying to fly you out of Saigon, but I have warned him that this won't be easy as you could be trapped between the fighting forces. The road between here and the Airport is under constant fire."

He looked at me questioningly before going on. "So it might be wiser if you were kept here a few more days for your own protection." I didn't say anything I was afraid to. "Until its safe for you to leave you will remain in your room, do you understand?"

"Yes sir." I replied. I felt utterly defeated and resigned myself that I would never leave this place. He pushed a glass of water towards me. "You are recovering from your sickness yes?"

"No!" I blurted out, and went on quickly afraid that my newfound courage would desert me. "I need to see a doctor I haven't any tablets left and have missed three injections, I am very ill and am scared I might die."

"We are short on medical supplies but I will see what can be done." He looked at me silently then went on. "When you leave in a few days you will get medical help then."

"But I need it now" I was pleading but didn't care.

"Anything else?" He asked in a bored voice.

"Yes I need cigarettes and soap." I wondered if I was pushing my luck, "Could I get some regular exercise to help me regain my strength?" He looked at me in a calculating way. "Have you any money?"

"No but my company will pay any receipts I sign." He laughed loudly. "Receipts no, money yes, we are at war, money only." I took my watch off and offered it to him.

"Two packets of cigarettes, box of matches and a bar of soap for this." He took my watch and examined it, smiled. "One packet cigarettes, one soap." putting my watch in his pocket. I nodded in agreement, disappointed in my bargaining skills. "See we treat you well, we have no quarrel with your Government." He waved his hand in dismissal indicating to the guard that the meeting was over.

"What about my cigarettes and soap?"

"Oh later." He replied. In my room I inwardly cursed myself for being a fool, now I didn't even have my watch never mind the cigarettes and soap, some wheeler-dealer I was!

The rest of the day I spent doing all sorts of things to try and relieve the boredom. I tried press ups but not having the strength gave that up I tried counting the tiles of the floor and gave that up. I was restless and kept looking at my watch only to see the white patch were it used to be, every time I did this I became angry with myself for being so stupid in letting it go so easily.

I needed a smoke badly to calm my nerves; I paced up and down muttering to myself until feeling tired and then stretched out on the bed. Sleep alluded me by pushing images into my mind, images of Chimp singing with me 'Maggie May' coming back from the docks, or dooks as he called them. I could see clearly the hard drinking Aussies, thinking they would be well underway to home now. *So would you if you had followed doctor's orders, eat and sleep, instead of being Jack the lad and drinking and doing other things.*

"What other things?" I said aloud.

You know well enough. Said my mind.

"No I bloody don't, tell me." I demanded irritated now.

Being sick and doing it. Mind whispered.

"Doing what?" I was shouting now.

SEX! Mind shouted back.

Laying there thinking of Smiler, thinking of us, the two of us dancing and she whispering in my ear for me to show her my room, our love-making…I closed my eyes in anguish hot tears welling in the corner of my eyes, tears for a lost love, for now I believed that I had lost her forever. Fumbling in the drawer for the bible I grasped it and waving it in the air shouted. "God, can you hear me?" Nothing…Raising my voice almost shrieking. "There is no sound on this earth that can be heard, until someone listens! Why won't you listen? The photograph fell onto my chest and I wept bitterly.

The guard pushed my tray into the room standing there just looking at me not saying a word. I was long past having any dignity left and buried my face in the pillow hearing the door close. Seeing that he had gone I approached the tray to see the same fish and rice. I ate what I could; it seemed to taste better these days. Maybe they were cooking it properly for now I had started to look forward to it, or maybe it was because now at meal times I propped the photo against the lamp on the bedside table and imagined her sitting opposite me and talking to me whilst I ate.

I told her many things. We would have lots more dinners together, that I would go to Lyon and get a job to be near her. She would smile at me as though in agreement. At the end of each meal I would clasp the photo to my chest and pretend we were dancing, with me humming the tune *We'll meet again…Some sunny day…*I desperately wanted to believe it.

CHAPTER THIRTY-ONE

Over the next few days I slept a little easier. I was continually drifting in and out of sleep and had become used to the dull ache at the back of my head, but I did feel a little stronger and even some times sparred up to myself in the mirror. My wound had healed. Just leaving a slight scar but my back was still tinged yellow and I itched all over my body, and as hard as I tried not too, I scratched. Parts of my body were red raw and were aggravated by my sweating, when the itching became unbearable I ran a cold bath and soaked in it.

It was while I was having one of my soaks that the guard appeared in the bathroom doorway. He held up a packet of cigarettes and soap grinning as he flipped the soap in the bath. I was dumbfounded, it was days ago since I had asked for them and I had forgotten all about them. I stood up in the bath the guard reached for the towel and handed it to me, then still grinning went into the bedroom. I followed him still wet with the towel around my middle. Opening the cigarettes I offered him one, he shook his head.

"Go on you ugly bastard, have one." I smiled awaiting his reaction. He just stood grinning and took one pulling a book of matches out of his tunic pocket and lighting us both, then threw the matches on the bed.

The first lung full of smoke sent me into a fit of coughing, just like at school when we had experimented behind the bike sheds. The guard laughed so did I, we smoked in silence and when we had finished the guard put his fingers to his mouth, listened at the door then opening it cautiously satisfied he nodded to me then slipped out locking it.

"So you didn't forget then." I said aloud. "But you bloody took your time didn't you!" I picked up the bible noting that eight pages were turned down.

Over my meal that night I told Smiler about the guard bringing me the cigarettes and my nearly choking with the first lung full. I laughed as I told her, she just smiled and in my head I could hear her say. *Oh, Moor-ise Cheri, you are so funny.* The radio had started to play Asian music instead of the continuous babble of jabbering voices, these interludes of music stimulated my brain and I was able to begin to rationalise as to what was what. I started to try to form a poem about what was what! But I couldn't get the words to run smoothly so just said aloud what was going through my mind.

"A politicians game of chess fuelling a civil war for their own greedy gains, sailing on a sea of deceit, letting the innocent sink to their death, whilst they floated on the ocean of life. The innocents could perhaps wonder. Who is that paddling in the tide of guilt?

My thoughts returned to my own Governments callous approach to its subjects, and could not get out of my mind the paltry sum of thirty shillings. Thirty pieces of silver! Picking up the bible I said loudly. "God, in here it says somewhere that you were also betrayed for thirty pieces of silver!"

Before putting the photo back in the bible I was surprised to see from the turned down pages the time I had spent alone in this room.

"How much longer." I asked her. "How much longer?"

When next the guard came with my meal he left the door open grinning at me. I weakly grinned back, thinking. *What are you up to you ugly sod?* I asked Smiler whilst eating, what was the guard up to? She didn't answer only smiled.

When I had finished eating, I put the tray down by the open door and cautiously putting my head out, peered down the corridor ready to draw back quickly if it was a trap.

The corridor was *empty!* I sat on my bed with mixed thoughts; the soldiers hadn't gone because I could still hear them outside, yet my door wasn't just unlocked, it was wide open? No guard? Why? I was still pondering when the guard appeared in the doorway beckoning to me, I was uncertain as to what he wanted me to do so stayed where I was. He beckoned me again and walked out of my sight. I walked out of the room; he was standing a little way down the corridor still with a big grin on his face. Watching him very carefully for any sign of a threat, I stepped out into the corridor, all he did, was to lean his rifle against the wall and with both hands shooed me away. I took some tentative steps away from him then stopped, looking back expecting something bad to happen. He was nodding his head grinning widely, I felt elated and walked as fast as I could manage to the end of the corridor then turning back. I walked right up to, and past the still grinning guard. Stopping at the head of the stairs I then looked back at him smiling, but straining my ears for any clues from downstairs for this luxury of being able to stretch my legs, my mind whispered so as not to be overheard. *You asked for exercise now you've got it, make the most of it!* I adopted the boxer's stance jabbing the air with my fists and trotted back past the guard into my room flopping on my bed laughing.

The door closed and the lock turned. Still laughing I lit a cigarette although I had rationed myself to two a day, and had had my ration, this was a special occasion, a special celebration. So I smoked the entire cigarette, instead of what I had been doing, smoking half and stubbing out. I was excited about the new dimension to my dull unexciting boring days, and of course it would be another topic of conversation with Smiler over my meal.

Still feeling elated I sat on the chair near the open balcony doors and tried to concentrate enough to read the Readers Digest. I didn't like to get too close to the balcony rail and take the risk of being shot at from the trigger-happy soldiers below.

My thoughts were racing and I couldn't concentrate on the words I was trying to read. Did the exercise in the corridor mean that I might eventually be allowed the freedom of the hotel? Did it mean I could go outside the hotel doors and breath fresh air and smell the flowers? The thought of me outside away from this hot confined room even for ten minutes a day got me all excited and my adrenaline flowing. I knew over excitement could bring on another attack but the thought of something new in my monotonous day, I threw caution to the wind.

Later in the bathroom I examined myself in the mirror, having stripped naked to enable me to see every inch of myself and was alarmed to see that the yellowish tinge had spread to almost the whole of my body. To make matters worse I was coming out in boils, the result that stared back at me was like looking at a paint colour chart, yellow skin, red raw patches through scratching, ugly looking boils and pallid face with dark holes for eyes. Sitting miserably on the toilet seat I wondered how long it would take for my legs to stop supporting me. I was starting to get paranoid. It was a long time ago since I had taken any medication and imagined going back into a coma and dying in this God forsaken room. This made me more paranoid than ever and to try and snap myself out of it, I busied myself in washing my clothes in the bath of cold water. No matter how hard I rubbed and rinsed, the sweat stains remained. My once white shirts and shorts still looked grubby, the bed sheets were dirty but I couldn't attempt to wash them for I had no way of drying them and I didn't dare hang them over the balcony rail.

I rubbed and rubbed, tears of frustration coursing down my face, until my knuckles were raw. Whilst I was struggling with my laundry, the guard had brought my meal. I noticed it when I came into the bedroom looking for a suitable place to hang my washing, I hadn't heard him and thought this wasn't the first time he had come without me hearing him and wondered if my hearing was going too! It was rice and fish again, I couldn't eat it in the state I was in so pushed it nearer to the open door. Peering out in the corridor I saw that it was empty and bravely stepped out walking towards the top of the stairwell, but hearing voices coming up the stairs I dashed back to my room. Moments later the guard appeared, picking up the untouched tray he beckoned, making walking motions with fingers of one hand. I stepped past him and walked the full length of the corridor then past him again back into my room, he grinned at me as he closed and locked the door.

Crouching down I sidled out to the balcony and sat with my back to the wall so as not to be seen from below. It was so stuffy in the room and to clear my head I needed what little air there was. I could hear but not see what was going on outside, muted voices from below, distant sounds of traffic and pungent smells wafted on the breeze. The heat from the sun, although going down, was still strong enough to create a muggy energy-robbing atmosphere that was lulling me into a form of a hypnotic state of mind. My thoughts wandered to my shipmates, what were they doing at this moment? Probably ashore somewhere in a dockside bar having a good time. I could hear Taffy complaining about the price of the beer, my mouth watered at the thought of a cool beer! I could see Chas chatting up one of the bar belles, with only one thing on his mind, I smiled to myself. "I bet you forgot your dreadnought Chas!" I looked around me guiltily in case someone had heard me, then laughed aloud.

"Stupid, who can hear you no one here but yourself, that's why you talk to yourself." The thought of a cold beer had me drooling; being without brought to mind the system in India, where they had what they call 'Dry Days'. On these days you could not get an alcoholic drink anywhere except in a Brothel. In Calcutta it was a Tuesday. So on Tuesdays these places did a roaring trade! Thinking about it, here I was trapped in a week of Tuesdays. Getting to my feet I went to my bed, undressing and draping my clothes over the chair near the open window then stretched out on the bed closing my eyes.

The next few days seemed an endless fruitless span of time. Eating or trying to eat fish, sleeping, walking in the corridor, talking to myself and crying over the photo of Smiler. I was in a complete state of nothingness and on more than one occasion had contemplated suicide, but the small rational part of my mind kept reminding that then I would never see Smiler again and the commies would have won. I couldn't remember if I had washed myself or if I had turned any more pages down. If I hadn't missed any then I had been here fifteen days.

CHAPTER THIRTY-TWO

I was beginning to shiver again. Each day for longer periods. When this was going on I could hear myself talking funny through chattering teeth. Even after taking the blanket out of the wardrobe and wrapping myself in it, hardly helped to alleviate my misery. I had even sat in the full sunlight on the balcony wrapped in the blanket to try to stop shivering but all it did was make me sweat more and that started me itching. So all I could do was ride the attacks off and hope that another wouldn't come with out giving me a respite.

It was on one of these days whilst huddled in my blanket on the balcony feeling wretched. I felt a hand on my shoulder shaking me, thinking it was Smiler with my medicine I looked up in joyous anticipation. Through bleary sweat stung eyes I tried to focus on the shape leaning over me and attempted to speak but no sounds came out, my throat was so parched. I tried to shout. "Don't leave me." as the shape moved away. I was frantically trying to keep it in focus, it was wavering and I began to think that my mind was playing tricks on me until I felt an arm supporting me and water trickling down my throat. I coughed and gagged bringing the water up and grasped desperately at the glass for fear it would be taken away gulping greedily slopping most of it over the blanket.

I still couldn't focus my eyes properly but gradually I glimpsed the face over me, *it was my guard!* Clutching his arm I frantically implored him to bring me a doctor, tears were mingling with the sweat on my face as I repeated over and over again. "Doctor...doctor...please." I felt myself being laid flat on the floor and his footsteps going away. I could feel myself drifting away and struggled to keep awake. The guard returned with another soldier, they lifted me up and placed me on my bed, I closed my eyes to ease the pain in my head. I could see Smiler coming towards me arms outstretched, nearer and nearer. She was smiling, her voice although fading in and out was still clear enough for me to hear her say. *Moor-ise cheri I am here, I will look after you...*I tried to lift my arms to her whispering her name but my arms wouldn't move. I could dimly hear other voices coming nearer and felt my arm being lifted. A sensation of a prick in my arm. Opening my eyes, expecting to see my Smiler, I saw the officer with another man before I passed out.

I became aware of movements around me but was reluctant to open my eyes because I was feeling so peaceful and mercifully free of pain. The thought of opening my eyes and the pain returning made me lie there eyes closed, listening to the sounds around me until I found myself straining to hear, when I couldn't hear anything.

I opened my eyes to find the room empty, I must have been dreaming I thought any moment now the guard will be bringing my tray. I found that I was sitting in bed propped up with pillows. My sheets had been changed they were sweet smelling and the sour smell of sweat had gone. My first reaction was that the French had retaken the city and I was back again in French hands. *The maid must have been in whilst I was asleep but how did she manage to change the sheets whilst I was in bed?* I wondered, trying hard to remember. Then it slowly came back, the guard helping me to my bed, the officer with another man, the prick in my arm *I've had a really bad attack and that must have been the doctor, maybe now I can have some medication.* I felt a little better with this thought.

The door opened and my guard came in, seeing that I was awake he grinned and came over to my bed placing a glass of whitish liquid by the table I thanked him as he went out of the room.

"How are you feeling now?" It was the officer and the other man whom I presumed was a doctor. They had arrived after the guard had left and again I presumed that he had reported back that I was awake.

"A little better thank you sir" I replied weakly. The officer explained that the man with him was a doctor and would examine me. *So I was right,* I felt slightly pleased about that.

The doctor seemed more Chinese than Vietnamese. He examined my temperature, pulse, blood pressure and my heart. It was a better medical than I'd had when joining the Merchant Navy! When he had finished he gave me a tablet.

"Quinine." He said in Pidgin English. "You take each day eat food and sleep." I thought to myself. *All doctors are the same; they all have the same remedies!* The officer paused at the door turned and said. "Is there anything else you need?" I nodded. "Yes sir, cigarettes and writing paper please." He didn't reply as he left the room.

I was dozing when movement in the room made me aware that someone was in my room. The guard had returned and was placing something on the bedside table, seeing that I was awake he pointed to the table grinning. The effort of turning my head caused me some discomfort, but when I saw what he was grinning about I forgot my discomfort and grinned back.

There on the table was writing paper, cigarettes and to my joy, my watch! Like a child at Christmas I reached for my watch and strapped it to my wrist, fitting snugly to the white patch as if it had never been off noting that it was afternoon, but what afternoon and what day? *I must count the pages when he goes.*

Lighting a cigarette and offering him one, he immediately went to the door and looked out. Satisfied he sat on the end of the bed and lit up; we sat like that in silence for awhile when suddenly he produced a grubby wallet from his pocket jabbering away all the time. He extracted a dog-eared photograph and pushed it towards me rather shyly, I saw it was obviously his family, a woman with the usual conical hat was smiling at the camera. With her were two children around Ten years old I quessed. Smiling at him I handed it back saying, "Very nice." He promptly put it back in his wallet and returned it to his pocket.

Not having any photo's of my own to show him, I didn't dare show him the one's of Smiler in her French uniform, for fear that he might mis-construe and think that I was after all, the enemy and confiscate them or worse. Instead I picked up the copy of the digest now itself dog-eared and flicked through the pages for something of interest to show him. I didn't want him to go just yet, enemy or not he was company, which I was desperately in need of, even though we couldn't speak a common language, I wasn't alone for these moments and it was like a tonic of sorts to me.

"England" I said pointing to a picture. I think he understood for he nodded, to make sure I pointed to the balcony where the skyline of Saigon could be seen saying. "Saigon-Vietnam!" Then back to the picture in the advertisement repeating "England" he nodded grinning at me. I was starting to enjoy this little interlude with him feeling rather like a school teacher with a backward pupil, and flicked more pages trying to show him how different my country was to his.

Being the Christmas edition and a year old, the digest was full of Christmas adverts and snow scenes, but didn't really depict the spirit of Christmas making it limited in what I could show him. One picture was a snow scene; children on sledges, Christmas trees lit up in gardens and lots of snow. This interested him because he studied it glancing at me and jabbered something. I smiled indulgently at him. I don't suppose he had ever seen snow and I made much from the picture. Adverts for Lemon Hart Rum brought back fond memories of ships I'd been on that issued the crew with a tablespoon of thick black rum like molasses which, when watered down and drunk below decks with my mates, gave rise to next days hangovers.

When I showed him an advert for Phillip Morris cigarettes, he promptly brought out his cigarettes and offered me one. I took it and tried to explain that wasn't why I had shown him the picture. We smoked in silence with him looking through the digest, my cigarette was absolutely awful but I smoked it rather than offend him. Surely he must have had them given to him, because no one would pay for them! After the smoke he indicated that he must leave, and left closing the door quietly behind him, I was a little sorry when he had gone because it had been a change from being alone and only having myself to talk to.

Taking Smiler's photo out, I told her about the guard's visit and that I had enjoyed it. She smiled and whispered in my ear. *Rest now, don't get over excited.* I took her advice and closed my eyes.

CHAPTER THIRTY-THREE

Over the next few days the guard had been leaving my door open and I had walked up and down the corridor with no guard in sight. Even my food had improved, I was now having a thick fish broth type soup and a hot drink, but most of all I was having my tablets and my health was improving, I knew because the attacks were shorter and not so intense.

I was surprised however when looking at the bible to see twenty pages turned down, I knew I had missed many but couldn't attempt to try and remember how many. I had seen the officer twice since my collapse; my anger had somewhat abated towards him and his army. After all he had seen that I had medical attention and was treating me to a great extent, kindly, he was not obliged to do any of these things other than through compassion, so I had a lot to be thankful for.

For the first time in a long time, I felt as though the worst was over and that I would get out of here and see my shipmates again. When that day arrived I resolved to block out this horrible chapter of my life before it did my head in altogether.

Although I was on the road to recovery, the fever attacks were becoming fewer and I could most times recognise an attack coming. I still wasn't fully ready when they did strike. It was on one of these days. I had been trying to write a poem, I couldn't really concentrate, my head was throbbing more than usual, I was never free from headaches, they were part of my daily life. So I didn't pay much heed to this one until I started to shiver and shake. The paper slipped out of my nerveless fingers. Clutching my head in both hands I rolled about moaning in abject misery. Faces flashed across my vision, voices in my head shouted, then whispered in my ear. The Aussies singing loudly their faces leering at me over beer glasses. Smiler's face swimming in and out mingling with the receptionists, who very pale with her clothes ripped off, was handing me something saying. *Two-O-Eight Sir, hope you enjoy your fish diet. Sir. Oh please help me Sir.* "I can't help you, I can't help myself." I heard myself shouting.

I will help you Moor-ise Mon Cheri. I looked up head to one side trying to see where her voice was coming from, I was crying, not just out of physical pain, that I could handle to some extent, what I couldn't handle were these torturous voices in my head, they seemed so real, but *what* was real and *what* wasn't.

"Where are you my darling? Are you safe?" I stood up and tottered to the wardrobe. "Please Smiler don't play tricks on me, I don't like this game." *I am here with you Cheri; I will always be with you.* I wrenched the wardrobe door open so violently that I almost pulled it over on top of me.

Then stepped back a scream strangled in my throat, the naked receptionist, bloodied with outstretched arms was smiling at me. *Please help me Sir…*I threw myself on the bed clasping my pillow over my head but couldn't shut out the voices. "Go away, leave me alone…Please…" my voice was only a whisper to theirs, they were getting louder and overlapping.

I sat up and scrambled to the top of the bed pulling the sheet and pillows on top of me to try and build a barricade. I was shouting loudly and wafting my arms about in a futile attempt to swat the voices. For one heart stopping moment I thought I had succeeded for they seemed to recede, the only noise I could hear now was my heart pounding violently against my chest in unison with the pain in my head. I was sweating so badly that my body itched with it, looking down at myself I saw that I had drawn blood with my scratching. Closing my eyes and clasping my arms tightly about my chest I rocked back and forth moaning incessantly to myself

I am here to look after you Moor-ise Cheri. I looked at her sitting on the end of the bed smiling at me. I reached for her crying with relief. "Oh my darling Smiler I have missed you so much." My arms went right through her…I stared numb with shock; she had changed into the receptionist who had her arms out to me.

"No—No—"I stumbled to my feet. *Yes my friend.* I turned then staggered backwards. Tommy still in bandages was coming towards me arms outstretched. *Friends eh?* Other voices joined in until they were shouting. *Friends eh?* The room was filling with them, Tommy. The Aussies. The giggling nurse. Chimp. They all had their arms out and coming towards me. They seemed as though they were there but not there, hazy like, but the one in uniform in the middle seemed a bit clearer, he seemed to be moving faster.

My back struck the balcony door. With a gasp I looked around to see Smiler standing on the balcony rail she looked so radiant standing there with her hand out to me, I could only stare and marvel at her beauty. I remembered the picnic in my dreams and how happy we were. *Come with me Mon Cheri, we will be happy again, I will look after you…*My heart was full of joy as I reached for her hand…

Then something pulled me back. I struggled and fought imploring Smiler to help me. She just smiled and seemed to float off the balcony rail. I screamed her name as I felt strong arms around me and was lifted off my feet. I couldn't fight any more and just sagged letting them take me wherever they wanted to. Voices were whispering all around me some far away some near. I just looked at the lights that were passing overhead not caring any more, just listening to my mind that was trying to tell me something. Irrational mind was arguing with lucid mind. *You must let him go the way he wants to go, and then he can be back with his friends.*

Shut the fuck up and let me help him, he goes nowhere without me.

You've not been much help so far, Its me that's had to do most of his thinking Yeah and look at all the pain you've caused him, I'm in charge now, I'm going to look after him from now on.

"Smiler." I shouted. Struggling again. "I want you to look after me."

More arms gripped me; more faces loomed over me. The officer's face swam in and out of my vision. I giggled as Twitchy's face looked at me, I wanted to shout. *They won't let me sign any chits, now are you happy?* But I couldn't stop giggling. They tried to stop my giggling by trying to drown me. Water was splashing on my face and some was going down my throat, no matter how hard I tried to keep my mouth closed tight. I was spluttering and trying to break free. I was shouting, crying, screaming, cursing then imploring, but all the time voices, but now they were fading and I felt myself falling into a void...

It was strangely quiet. I opened my eyes. This wasn't my room? My room didn't have a desk and filing cabinets? I was lying on a couch with a blanket half draped over me; fearfully I glanced at the floor expecting to see a river of blood. Why did I expect to see a river of blood? I didn't understand my tongue felt sore and swollen, I could taste blood in my mouth. *Oh my God I've been drinking the river.* I panicked and tried to sit up. I couldn't move. *I'm dead and I am in Gods office waiting to be allocated, I must ask him to put me with Smiler.*

Smiler! I came fully awake and strained against whatever was restraining me...I was tied hand and foot to the couch! I was trying to rationalise my situation when the door opened, and a soldier came in. I stared at him thinking. *I've seen you before but where?* He straightened my blanket then left the room. I don't know how long I was left alone because I was drifting in and out of consciousness, and was only aware that someone was in the room when I felt my bonds being taken off. I lay still waiting to see what was to follow. My plan was to give as good as I got if they attempted to hurt me again.

I was lifted into a sitting position and a glass was put to my lips. I clenched them together, keeping my eyes shut. *I know your game; you want me to think its water so I will drink it, when it's really poison! Well I'm to clever mate, you'll have to do better than that.* I felt pleased with myself and giggled. Fingers were at my mouth I could feel it being prised open and water trickling in making me choke. *Ok, Ok I was only joking, keep your hair on!*

Opening my eyes I saw the Officer and Twitchy standing over me. Twitchy looked tired and concerned. I tried to smile at him, to reassure him that Yes, it was me, albeit a little worse for wear but my brain didn't function properly. Instead of my lips curling into a smile, my eyes watered spilling down my cheeks.

Twitchy was saying something, I didn't understand so all I did was nod my head, I didn't want him to get angry and go away. His voice sounded far away and I wondered if I was going deaf. I giggled again I could hear that. I felt myself wetting myself, and giggled louder. It was their own fault for pouring water into me; it has to go somewhere. I giggled louder again and then heard myself laughing, and then great sobs were making my chest hurt so I lay there crooning to myself listening to lucid mind telling me to hold on not to let go. I lay there looking at Twitchy and the Officer. Smiling at them through my watery eyes, willing them to believe it was all right and that I forgave them.

CHAPTER THIRTY-FOUR

The doctor had gone and I was alone in the foyer, the injection he had given me was starting to take effect I was feeling drowsy, *who was it that said that this would happen?* I racked my brain but couldn't remember. I was sitting in one of the chairs near to the bar wrapped in a blanket. The maids had done a good job in cleaning it up, it was very nearly like I remembered it. I was dreamily looking around me and thought that the staff had changed their uniforms, but I didn't like the change, they all wore brown now. *I must complain to the manager and have their old uniforms back.*

I looked at the table near my chair and saw a glass of orange juice and a packet of cigarettes, I had to grasp the glass with both hands before I could lift it and spilt half of it on my blanket. My hands were shaking badly and I glanced around fearfully in case anyone had seen me. I left the cigarettes alone I was afraid I might set myself on fire although I felt I needed one badly.

Something was niggling in my mind about the table and the glass, flashes of things that had happened at these tables were struggling to stay, but my mind wouldn't dwell long enough for me to remember, I was getting a headache just trying, so gave up and dozed.

"You almost had a complete breakdown." I was sitting in the lounge. The officer had agreed for me to come down for an hour each day; he had seemed concerned over how ill I had been and said that he was doing all he could to co-operate with Mr Evans to get me out of Saigon.

He had even allowed me to have a cup of coffee with my cigarette when I was in the lounge. It was sheer luxury for me and in my confused mind I often thought I was back in my ships mess, until I was rudely made aware of the soldiers, and then from euphoria I was plunged back into despair.

"Yes, if it wasn't for your guard grabbing you, you would have gone over the balcony—" He paused. I was listening to him on the telephone. The officer had brought it out to the lounge and after plugging it in behind the bar had handed it to me saying.

"Your Mr Evans wants to speak to you." Before walking away leaving me alone, well almost, my guard was sitting a few tables away pretending he wasn't there.

"—when I heard I was so shocked, I asked could I come over, when I arrived you were almost frothing at the mouth and delirious they had to subdue you—" I mumbled something down the `phone I was in a dream like state and wasn't really listening.

"—What was that? I didn't reply, I was watching the guard. So he grabbed me did he, to save me, save me from what? He saw me watching him and grinned at me. I raised my hand and gave him a limp wave, my arm felt heavy and I put the phone down on the table. Slowly things were coming back to me and they frightened me, I was sobbing quietly to myself I felt a broken man.

The phone was making tinny noises besides me; I looked at it for a minute puzzled, then picking it said. "Hello?" "There you are, I thought you had gone, are you all right?"

"Yes, its just that I'm tired and want to sleep, I'm sorry what were you saying?" "I'll make it brief, then you can lay down, I am making positive headway in getting you out of here, it could be any time now so be ready for when I tell you to go…do you understand?

"Yes I understand." My lucid mind was telling me to be happy that I would soon be going home. I wasn't convinced, I'd never spoken to Twitchy on the `phone before It might not be him.

"Hello are you still there?"

"You are Twi…I mean Mr Evans aren't you? This isn't a cruel joke being played on me is it?" I was almost pleading

"Of course its not a joke, what do you take me for? Look I must go now, be ready for when I contact you again. Ok?" "Ok thank you." I replied.

"Look after yourself. Bye then." The line went dead. I sat there holding the dead phone in my hand thinking of what Twitchy had said. Hope was slowly rising within me as realisation set in; I could soon be out of this nightmare, back with my shipmates again, back where I belonged.

I felt exhilarated and smiled at my guard, he smiled back. Putting down the phone I wearily made my way back to my room, my guard a few paces behind. Safely in my room I took out the photograph and told Smiler about the phone call, whispering to her, for her to phone me.

The next day I was summoned to see the officer, I was feeling a lot better after good nights sleep no dreams, no voices, and a peaceful night for a change. "You may smoke if you like. "He shuffled some papers. "I have spoken with your Mr Evans and have agreed to give you the safest route to the Airport that I can, but I can't guarantee anything as fighting is fierce around the Airport, but we are winning." The last bit said a little smugly. I nodded. "I would like to thank you sir for all you have done for me. "It wasn't much, we are at war with the French not the English, I am sorry that you have been ill and been caught up in it." He said this as if he meant it. I believed he did.

"I have taken the guard away you may use the downstairs, but if you attempt to go outside, I will bring him back and you will be confined to your room again, is that understood?

"Yes thank you sir, would you please thank the guard for me for stopping me doing something foolish the other day."

"Yes I will, I'm sure he will be pleased, he is not a fighting soldier, he is a staff soldier and has been concerned over your health." He stood up shaking my hand, indicating that the meeting was over.

I wandered about the foyer in a state of euphoria, so it was going to happen at last, after hearing what the officer had said, I now really believed it and couldn't wait to get to the airport

I stood with the wardrobe doors open and viewed my meagre possessions. Seeing the shirt and slacks on the hanger brought back memories of my dinner date with Smiler. How happy we had been, with a lump in my throat I went to the bedside cabinet and took out her photo, in doing so I was shocked to see twenty eight pages turned down. I knew that I had stopped doing it since my breakdown and found it hard to believe that I had been cooped up in this room with very little human contact for so long. I kissed her photo and carefully placed it back in the bible. Returning to the wardrobe, I packed my few things in my bag then closing the doors sat on my bed, and reflected.

The first thing I'm going to do when I rejoin my ship, is to have some beers, the image of Tommy Aussie popped into my mind. The two of us pissed and laughing over the joke of 'My company pays my company.' It was a joke all right because my Company will be paying no one, because all my chits must have been destroyed along with the other hotel records!

I laughed at the irony of it all, on one hand Twitchy throwing a wobble over my spending, and me shouting at him for it, whilst on the other hand with hindsight I could have thrown a big dinner party and invited Twitchy! The more I thought of this the more relief I felt because all the chits I'd signed for food, drinks, clothes and all the sundry stuff must have been well over a hundred pounds, more than a years wages for me!

I ate my meal that night with relish, I hadn't seen who had brought it because I had left my door open more as a gesture of defiance than anything else. It must have arrived whilst I was in the bathroom. I wondered if it had been my normal guard? I had now moved the chair to the bottom of my bed and placed my bag on it ready to grab it on my way out, day or night.

I was restless but excited awaiting Twitchy's call, and kept going to the balcony, brave now I went to the rail and looked out. Everything seemed the same. The same noises of city life. The same noises of distant gunfire, the only noticeable difference was the soldiers and their uniforms, but even they seemed different now, not as agitated and vociferous as I first saw them. None of them challenged me for being on the balcony. I lit a cigarette and smoked contentedly enjoying the night air, which was considerably cooler than in my room. Stubbing my cigarette out and not chancing my luck any further I walked to my bed and fully dressed in case I was called in the night I lay down and attempted to sleep.

I awoke to full sunlight beaming through the room. Already it was getting warm and I groaned at the prospect of another sweltering day cooped up. Getting up and having a cold shower, which didn't help to cool me, I examined myself in the mirror,

I was losing that haggard look although my face still had hollows and was pale looking, but my body seemed to be filling out which pleased me. I was still full of optimism that my days here were numbered and that I would hear from Twitchy soon. The thought of being again with my shipmates filled me with such excitement that I was worried that I may bring another attack on.

Going down to the foyer I sat in the seat by the bar and lit a cigarette, moments later my guard came up to me and handed me a note, he was grinning all over his face as if he knew what it contained. Before I read it and he went away, I stood and shook his hand and did my best to thank him, he seemed to understand what I meant, I dearly hoped so. The note was from Twitchy saying to be ready for pickup at a moment's notice to the taken to the Airport, a car would be sent to the hotel. I was surprised when I saw the date. March 16 1954! March 16? We had sailed into Saigon the middle of January that meant I had been here over two months! It wouldn't sink in that I had lived in a nightmare of misery and pain for more than two months?

Returning to my room I doubled checked my belongings and moved them nearer to the door, then stood on the balcony watching for the car from the Embassy

CHAPTER THIRTY-FIVE

The car was jolting over ruts in the road. The driver was cursing to himself as he swung the wheel to avoid an overturned cart with the dead ox still in the shafts, its load of vegetables were strewn across the road and the car made squishy sounds as the wheels went through them. My driver hung on grimly to the wheel as the car swayed from side to side, zigzagging through debris.

I was in my room when the guard burst in gesticulating for me to follow him and pointing to my bag; down in the foyer the man from the Embassy was standing there looking apprehensive. He was somewhat dishevelled and pinned to his crumpled suit was a badge showing his name and the Embassies.

He approached me asking Mr Tudor? When I nodded he urged me to follow him saying that we must be quick and get to the Airport. I noticed that the few remaining staff were huddled in a corner and looking frightened. I told him to wait, I had to see someone, he wasn't very happy and told me so.

"Tough." I said surprised at the vehemence in my voice walking away in search of the officer. I wanted to say good bye, he had shown me compassion, and the least I could do was to say good bye.

Entering the dining room I saw a group of officers around a table seemingly poring over a map. Looking up the officer seeing me came over and with a wry smile said.

"You will soon be on your way, I hope you have a safe journey." With that he put out his hand which I clasped with both hands saying in a choking voice. "Thank you sir for looking after me…

I truly hope you come to no harm." Thinking to myself as I walked away. *In better times and different circumstances we might have been friends, who knows you are not much older than I am.*

The driver was still muttering to himself leaning over the steering wheel nose almost touching the windscreen, the masked headlights cutting a feeble swath through the darkness. The city was behind us and all around was jungle, which in the darkness felt ominous and claustrophobic.

I wondered how far the Airport was because by now I was in a strangle hold of anxiety, and felt for sure that we would crash at this speed, and without adequate lighting on the car, and the driver swerving all over the road, at times I had to grab hold of the strap.

"Hey driver slow down will you, you will kill us and I've not come this far to have that happen." The driver still muttering turned and said. "Ok." turning back to his driving but seemed to go faster not slower.

As we neared the Airport it was evident that the war was still going as fiercely as ever. The sky was lit with arcing lights and the noise of gunfire was deafening. A bomb or something exploded nearby, the shock waves sending the car lurching to one side of the road. For one awful moment I thought we were going to topple over, but the driver was good, he just wrestled with the wheel and kept us on four wheels, I almost wished that I was back at the hotel.

French soldiers at the Airport waved us through banging on the car as if it would make it go faster! The driver weaved his way through wreckage of vehicles and gun posts towards a darkened hanger with his horn blaring. As we approached its doors opened and we shot through.

Gratefully I stepped out and stretched myself. My bones were aching after the gruelling journey. I looked around me my nose twitching. A most appalling smell assailed my nostrils; it threatened to engulf me completely and attempted to enter my stomach via my mouth. I gagged putting a handkerchief over my mouth that helped a little. This was worse than Garlic Breath and the Latrines put together, they were roses compared to this! It was a mixture of human sweat, animal droppings; spicy cooking and vehicular fumes all mixed together in a concentrated cloying soup of stink.

I could hear the noise of chickens and on looking round through watery eyes, I saw that the hanger was filled to overflowing with people of all ages, most had suitcases and nearly all had crates of chickens and some goats! People were in all sorts of postures, some trying to sleep whilst the noise of others around them in animated conversation with plenty of arm waving must have made it impossible. Others were eating rice dishes of some kind wrapped in palm leaves. All this I took in whilst stretching my limbs

A hand touched me, turning I saw it was my driver, he pointed to a shed like building in the corner, walking towards it I had to step over prostrate forms. *Sleeping I hope.*

Twitchy was in the hut. He looked strained and tired. His shirt was dirty and he hadn't shaved for a day or two by the look of him. He explained that I was going on the first available plane to Korea and that my ship was expected to arrive there in a day or two, nothing was flying out tonight he added. "Maybe tomorrow when the fighting has died down, it's a mess I think the French have finally had it." He said miserably.

"What will happen to you?" I enquired.

"Oh I will fly out eventually and go back to London."

"Don't give my regards to Churchill." I said sarcastically. He looked at me hard but didn't say anything. Instead he talked about how he thought the war was going. That the French were just about holding the Airport, but the Vietminh were closing all the time and that it was just a matter of time. Pockets of the area and the landing strips were being fiercely held by the French who were flying their wounded out on any available plane. "That's were you will fly from." He told me. I asked if any of the hospital staff were still on the Airfield. He didn't know as they were at the other end of the field.

"Have you seen my nurse since you have been here? Is she safe?"

"I don't know I have been too busy here to know what is going on there."

"But could you find out if she flew out with the wounded? I need to know that she is safe." Looking at his face I knew he couldn't or wouldn't. I tried again.

"Could I go over there and find out for myself?"

"Certainly not—" He was almost his Hoity Toity self again, "—you will remain here, any moment now or tomorrow we could get the signal for you to go, there is no second chance." Pointing to the crowded hanger through the window added. "See those poor bastards, most of them will never leave here, not enough planes you see, they have come here for refuge."

I went to the window and saw the dejected faces and felt humble that I was one of the chosen ones. Twitchy was still talking.

"Its dog eat dog out there, money talks and most of them have none, its who you know not what you have, so if you leave this hanger you might as well join them because I couldn't help you any more."

I turned to him incredulously. "But what will happen to them when we have gone?"

He shook his head. "God only knows, some will be able to fly out but the others…"

I stared out of the window miserably, Smiler may be only a few yards away and I will never know I reached in my pocket for her photo and to my utter horror it wasn't there. In my haste to get away I had left it in the bible and that was back at the hotel!

After a fitful nights sleep in a hard chair and a mug of hot tea? Whatever it was I needed it, if only to wash my tablet down. I was upset over leaving Smiler's photo behind it was like an omen that I would never see her again. I had remembered my tablets but not the photo? My only hope was that she having my address would write to me.

Going to the window with a heavy heart I saw that the vehicles that were in the hanger last night, were gone. A ragged queue was forming at the hanger door, which was still closed. I lit a crumpled cigarette from a nearly empty packet and looked for Twitchy; he was nowhere to be seen. The heat in the hanger was stifling and my head was aching dully, after the events of yesterday and the disappointments, I hoped and prayed that I wasn't in for another attack. I walked over to the hanger door to try and get some fresh air ignoring the tugging and pushing of these wretched people. I stood there in a kind of daze, everything and everyone seemed to be going at a fast pace, even standing still, seemed standing still fast? Soldiers seemed standing still at full speed! It was weird!

From time to time I saw Twitchy but not to talk to. He too was bustling at top speed, at times it was comical, but I couldn't laugh because I felt that I had joined this tide of bustling people in this trepidation which seemed to emanate from the very walls of the hanger itself...

Tired of watching all the panic around me, afraid that I would succumb to the level of a headless chicken running around in circles going nowhere, I opened the hanger door a little and finding a box to sit on, sat with my back to the crowd and looked out at the sun drenched runway blocking out of my mind all the pathetic activity behind me.

I tried to remember some of the poems I had written at the hotel that would sum up this terrible horror that mankind inflicted on each other. I remembered one and recited it aloud.

Politicians emerge and look into the eye of shame.

Release the grip of the chain-mail fist and offer instead.

Salvation-by admitting, that you are partly to blame.

Governments should think, would they, if they could see this carnage, so eagerly go to war? Or will they as always put power first before human life?

"Come on its time to go." Twitchy was looming over me. A weary smile was etched on his face. A pang of regret stabbed me as I thought of how I had treated him, how I had, to myself anyway, made fun of him and had shouted at him. Looking at him now I felt ashamed of myself and wanted to tell him so, but didn't because I didn't think he would believe me. "Follow them." Pointing to a ragged column of running people. He seemed embarrassed as I shook his hand thanking him. He shrugged his shoulders twitching at the same time which made him look more funny than normal that I couldn't help myself and burst out laughing, then instantly regretting it. I hugged him to hide my own embarrassment.

"Go Go." He sniffed pushing me away. I hurried after the others, crouching as I ran towards a sorry looking 'Dakota' which loomed ahead of me shrouded in smoke which was drifting across the airfield and being dispersed in swirling clouds as it mingled through its massive propellers. Together with the excited shouting of the milling crowd around its open door, the willing hands reaching down and pulling the slower ones on board. Crates of chickens were being pulled up to! The whole atmosphere was electrically charged with agitation, apprehension but above all exhilaration.

A sweating French soldier unceremoniously pulled me up and before the door was pulled shut I glanced at the hanger and waved hoping that Twitchy would still be watching. The insides of the plane had been stripped completely and every available space was packed with refugees together with their pitiful possessions. Some were sitting on the crates of chickens, whose occupants were screeching and shooting feathers out!

Sitting with my back against the fuselage I breathed a sigh of relief, even amongst chickens my nightmare was nearly over, *I was free!* I would now be able to have regular treatment and get better from this accursed Malaria. Relaxing, letting the vibrations and motion of the aircraft soothe me as it gathered speed and lifted into the air, I thought with an aching heart of Smiler. Would I ever see her smiling face again?

Would I ever hold her in my arms again? I consoled myself that wherever she was; she had my address in England and would write to me, I knew I would do my best to locate her.

In the soothing state my mind was in through the rhythmic vibrations of the plane. I mentally formed a short poem and through the drone of the engines I whispered aloud.

Carry my thoughts and voice wild wind.

Carry them to Smiler for me.

Place my kisses on her lips.

Make her remember, and write to me.

CHAPTER THIRTY-SIX

We landed in Korea. The jolting of touch down brought me out of a sound sleep, moments later the aircraft came to a stop and the door was opened. Soldiers helped everyone to disembark and shepherded us to waiting trucks, which were lined up in convoy. Standing in a state of bewilderment on the runway not knowing whether to join the throng of refuges boarding the trucks or wait to see if anyone turned up for me. I lit a cigarette noting that it was my last and watched the wretched straggle boarding the last remaining trucks.

I was just about to join them when a car pulled up and the driver asked my name. It was an Embassy car but I couldn't make out whether it was British, French or Korean. I opened the door and got in, we sped off towards the Airport buildings without saying a word.

Entering the Airport building I was met by a loud noise of agitated and excited people. Tables had been set up and harassed looking officials were attending to queues of people waiting to be admitted. Korean and French soldiers were everywhere, standing guard at all the doors, keeping the queues in line and escorting those who had been dealt with at the tables to other parts of the building.

"You go over there." My driver was pointing to a table a little way from the main stream. It looked like Europeans manned it, I saw that my driver was Korean and wore an Embassy badge, following his outstretched arm I approached the table.

"Mr Tudor?" He looked at me smiling. I didn't recognise his uniform and assumed he also was from the Korean Embassy. Beside him sat a nurse, who, judging by her uniform was French. My heart leapt for joy; she would surely know what happened to Smiler!

"Yes." I replied.

"I have here—" looking at some papers. "—that you may need some medical attention." Raising his eyebrows enquiringly. "Do you?"

"Yes, I need to see a doctor for an injection and to obtain Quinine tablets." I said still staring at the nurse.

He smiled again. "Yes of course, nurse will take you and welcome to Korea you are safe now." He stamped some papers and handed them to the nurse still smiling. She stood up and asked me to follow her. I was led into a small room and as she was about to leave me, I grabbed her arm and spoke in a rush. Had she any knowledge of the Saigon Clinic staff, nurses, doctors, anybody who had escaped, if so where could I contact them? She listened sympathetically shaking her head, then patting my arm moved away.

The doctor asked me a lot of questions as he examined me; Tut Tutting to himself as he looked at my back, then gave me an injection. I asked him the same questions as I had asked the nurse indicating that one person was especially important to me. He didn't know either, indicating that so much was going on that he couldn't keep track as to what was going on, but yes a lot of medical staff had been repatriated to France over the last four or five weeks, maybe she was amongst them he said hopefully. Amen to that I thought.

The next day I was driven to the docks. On first sight of my ship, emotions ran high; I read and re-read the stern. 'M V Hartismere.' London. Now I knew that I was home and free.

THE END

ABOUT THE AUTHOR

Secondary Modern Schooling leaving at age 14

Running away to sea at age 15.

Time as Merchant Seaman 6 Years

Coal Miner for 18 months to avoid National Service.

Spent 3 1/2 years in the R A F until invalided out.